FOR RICHER FOR POORER

By Danielle Steel

For Richer for Poorer • A Mother's Love • A Mind of Her Own • Far from Home
Never Say Never • Trial by Fire • Triangle • Joy • Resurrection • Only the Brave
Never Too Late • Upside Down • The Ball at Versailles • Second Act • Happiness
Palazzo • The Wedding Planner • Worthy Opponents • Without a Trace • The Whittiers
The High Notes • The Challenge • Suspects • Beautiful • High Stakes • Invisible
Flying Angels • The Butler • Complications • Nine Lives • Finding Ashley • The Affair
Neighbours • All That Glitters • Royal • Daddy's Girls • The Wedding Dress
The Numbers Game • Moral Compass • Spy • Child's Play • The Dark Side • Lost and Found
Blessing in Disguise • Silent Night • Turning Point • Beauchamp Hall
In His Father's Footsteps • The Good Fight • The Cast • Accidental Heroes
Fall from Grace • Past Perfect • Fairytale • The Right Time • The Duchess • Against All Odds
Dangerous Games • The Mistress • The Award • Rushing Waters • Magic • The Apartment
Property of a Noblewoman • Blue • Precious Gifts • Undercover • Country • Prodigal Son
Pegasus • A Perfect Life • Power Play • Winners • First Sight • Until the End of Time
The Sins of the Mother • Friends Forever • Betrayal • Hotel Vendôme • Happy Birthday
44 Charles Street • Legacy • Family Ties • Big Girl • Southern Lights • Matters of the Heart
One Day at a Time • A Good Woman • Rogue • Honor Thyself • Amazing Grace
Bungalow 2 • Sisters • H.R.H. • Coming Out • The House • Toxic Bachelors • Miracle
Impossible • Echoes • Second Chance • Ransom • Safe Harbour • Johnny Angel
Dating Game • Answered Prayers • Sunset in St. Tropez • The Cottage • The Kiss
Leap of Faith • Lone Eagle • Journey • The House on Hope Street • The Wedding
Irresistible Forces • Granny Dan • Bittersweet • Mirror Image • The Klone and I
The Long Road Home • The Ghost • Special Delivery • The Ranch • Silent Honor
Malice • Five Days in Paris • Lightning • Wings • The Gift • Accident • Vanished
Mixed Blessings • Jewels • No Greater Love • Heartbeat • Message from Nam • Daddy
Star • Zoya • Kaleidoscope • Fine Things • Wanderlust • Secrets • Family Album
Full Circle • Changes • Thurston House • Crossings • Once in a Lifetime
A Perfect Stranger • Remembrance • Palomino • Love: *Poems* • The Ring • Loving
To Love Again • Summer's End • Season of Passion • The Promise • Now and Forever
Passion's Promise • Going Home

Nonfiction
Expect a Miracle
Pure Joy: *The Dogs We Love*
A Gift of Hope: *Helping the Homeless*
His Bright Light: *The Story of Nick Traina*

For Children
Pretty Minnie in Hollywood
Pretty Minnie in Paris

Danielle Steel

FOR RICHER
FOR POORER

MACMILLAN

First published 2025 by Delacorte Press
an imprint of Random House
a division of Penguin Random House LLC, New York

First published in the UK 2025 by Macmillan
an imprint of Pan Macmillan
The Smithson, 6 Briset Street, London EC1M 5NR
EU representative: Macmillan Publishers Ireland Limited, 1st Floor,
The Liffey Trust Centre, 117–126 Sheriff Street Upper,
Dublin 1 D01 YC43
Associated companies throughout the world

ISBN 978-1-5290-8598-3 HB
ISBN 978-1-5290-8599-0 TPB

1 3 5 7 9 8 6 4 2

A CIP catalogue record for this book is available from the British Library.

Typeset in Charter ITC by Palimpsest Book Production Ltd, Falkirk, Stirlingshire
Printed and bound in the UK using 100% Renewable Electricity by CPI Group (UK) Ltd

Visit **www.panmacmillan.com** to read more about all our books
and to buy them.

To my beloved children, Beatie, Trevor, Todd,
Nicky, Samantha, Victoria, Vanessa, Maxx, and Zara,

May you each find the right person to love
and be loved by, to hold and cherish, a fair exchange.
May you get as good as you give, don't settle for less,

and if you get it wrong the first time or the tenth
or hundredth time, be brave enough to try again,
until you know you have found the right person
to love you as you love them,
fully, wholly, with all your hearts,

and when you do, cherish each other forever,
and you will be forever blessed,
just as you deserve.
I love you,

                                        Mom/DS

FOR RICHER FOR POORER

Chapter 1

Eugenia Ward had spent the morning minutely going over her personal accounts and all her accounting records online, the same records that had been causing her endless anxiety and sleepless nights for the last eighteen months, ever since the pandemic began. She was a tall, slim, blonde, serious-looking woman, impeccably trained as a fashion designer, and had been in the business for thirty-three years. She checked her accounts diligently, while making notes on a yellow legal pad of things she wanted to move and change and watch out for, expenses she could carve out of her overhead, and others she would eliminate from her life if she was forced to. It had been a long, slow process as she did everything to keep her business afloat. She was divorced with five adult children, two of whom she still helped to support. She had started her own company fourteen years before, when she turned forty. She made the most elegant, luxurious evening gowns and wedding gowns. They were ready-to-wear that looked like haute couture. They were worthy of the finest design houses and high-end labels in Europe and the U.S., and a year after she'd opened the doors of her Eugenia Ward stores, she added another dimension, her own haute couture line of evening and wedding gowns, which was her dream come true. They were made to order, entirely by hand, in her own ateliers by sewers who had been trained in Paris. Like some of the finest French designers, she now created both ready-to-wear clothes and haute couture. Her made-to-order handmade gowns were shown, ordered, and fitted in her exclusive private salons. She made it a memorable experience for her clients.

Her business had been a brilliant success and had taken off like a rocket, and much to everyone's amazement, Eugenia had been able to pay off her investors in five years. She had loyal clients around the world, and had had several offers to buy the business, but she had always refused. Both arms of the business were a gold mine, and she loved what she did. Eugenia was involved in every aspect of the business, with her haute couture gowns made under the label Princess Eugenie and her ready-to-wear line eponymous, as Eugenia Ward.

For Richer for Poorer

As a respected American designer, she showed her next season's line of ready-to-wear gowns at Fashion Week in New York twice a year, in February and September, and her haute couture line in Paris, with the other remaining couture houses, in January and July. She had a store in the Seventies on Madison Avenue in New York for her ready-to-wear gowns, and above it her very elegant haute couture salons, where they had fittings. She also had an office on Seventh Avenue where they took ready-to-wear orders. She had a store on the Avenue Montaigne in Paris, and a business office above it for orders in Europe. It was an impeccably run operation, and extremely lucrative for Eugenia. Until the pandemic hit them like a bomb. The entire world had been in lockdown for months, repeatedly, and curfews were in force around the globe. Social events, even small dinner parties, were canceled, as well as every socialite jet-set wedding. No woman in any city in any country had worn an evening gown in almost two years. Evening wear and the events where one wore it had vanished overnight. Eugenia was one of the most famous and successful designers in fashion history and poured much of what she made back into the business, and in the blink of an eye, she had become obsolete. Now women were wearing yoga pants, exercise clothes, blue jeans and sweatshirts, fleece-lined slippers and running shoes, and down jackets instead

3

of satin evening coats. Their jewelry to go with the evening clothes had been in vaults at home or the bank for almost two years, and the calendars of the most popular socialites were blank.

Eugenia hadn't arrived at the pinnacle of her success by accident or casually. Her father had wanted her to get a law degree, and her mother thought she should study art history and work at the Louvre in Paris or the Metropolitan Museum in New York. Her parents were serious, conservative, well-educated people from respectable families. Her mother had gone to Vassar, her father to Yale. Her mother had never worked. She played bridge, served on charitable committees, and oversaw their only daughter's education and well-being. They were good parents. Her father was the president of a New York bank, and both came from solid but not wealthy families. Her mother had gotten a master's in Renaissance art at Columbia, and painted still-lifes and landscapes in the style of the Old Masters as a well-executed hobby. The walls of the Park Avenue apartment where Eugenia had grown up were covered with her mother's art.

Eugenia had been passionate about fashion all her life. It fascinated her, particularly the glamorous gowns created for movie stars and famous women. Creating them herself was all she wanted to do. It was her dream. Her parents thought it undignified, irrelevant, and frivolous, but they couldn't stop her.

Her mother had tried to redirect her artistic impulses into a more educated, intellectual career, and her father thought she would do well as an attorney and tried to convince her to go to law school. But Eugenia's passion for the fashion world was limitless. She was constantly sketching clothes, and fascinated by the history of fashion and great designers, both in France and the U.S. She made her mother an evening gown for Christmas when she was sixteen. It was inspired by a gown designed by Christian Dior in the 1950s, and she sewed it herself. Her mother was bowled over by it and it fit perfectly. Even her parents didn't deny she had talent, though they wished she would turn it in a more intellectual direction. But all Eugenia wanted to do was design beautiful clothes for real live women to wear, to make them look like movie stars. Before that, she made clothes for her Barbie dolls that were miniature works of art. She turned them into an art project in college and made a video of them. She had spent hours dressing her dolls as a child, and making their clothes by hand. She made clothes for her friends in school. She was obsessed with fashion.

Her determination to work in fashion was the cause of the first major disagreement she and her parents had ever had. Their relationship had been strong, easy, and harmonious before that. Her mother was properly dressed, but not interested in fashion.

After tearful battles with Eugenia, they had finally given in, and Eugenia had gone to Parsons School of Design, as well as NYU, majoring in fine arts, with a minor in art history to satisfy her mother, and graduated at the top of her class with honors. It had calmed her parents down for a while.

She had done an internship in the haute couture ateliers of Valentino in Italy, right after she graduated, and then worked at Dior in Paris for two years, at first in ready-to-wear and then in the sacred halls of haute couture. It was the high point of her time in Paris.

She came back to New York after two years at Dior, and at twenty-four, was hired by Oscar de la Renta, where she became his head designer and stayed for sixteen years, until she started her own business with his blessing. He was her mentor and advisor, and the man she respected more than any on earth, other than her own father. Oscar thought her immensely talented, which no one denied, not even the critics, who worshipped her and rarely criticized her work. They said she was "inspired," with an undeniable gift for creating the most glamorous gowns in the last thirty years, gowns that no one wanted now, because they had nowhere to wear them. Eugenia knew they would come back eventually, when the last of the pandemic had skittered away like a rat off a ship, but in the meantime, no one was there yet. People were depressed and suffering the effects of PTSD, after a year and a half of fearing for their lives and watching the world crumble around them.

The kind of women who wore Eugenia's dresses and didn't shrink at her prices had fled to their country homes when the first alarms sounded, and most of them were still there. New York had been a ghost town for more than a year. It was finally reviving slowly, but a third or more of the shops were boarded up. Stores that had existed for decades had gone out of business. In good weather, people were eating in jeans at casual restaurants with outdoor terraces. In bad weather, they stayed home. Most of Eugenia's clients were hidden away in Connecticut, Long Island, or the more elite areas of New Jersey with stables of horses on their estates. In Paris they were in their châteaux that dotted the countryside in Normandy and other regions. In England, they were in their country manors and on grand estates, and even those who gave hidden, forbidden parties in the privacy of their homes weren't doing it in black tie and ball gowns. There were no debutante balls and cotillions, nor fairy-tale weddings. Fashion Week had been canceled season after season for two years, fashion shows were virtual, and plans for the coming seasons were still tenuous. Large gatherings were strictly forbidden. Eugenia had kept her shops open in New York and Paris, with one or two employees, but she had no customers, and her overhead was crushing. She was hanging on by her fingernails, and didn't want to lose everything she had built. Supporting and educating five children, plus her own expensive husband and the divorce, had all been costly. She spent a fortune on rent, payroll, and exquisite fabrics, and the fashion shows she put on four times a year had all weighed heavily against her greatly reduced profits. It all worked as long as the money kept rolling in. And now it had stopped. The pandemic was strangling her business and she was hemorrhaging money. Her business was gasping for air and she was determined to hang on.

Fashion Week in New York was going to happen in a month, in September right after Labor Day, and in a daring move, fighting for survival, Eugenia was going to try something different. She had gone through all the fabrics she had in stock, trying to use what she already had, and was making a small selection of exquisite satin and lace and silk tops that her customers could wear with leggings or jeans. She was designing cozy wraps and double-faced cashmere jackets with the exquisite trimmings she had been saving for years to put on evening gowns with matching coats. She was trying desperately to raise her clients' spirits, and give them glamorous, fun things to wear that would make life seem less dreary and keep her in business. She couldn't charge her usual high prices for what she was going to show this time, but everything helped. She had ordered commercial down jackets, which was all anyone wore now, and added fabulous patterned silks as the linings and exquisite French "frogs" as the closures. As an experiment, she had been personally hand-sewing jeans she bought commercially, decorating them with rhinestones, synthetic pearls, and colored beads in exotic patterns and using braid, gold tassels, and trim to dress up the jeans and make each pair a unique creation. She was selling them for five thousand dollars apiece, ten in some cases, and her clients were eating them up. She had bought bolts of denim from merchants who still had it in stock, and sewed it herself into suits and pants with tops. She had let all her sewers go, and they were at home on unemployment. In the meantime, she was selling what she had. And now she was creating a most unusual line for Fashion Week this season, with white jeans encrusted with pearls and rhinestones for the spring/ summer. It was a valiant effort to keep her business alive, after it had been on life support for months. She was using as much as she had in her stock and storerooms, to minimize her purchases. She was trying to be as careful and creative as she could.

Eugenia herself was wearing nothing any different from her clients. She was living in jeans and sweatshirts. She had noticed that during the worst of it, she felt better when she wore color, and she was making sweatshirts in vibrant tones that made her happy just looking at them. Hopefully they would make her clients happy too. It was a long way from her training in traditional design and haute couture, and what she usually created, but these were special times that required desperate measures. In the scheme of real life, fashion had shrunk to invisible proportions for everyone, and yet wearing clothes that made one feel ugly on top of it was even more depressing. There was a happy medium somewhere that would meet the current need and she was determined to find it. She wasn't going to gouge people when she priced the new daywear line, except for the handmade one-of-a-kind items, which were of the highest quality and virtually priceless, made by the designer herself. There was a lot of hand-stitching involved in what she was doing now, and that was worth something. But she wanted her designs and creations to be mood elevating, to make people feel hopeful and happy when they wore them. Each piece was unique.

They looked expensive. Some were, but most weren't.

She wanted them to be fun to wear. It was an odd time for everyone. She had no idea how the collection would be received. The critics might blast her off the runway. But she had to do something. She was born to create. She even covered one sweatshirt with tiny feathers. It was a work of art as much as a piece of clothing, which was how she felt about fashion. To Eugenia, fashion was an art form, like music or dance or painting. And people's bodies were the canvases she worked on. She was almost ready for the runway show after Labor Day, and she was taking some time off in August to spend with her children. Her five adult children were her greatest source of joy and the center of her private universe.

She was one of those women who had thought she could have it all, a husband, a family, children, and a rewarding career, which in her case had supported them all for three decades. Three of her children were self-supporting now, her oldest child and only son, Stefano, her middle child, Daphne, and her youngest, Sofia, an independent spirit who danced to her own tune and thought fashion was defined by army surplus. Her other two daughters, Eloise and Gloria, couldn't live on what they made and needed assistance, so she helped them with additional support. They were underpaid in their jobs. She was the safety net under all of them in one way or another. They ranged in age from twenty-six to thirty-one. They were her masterpieces, and she couldn't let them down by going bankrupt. They counted on her, and she tried to provide them with a role model, proving that hard work was its own greatest reward.

She felt she had failed them during the pandemic, by nearly running aground. The tidal waves of the coronavirus had all but swept away the success she had built and enjoyed, and the life she had created for her family and herself through her business. She was hanging on, but when she studied her accounts, as she did regularly with overwhelming anxiety, she was desperate to find a way to shore up her failing business until normal life returned. She was running out of money. And she was determined not to lose her business.

Lately, she'd been considering looking for investors again, as she had in the beginning to get started, to tide her over this time and keep her from drowning. She had had four solid, faithful investors when she established her brand, and she hadn't let them down. What she had sold then made sense at the time, but how could she convince anyone now of the importance and validity of expensive evening gowns, when there was no opportunity to wear them, and might not be for many years, if the scientists didn't get a grip on the pandemic situation. Things had improved considerably, but there was still danger lurking that no one could deny, and the pandemic was not yet over. She had to hang on until it was. She felt certain it would end, as the Spanish flu had eventually slunk off into the mists. But after what they'd all been through, would women still want evening gowns? Would anyone care?

Of her four original investors, two had died, one had moved back to China and retired, and the fourth had suffered severe reversals of their own. None of them were still an option.

There had been blessings in the pandemic too.

The dangers of the pandemic had brought people back to basics, reminded them of the importance of family. Some of her clients had gotten to know the children they barely knew before and had spent too little time with. There was nothing to do at night in the first year. People actually talked to each other, spent time together, helped their kids with online school and homework, went for walks. They slowed down after having run a race for years, a race to be the biggest, fastest, richest. Now they were all at home on "pause" and they didn't need an haute couture evening gown, or even a ready-to-wear one, for that. All the men dressed like lumberjacks now in the winter and campers in the summer, and the women dressed like schoolgirls. There were no fancy hairdos, and their jewels had been in the safe or at the bank for two years. Eugenia had dressed them for the life they no longer had, not the one they were living now. She was hoping that her upcoming runway show would change that. She wanted to play too. She had no idea how the fashion critics would react to it, and she was afraid they would deal the final death blow to her business. It wouldn't take much. She had little money left of what had been a very sizable fortune she had made herself, having poured most of it back into her business and spent the rest on her kids. Who else would she spend it on? And the divorce had hit her hard before Covid. She had wanted to be fair to her husband, and he had kept pressing for more. She didn't want a big battle, all in the press. She had paid a high price for discretion and fair play. Her ex-husband was a taker, not a giver, and had cost her a fortune for years before the divorce. He had taken full advantage of her success, and contributed nothing to it.

Sometimes she cried in her bed at night, terrified of the future. She hadn't been this frightened since she was a child, afraid that something bad might happen, or when her parents died within a year of each other when she was in her twenties with five young children, but she had her husband, Umberto, then, and the illusion that he would always be there for her. She'd been frightened when they got divorced too, although she was the pillar that had held up their world. Her parents and grandparents had left her a little money, but it had finally run out, just as her business took off. The timing had been providential. She had never been as frightened as she was now, afraid her whole world was caving in. She couldn't see a light on the horizon. She knew it was there, like the darkness before the dawn, but she couldn't see it yet. She had to find it soon, before the ship she had built with her own hands ran aground, and it would soon if she didn't do something dramatic. Of that she was certain. She just didn't know what. She had no one to talk to about it. Covid had separated her from her friends, with all the lockdowns and restrictions. Most of the people she knew had left town and were isolated in their country homes. She had never felt so alone in her life. With no partner and her kids grown up, her business was failing and her money running out.

Everything she had ever done seemed fated, like part of a plan, with perfect timing. As one thing ended, another started. Her first internship, her jobs, her business. She had met her future husband when she did her internship at Valentino in Italy. He was an Italian prince, a descendant of the royal house of Florence, which had existed when Italy had been divided into states and principalities for centuries, which it no longer was. Umberto was the most elegant, charming, aristocratic man she had ever met, and the most beautiful. He made her feel like Cinderella. Shy as a child, and in a foreign country, she had never met anyone like him, and innocently had had no sense of her own beauty and strength, only confidence in the designs she created. She was certain of her designs and never doubted them. She was naïve, talented, and young, and he was so sophisticated. Umberto was magical. She was twenty-one when they met at a ball in Venice. Someone from Valentino had taken her to it. It was the most extraordinary setting she had ever seen, a fifteenth-century palazzo, with candles everywhere. Umberto caught her when she tripped on the dress she had made. She hadn't had time to finish the hem properly and had taped it, as they did with the models sometimes when a dress wasn't finished right before a show. Umberto had been struck by her innocence and vulnerability and natural beauty. He was forty-five years old, one of the most desirable men in Italy. He oozed aristocracy and charisma. Her discreet, conservative, respectable parents and their world were of an entirely different breed. They seemed dull compared to Umberto. He was so glamorous. She felt like a princess in a fairy tale when she was with him, and he wisely sensed that with her talent, passion, and energy, she would go far. He had good instincts about people and how they could be of use to him. Umberto was showy without appearing to be, and dazzling. He lived in Rome, and took her under his wing, which was flattering and exciting. He took her to parties all over Europe, and introduced her to people she had read about and never dreamed of meeting. He had a reputation for dating models and movie stars, and rich and titled young women. He had endless charm but not a penny. He told her she would be famous one day, he was certain of it, which seemed absurd to her. She wanted to create gorgeous designs, she wasn't seeking fame. Fame was for other people. She didn't care about fame, she just wanted to make beautiful clothes.

Her parents objected to Umberto when they met him, because he had never had a real job. He "connected" people, brought them together in the most elegant, gracious way and helped them buy houses, meet jewelers, charter yachts or buy them, and he made a commission on every transaction, doing it so smoothly that no one objected to how much he charged them. He was a very special European breed where a title became a job and was turned into a handsome profit, especially by a prince. He had a talent for pulling money out of thin air and other people's pockets painlessly. Her parents thought none of what he did was respectable. Her father called him an operator and a con man, which he wasn't. Umberto wasn't dishonest, he was just clever, greedy, and charming. He was like a magic trick that everyone loved and watched with admiration. They got what they wanted, and so did he.

Despite her parents' objections, Eugenia married him less than a year after they met. He followed her to New York to close the deal. They had a small wedding, commensurate with her parents' displeasure, and she became a princess. Afterward, she was never sure why he'd married her. She only had a very small inheritance from her grandparents, and later a barely larger one from her parents, but he saw the potential she had and her money disappeared quickly in his hands. She got the job with Dior in Paris after they married, and he didn't object to her working. Umberto was absolutely certain Eugenia would become a success, with her talent. She was delighted because she loved her job and was learning everything she would apply later to her own designs, all the techniques of haute couture. Everyone who worked with her saw her potential too.

Umberto di San Benedetto was a passionate man, and Eugenia was madly in love with him. She got pregnant three months after they married, which dashed her parents' hopes that she would come to her senses, see him for what he was, leave him, and have the marriage annulled. He had her in his thrall. She was young and healthy, worked hard in the daytime, and went to parties and danced with him at night. Their son, Stefano, was born on their first anniversary. Eugenia was twenty-three, and Umberto was now forty-seven, wildly proud of his firstborn, his son and heir.

All his father had to give him was his title, which meant everything to Umberto, and little to her. Much to Eugenia's amazement, they lived in a very grand apartment in the 7th arrondissement, which a friend had loaned to Umberto in exchange for a favor. It came with two servants who took care of the baby too. Eugenia loved the glamorous life Umberto created for her, and she made enough to support them between his "commissions." They never had a lot of money, but Umberto was always able, with his connections, to create a grand lifestyle out of thin air. Her parents disapproved of everything he did.

When Stefano was a year old, they moved to New York. Her father had just died suddenly and her mother was ill, and Eugenia wanted to be near her in New York. She was already pregnant with their second child, Eloise. Eugenia got an amazing job immediately, working for Oscar de la Renta, who recognized her talent. It was a bittersweet time. Her mother died of cancer and grief after losing her husband, weeks after Eloise was born. It was a time of sorrow mixed with joy. The baby was beautiful, with her mother's exquisite, delicate features and her father's noble bloodline. Umberto was once again very proud. And Eugenia made enough by then to hire a nanny so she could work.

Eugenia didn't quit her lucrative job with Oscar de la Renta when Eloise was born. She couldn't afford to.

Umberto had rapidly made the same profitable connections he'd had in Paris, and used them well. There were always homes in Palm Beach being loaned to them for vacations, trips to the Bahamas on yachts and to Europe on private planes, free clothes, and free hotels. And Eugenia's salary supported them, along with the inheritance her parents and grandparents had left her. Umberto was very grand, while Eugenia managed it all, two young children, a demanding job, an expensive social life that kept them out every night. The nanny Eugenia hired helped her deal with the children. Her life was a juggling act. Eugenia spent as much time with the children as she could and Umberto would allow. When she insisted on staying home with them, he went out alone, almost every night in black tie. Eugenia was still desperately in love with him and under his spell. He was cavalier about their love life, and she got pregnant accidentally when Eloise was three months old. Daphne was the result nine months later. Stefano and Eloise looked like blond cherubs, and Daphne was a beautiful baby with dark hair. Eugenia was back at work in a month. Their constant social life continued, although Eugenia couldn't keep up anymore with three children and her big job with de la Renta. She was increasingly being noticed in the fashion milieu and by the press, and Oscar was very good to her, allowing her to shine. Eugenia had two more babies after Daphne, Gloria a year later and Sofia ten months after that. She'd had five babies in five years, was Oscar's chief designer, and was twenty-eight years old, with a highly coveted job. Eugenia was keeping them afloat. Somehow, they always managed.

By the time Sofia was born, they had lived in New York for four years, and Umberto was homesick for Europe. He began to travel more and more to balls in Italy, weddings in Paris, shoots and house parties in England with his international friends. He would come home to Eugenia from time to time, and take off again. He spent no time with their children, and very little with her. She spent the weekends with the children, after working all week, all of which bored Umberto. He loved the idea of the children, but not the reality. He loved showing them off when they were clean and dressed beautifully in matching outfits Eugenia made for them when she had time, or sketched and had one of the design assistants make. They looked like the little prince and the four little princesses they were, but she wondered sometimes if Umberto could even tell them apart. He was proud of them, but barely knew them. Years slipped by and with what was left of her own money, and her salary, Eugenia put them in the best private schools in New York. Her life was a relay race of children and work, and it was Oscar, her mentor and friend, who finally encouraged her to find investors and start her own brand. He became one of the investors, because he had so much faith in her, and he guessed easily the burden she was carrying, with five children and an absentee husband. He had seen Umberto at enough parties around the world, without Eugenia, to understand what was going on. Eugenia suspected by then that Umberto wasn't faithful to her, but she didn't have the courage to ask, and really didn't want to know. The children needed at least the illusion of a father, and she didn't want a painful and embarrassing divorce, or to be completely on her own. She realized by then what she hadn't understood before. The worldly women he knew had recognized him for the opportunist he was, and never married him. He had needed an innocent like Eugenia when they married. She was destined for success, and followed him with stars in her eyes. She worked hard to provide everything he wanted, and a family, but she wasn't naïve anymore.

When she'd left the job with Oscar and opened her own business fourteen years before, she had laid the groundwork so carefully that it was almost an overnight success. Within a year, she opened the haute couture arm. Oscar was the first of her investors whom she paid off, out of gratitude for all he had done for her. She could never have done it without his help. He had replaced her with a very capable designer, and Eugenia and Oscar remained friends. Umberto showed up for her opening parties, but very little else. They hardly saw each other anymore. It wasn't a marriage. He was more like a houseguest, an occasional visitor. She didn't cheat on him. She didn't have the interest, the energy, or the time. Her children and her business took up all of her attention. She had a marriage in name only, which suited Umberto. Eugenia had served her purpose, giving him the life he wanted. And after Sofia was born, the physical attraction between them came to an end. Eugenia began to hear about his affairs, which ended it for her. She couldn't handle or afford more than five children. Umberto had started traveling more then, and spent more time in Europe than New York. He said he had never felt at home in New York, although he had many friends there. And the women he pursued were mainly in Europe.

Four years after Eugenia opened her business, Umberto asked her for a divorce. It wasn't a heartbreak, but it was a sadness and a disappointment that he wasn't better than he was. They had been married for twenty-two years. The time had flown. It had been ten years now since the divorce. She had paid less than the settlement he demanded, but much more than she should have. He wanted half of her business, which she refused, but he hired a very aggressive lawyer and drove a hard bargain. He was sixty-eight years old, had no money or profession, and said he was too old to get a job and work, and the judge agreed. Umberto had no skills or training for anything. He always came out ahead in his deals, and he did with her as well. She knew she would never recoup what she had given him in the divorce, but her business was solid at the time, she managed to pay her investors back in spite of it, and she was able to support herself and their children until they grew up.

When the pandemic happened, the bottom dropped out of everyone's world, and no one wanted to buy evening gowns. No one could have predicted or even imagined it. The bulk of her income stream dried up, and she had no way to recoup her losses for the moment. But she was determined to hang in and work her way back to the top. She was never afraid of hard work.

She had heard that Umberto was still living like a prince in Italy, and she had no idea if he was living on new deals he made, or simply on what was left from her settlement. He visited their children once or twice a year, took them out for glamorous evenings, and was always charming and fun. He turned his visits into an adventure of some kind and then floated away, while she lived the day-to-day existence of running a business and being the mother of five young adults who barely knew their father. She was too gracious to malign him to the children, and she didn't want to upset them, but she had lost any semblance of respect for him years before. Her father had been right. Umberto was an operator, brilliant at what he did, and how he achieved it. She doubted now that he had ever loved her. She was just a convenient opportunity he could tell would turn into a gold mine for him one day, and she had. She had provided a stable base for him to operate from and eventually a golden life he felt entitled to, and five wonderful children, all of which gave him an aura of respectability that was undeserved. It didn't matter anymore, the past was the past, and she felt nothing for him by the time they divorced. Everything she had felt for him was dead. He was seventy-eight years old now. They had a long history together, and five children, and she was grateful for them. She regretted their settlement, with the effect of the pandemic on her business. All she could think of was how to stop the ongoing loss of money, how to shore things up and fight her way back to financial stability. There had to be a way, and she was determined to find it. She refused to give up.

She sat at her desk for a moment, pondering the figures she had just studied again. She was taking all her children on vacation for a week, as she did every summer. She had rented a compound of small houses in East Hampton. She had visited the property in February, and had set the money aside for it, as she always did. It was a treat for all of them.

She was driving to East Hampton that night and her children were due to arrive the next day. Daphne and her husband, Phillip Brooke, had a beautiful estate in Southampton that he had inherited from his parents. Daphne had followed in her mother's footsteps with an older husband, and four years ago had married a man twenty-two years older than she. Eugenia was twenty-two when she married Umberto, but Phillip was nothing like him. He was a rock-solid, responsible, kind man, a good husband and father, who had inherited an enormous fortune and had made a career of running his own investments. He provided Daphne a lifestyle that none of Eugenia's other children had, and she handled it well. She was a wonderful wife to Phillip, and mother to their three-year-old son, Tucker. Eugenia knew she would never have to worry about her. Daphne was set for life. She was a sensible, intelligent, responsible, loving, good person, and a joy to be around. It was her other four children that Eugenia worried about, none of whom were as comfortably set as Daphne and never would be. Fortunes like Phillip's were inherited, not made.

Eugenia got up from her desk, turned off her computer, and left her office. She still had to finish packing before driving to the Hamptons that night. She was looking forward to the week with her children. Her business problems could wait while she took a week off. And a week before the Labor Day weekend, they would get together again for Gloria's elaborate, very expensive wedding that they had been planning for a year, waiting for Covid to subside. The time had finally come, and it seemed safe. Gloria was marrying a young lord from England, who, like Umberto when Eugenia married him, was rich in blue blood and short on funds. Geoffrey and Gloria were both writers, and Gloria had a job at a publishing house in London to support her. Eugenia wasn't crazy about Geoffrey, but it was Gloria's life and what she wanted. Gloria was twenty-seven and Daphne was twenty-eight now. The two women couldn't have been more different. Geoff and Gloria were flying in from London to join them, at her mother's expense, as they couldn't have come otherwise. And Eugenia wanted the week with her children. It was sacred to her.

Eugenia left her office, exiting through the separate doors to the haute couture salon. She walked past her store and saw the single salesclerk she still employed, in spite of having no clients, but she didn't want to just close her doors. Eugenia waved, and the young woman waved back and smiled. Eugenia walked the two blocks to her apartment on Fifth Avenue in the Seventies. She had been thinking about selling it if her business didn't recover. There were so many changes in store. She tried not to think about it, and to focus on the week ahead with her children. None of them knew how frightened she was. She always tried to model strength to them, and calm. None of them had guessed the waves of panic that seized her at night, or the weight of carrying all the burdens alone. But they were her children, and she felt she owed it to them to be strong, or at least appear to be. She couldn't wait to get to the Hamptons and relax for a week. She hoped that everything would go smoothly, but the one thing she had learned in the past eighteen months was that nothing was ever sure. Everything in life, both good and bad, was a surprise and totally unpredictable.

Chapter 2

It only took Eugenia an hour to finish packing when she got back to the apartment from her office. She had three bags full of clothes for every eventuality, evenings at home, days at the pool, a few fancier things to wear out to a restaurant, or a party, if they were invited anywhere dressy. Daphne and Phillip were giving a small outdoor party for them in two days, and Eugenia had hired a cook to make lunch and dinner at her house so they could enjoy their time together and relax at meals. It would be a real vacation for everyone, even for Eugenia, not having to wash dishes or prepare meals to everyone's liking.

The house came with two maids to make their beds and keep everything clean and orderly. It was going to be a week of luxury, maybe for the last time. She usually met all her children in Europe for the week's holiday, at her invitation and expense, at some of the best hotels, in rented villas, or on chartered boats. The six cabins on a standard charter were perfect for them. But with the pandemic not quite over yet, it seemed easier to stay in the States. Daphne was heavily pregnant and couldn't travel, and Eugenia wanted her to be with them too. So the property she had rented in East Hampton, near the Southampton home where Daphne and her family had spent the pandemic, seemed the right choice. Eugenia was looking forward to it, and hoped that everything would go smoothly, and was as nice as she remembered when she visited the house. She'd rented it because it had a main house and three smaller guesthouses and would accommodate them all.

She had a salad after she closed her bags, and was on the road by eight o'clock. The doorman loaded the suitcases into her car, along with a few shopping bags filled with loose ends. The Friday night traffic was light by then. At the height of the summer, as it was now at the end of July, it could take four hours to get to the Hamptons in heavy traffic. She made it in two and a half, and found the keys to the main house easily, where the realtor said she'd left them in a box on the porch. There were handsome gates to the property, and a long driveway.

The main house had three bedrooms on the upper floor,

in addition to the master suite, which Eugenia remembered as spacious, airy, and lovely. Every bedroom had its own bathroom. Downstairs on the ground floor there were two living rooms, a den, a dining room, and an enormous kitchen with a big table where they could all eat together informally. It suited all their needs to perfection, with the three smaller guesthouses, the pool, and a dressing room. There was a downstairs playroom in the main house with a pool table, a movie room, and a huge library of films.

Her children with partners would each have a guesthouse of their own, each with two bedrooms. Gloria with her fiancé, Geoff, and Sofia with Bradley Jackson, a man they were meeting for the first time. He was a young doctor at the hospital where she worked as a nurse practitioner and midwife. The third guesthouse would be occupied by Stefano and his wife, Liz. Eloise was staying in the main house with her mother, since she was on her own. Eugenia was curious about the man Sofia was bringing. She was extremely private about her life, and she had said little about him, except that he was a very talented doctor. But if she was bringing him on their family vacation, Eugenia knew he was important to her, so all eyes would be on him. And Sofia never brought men home. Being together on vacation was more challenging now that most of her children had partners. There was more opportunity for dissent and conflicting opinions, provoked by their partners. It was a lot easier when they were younger and came alone, but this was the way it was now, and Eugenia had adjusted to it. Daphne was the peacemaker, and Phillip seemed to make every situation easier in a fatherly way with unlimited patience, and knew when to withdraw when family discussions became heated. He was an asset, not only for Daphne, but for all of them. He was older and knew better than to enter the fray when things went off the rails. They were a lively group with different personalities and strong opinions, and expressed them freely.

Stefano's wife, Liz, was exactly the opposite of Phillip. She was famous for making some caustic, controversial remark or harsh criticism her in-laws took exception to, and Stefano then had to defend his wife, when his sisters challenged her and complained about her later. She came from a very simple background, having grown up in Queens, and had some rough edges, and was occasionally aggressive when she felt threatened by Stef's sisters. She was extremely bright, had paid her own way through business school, and was politically very liberal, which some of the others weren't. She didn't like snobs and she thought it was ridiculous that Stefano had an inherited title and was a prince. She made fun of him for it, although none of them used the title, and Eugenia never had either except when she was out with

Umberto socially, when they were married. He expected it and took the title very seriously, although he was the prince of nothing now, with no throne for a royal to be on in Italy. Princes in Italy were a dime a dozen, although Eugenia would never have said that to her husband. She used the title for her haute couture line, but not personally. It was just part of Umberto's mystique and meant more in Europe than in the States, which she always thought was part of why he moved back to Europe. There he could be Prince Umberto of Florence, and not just Eugenia Ward's husband, which sounded common to him, and demeaning. He never felt denigrated by spending her money, however, by any name.

The family jury's verdict was not yet fully in on Geoff, Gloria's fiancé. He was from an aristocratic family and Eugenia had found him snobbish when she met him. He was also very attached to his title. His father was an earl, although penniless, with a threadbare, crumbling estate in Sussex, a drafty, dreary manor house Geoff made sound like Buckingham Palace. Geoff was always aware of who had money and who didn't. It mattered to him. He could be fun when he'd had a lot to drink and took himself less seriously. Eugenia found him pompous and irritating, with enormous literary pretensions about the novel he'd been writing for as long as Gloria had known him, two years now, nearly three. He never seemed to finish the book.

33

Eugenia knew that Gloria was impressed by him, though her mother was not entirely sure why. Gloria was a very serious writer, and Eugenia thought she would become successful at it in time. She wasn't as sure about Geoff. He was all talk, bragged about graduating from Oxford, and as an only child was not used to fitting into a big family.

He and Gloria were treating their wedding as the event of the century, which worried Eugenia. The expenses kept growing, and while she had set a large amount aside to pay for it, a huge stretch for her at the moment, they were already at twice the original budget, which Gloria was completely oblivious to, as was Geoff. They never mentioned the expense and expected Eugenia to put on a grand event and foot the bill for everything. It never occurred to them that business might be bad and it might be hard for Eugenia, and she never said it. The dress she had designed, according to Gloria's wishes, was fit for a queen, or a Saudi princess with a very rich father. The dress was entirely made of antique lace, with a matching coat, a ten-foot train, and an exquisite veil. It was encrusted with tiny pearls and had taken a year to make, and Gloria was going to look gorgeous in it, in exactly four weeks. Umberto hadn't contributed a penny to the event, of course. Eugenia didn't expect him to, but some fatherly gesture might have been nice, and would have been appreciated. It never occurred to Umberto or to Gloria that he should contribute. She was used to her mother shouldering the full load for everything, alone. They all were. It was what she had always done, since Umberto wasn't going to, and until recently she could afford it. Now it was another story, and from the look of her accounts, the vacation in the Hamptons and Gloria's wedding seemed like they might be the family's last moments of ease and luxury, but they didn't know it yet since Eugenia hadn't told them, and didn't intend to for a while. She was still hoping for a miracle to help turn things around.

She took a quick tour of all the houses when she arrived to make sure that everything was in place for their arrivals the next day, and it was. The houses were spotless, the beds perfectly made with beautiful Porthault sheets from Paris. The furnishings were modern and well chosen from Italian designers by a well-known decorator. It was just as Eugenia remembered it, only better. There were even flowers placed in every room, and Eugenia settled into her own suite at midnight, turning on the large screen TV in her bedroom when she got into her bed in the perfectly pressed sheets, and minutes later, she was asleep. The vacation had begun.

The sun was streaming into the room when Eugenia woke up the next morning, and the TV was still on. She turned it off and opened the windows, as it was warm with a light breeze. She could see the ocean in the distance, and they had access to the beach down a private pathway which she wanted to explore later. She went downstairs, and the maids were busy, vacuuming the living room. They seemed like pleasant young women and one of them offered her a cup of coffee, which she accepted gratefully, and then she went to sit on an old-fashioned porch swing as she surveyed her temporary domain with pleasure. It was a little piece of heaven, and she was grateful to be able to do this for her kids, in spite of the last eighteen months. She felt lucky to be there. She was smiling, thinking about it and enjoying the peaceful moment, when a station wagon drove up the driveway and stopped in front of the main house, a dozen feet from where Eugenia was sitting, swinging gently.

Her smile broadened immediately when her daughter Daphne emerged from the car. She looked like a cartoon of a balloon with pretty face and legs attached. She was almost eight months pregnant with twins, with six weeks to go, due the week after her sister's wedding, and hoped she'd make it until then. Twins were likely to come early, which would be all right too, and almost welcome. Daphne smiled as she made her way to her mother, climbed the steps to the porch, and collapsed in a big wicker chair next to the swing. She looked as though she would explode if she got any bigger. She'd been shocked when she learned she was having twins, but now she thought it would be fun, after she got the delivery behind her. Like her mother, she'd had easy pregnancies, for her first child and even the twins so far. Eugenia was happy to see her, and Daphne was smiling and a little out of breath.

Eugenia leaned over to kiss her. Daphne was twenty-eight years old with dark hair in a braid down her back, big green eyes, and a tan from the summer in the Hamptons. They'd been living there on her husband's estate since the pandemic started. It had been easy and relaxed and felt safe. They were planning to move back to the city after the twins came, since the city seemed safe again and Tucker was starting nursery school in September. They lived a few blocks from Eugenia's apartment in an elegant town house Phillip had bought when they married. But in the meantime, they were enjoying the summer, and now her family's visit for a week. It was the first time they would be together since the pandemic started, and they were all looking forward to it, especially Eugenia.

"How do you feel?" Eugenia asked her.

"Huge. If I drop something now, I can't pick it up. If I did, I'd probably fall over and never be able to get up." Daphne laughed, but she looked happy and relaxed. "They feel like baby elephants." They knew that the twins were fraternal, a boy and a girl, so she and Phillip would have

two sons and a daughter. And fraternal twins were heredi-
tary. Umberto vaguely remembered twins somewhere in
his family tree, but couldn't remember who. Phillip and
Daphne were delighted, and Eugenia was happy for them.
"When is everyone arriving?" Daphne asked, pleased to
have her mother nearby for a week, and then again for the
week of Gloria's wedding before Labor Day. Although
Eugenia always firmly insisted that she had no favorites,
she and Daphne had the easiest relationship, the most in
common, and were closest, now that all her children were
adults.

Daphne had such a stable carefree life, because of Phillip
and a solid marriage, that her life was less stressful than
that of the others, and she was a good-natured, upbeat
person. Phillip took care of everything for her, and his main
goal in life was to protect, love, and please her. Eugenia
had no worries about her. Sofia was content in her life too,
although it was very different. But Eugenia wasn't as sure
about the others. Stefano was wound very tightly, very
driven and ambitious, and always seemed tense to her, and
Liz pushed him hard too. Eloise was perennially anxious
and extremely stressed by her career. Gloria appeared to
be heading toward a potential disaster with her choice of
husband, but Eugenia knew there was nothing she could
do about it. At least Daphne and Sofia seemed to have found

their niches in life, which was something. Hopefully, the others would get there too.

"Eloise's plane from Paris lands at eleven," Eugenia answered. "With baggage, customs, and the drive here, I figure she'll be here around two-thirty if the plane is on time. Sofia's plane from Memphis lands at one, so she could get here about an hour after Eloise. Gloria and Geoff said they would be here in time for dinner. And I don't know what time Stef and Liz are leaving to drive up from the city. He said they both had work to finish."

"That sounds like him," Daphne said easily, admiring the property around them. There were three gardeners tending to the lawn and flowerbeds. "What about you, Mom? Can you take a break while you're here?" It was no secret that Stefano and Eloise got their intense work ethic from their mother. Daphne had worked at a magazine briefly before she married Phillip but had no aspirations to have a career. Eugenia was always working, either sketching or in meetings on the phone, lately more so with attorneys and accountants.

"I'm planning to take the week off," she assured Daphne.

"Until Gloria arrives with another thousand requests and changes for the wedding of the century," Daphne commented. She had had a beautiful wedding four years before, and was far more relaxed than her sister was now. The wedding had seemed like an additional joy for Phillip and Daphne, not the be-all and end-all it was to Gloria and Geoff, as though they had to prove something and validate their relationship by how elaborate their wedding was. It added an additional layer of stress to everything about it, and made it much less enjoyable to plan with her. They were all tired of hearing about it. It was all Gloria had talked about for a year. And Geoff wasn't shy about wanting the best and most expensive of everything, as if to prove how important he was, as long as Eugenia was paying for it. And he never stopped talking about all the fancy aristocrats on his parents' guest list.

"Gloria texted me last week to ask if I would consider wearing a special matron of honor dress," Daphne said with a grin. "She said she was sure you wouldn't mind making one for me. I told her it would have to be made by the same people who are making the tent, and no, I don't want one. With any luck, the twins'll come early, and I can actually wear something human scale, and not a circus tent," she said with a sigh.

"Don't do anything silly to provoke it," Eugenia warned her.

"I won't. I'll come over after dinner tonight to see everyone. Phillip said he'd drive me. He doesn't want me driving at night anymore. I can hardly get behind the wheel anyway. My arms aren't long enough."

"He's right," her mother confirmed, "and it won't be long now."

"I don't know how you did it five times in five years," Daphne said admiringly. "This is only my second time, and I'm not sure I'd do it again. Three children might be enough. I love Tucker madly, but I feel like the whole last year has revolved around my belly. It seems much longer than last time."

"I never had twins," Eugenia reminded her, "and I don't know how I did it. I was on a roll. I was young, although you are too. Your father wanted lots of children, and I thought I could manage it. It was a major juggling act with work, though," and Umberto never lifted a finger to help her. Italian princes didn't, and he was in his fifties by the time Sofia was born. He was not about to change diapers or take the children to the park to play. He liked showing them off in their matching outfits before a dinner party, but not much else, and never for more than a few minutes.

"I couldn't do this if I had a career too. I don't know how you did, and with a big, demanding career in fashion too."

"Oscar was very understanding when I worked for him. And I just managed somehow. I was crazy about all of you so it seemed worth it, and I was pretty well organized." Eugenia knew that Phillip didn't do a great deal more than Umberto had, and was also twenty-two years older than

Daphne, having just turned fifty. But he provided Daphne with all the help she wanted, which made things easier, and he was great with their three-year-old son, and would undoubtedly be with the twins too. They were a sweet family. It warmed Eugenia's heart to see them together.

"That's why Eloise always says she doesn't want kids. She says she can't have children and a career, and it's too stressful as it is, with only her career," Daphne said.

"She might change her mind later, if she meets the right man," Eugenia commented.

"I'm not so sure. She's so anxious about her job all the time, I don't think she could manage kids too. I think Stef and Liz feel the same way. Liz is a lot more interested in her job than having children, and they think the planet is too screwed up and overcrowded to bring more humans into the world." Stefano was thirty-one, and Liz was five years older at thirty-six. Her biological clock not only wasn't ticking, it wasn't making a sound. Neither of them wanted children so far. And Eugenia felt it was entirely up to them.

All of Eugenia's children were so different. None of them had taken on the challenges she had, with a mammoth business and career and five children. She wasn't sure anymore if she would do it again, but she was glad she had. She hadn't even remotely guessed what a huge stress it could be if something went wrong with the business. She hadn't foreseen it, few had. Nor had she understood at twenty-three or even twenty-nine what an overwhelming responsibility it was being the parent of five adults with problems and needs and crises of their own, with only one parent to guide them, because of an absentee father who was only interested in going to parties and playing prince for his entire life. She had taken a lot on, and managed it, but she was paying a high price for it in the quality of her life now, which Daphne seemed to understand better than the others. She worried about her mother and all she was carrying, and she didn't know the half of it, but she could guess. The others thought of themselves more than they did their mother. That was the nature of children until their parents got too old to take care of themselves and became a burden to them—a time in her life that Eugenia dreaded, and had never thought of until now, especially if she lost everything and couldn't support herself, which seemed like a real possibility. She was going to do everything humanly possible to avoid having that happen.

Daphne left shortly before lunchtime, in order to have lunch with Phillip and Tucker, as she did on most days. She had an exceedingly pleasant, low-stress life. She couldn't wait to see her siblings that evening.

After she left, Eugenia checked her emails and answered the most pressing ones. She was trying to buy more denim, which was hard to get, in case the pieces in her show were a hit and she got a lot of orders for them. She knew more about denim now than she ever had. Japanese denim was considered the most high-quality and desirable, with the most body to it. She had put several denim pantsuits in the next show, which were exactly what women wanted now, and hers had a high fashion look. Haute couture jeans. Eugenia smiled as she finished her emails and went to meet the chef she had hired for the week, who turned out to be an enterprising young Frenchwoman who was delighted to hear the list of favorite meals Eugenia wanted for them. She was going to prepare lunch and dinner every day, except for the nights they went out.

Eugenia took a quick swim in the pool, and was just getting out and drying off when she heard a car on the gravel driveway, and looked over a hedge to see a black Cadillac SUV stop in front of the house, and a chic young woman jumped out. She had long blonde hair like Eugenia, and was wearing head-to-toe black, with jeans and a black cotton blouse, and carrying a large black alligator bag. Eloise looked very French and she was wearing a wide gold cuff on each arm. She was smoking, and looked pale and nervous, but she was undeniably fashionable and very beautiful.

Eugenia called out to her and ran to meet her, wrapped in a towel, with her hair wet, and Eloise grinned broadly and gave her an enormous hug when they collided.

"How was the flight?" her mother asked her, so pleased to see her. They had only seen each other once during the pandemic, and the week together would be a gift. Eloise had been very close to her mother growing up, but had lived in Paris now for eight years, since she had graduated from Parsons, like her mother, and in Eloise's case, she moved to Paris and stayed there. She had been working for Balenciaga designing streetwear and had made a name for herself. She and Eugenia usually saw each other during Paris Fashion Week, but there had been none for almost two years now. Eloise was rail-thin, like a model herself, looked the most similar to her mother of all the children, and was proud of it. She admired her mother and thought she was talented and gorgeous. She was a hard act to follow, particularly since they were in the same field. She wasn't jealous of her mother. Eugenia was her role model.

"I slept the whole way. It's been crazy. I was exhausted," a standard response for Eloise. Her life was constantly high pressure, working for a major luxury brand.

Eugenia showed her to her room, next to her own, and the driver brought up her four bags, and Eugenia already knew that every outfit in them would be black and killer chic and very fashion-forward. Eloise's face clouded immediately as soon as they were alone.

"I think they're going to fire me, Mom," she said, on the

verge of tears. "Business has been terrible in Europe until they started letting Americans into the country again a few weeks ago. Our stores in Asia have been saving us, and keeping us afloat. But they're talking about severe cutbacks, and I'm sure I'll be on that list." Eugenia smiled, looking at her. Eloise was even taller than her mother and a beautiful young woman, despite the anxious expression. Eugenia had heard it all before.

"You've been saying that since they hired you. They need you. They're not going to fire you." Eugenia was sure of it. Fashion was a cutthroat business, but Eloise had a huge talent and her job was secure.

"This time I think they are. I hate the new director of marketing and he hates me. He says my vision isn't global enough, and too traditional."

"They'll probably fire him before they fire you. Can you try to relax for a week?" Eugenia asked her gently, and Eloise nodded hesitantly. She lived on the edge of her nerves, and she was anxious every hour of every day in an extremely stressful job. She paid a high price for her success. She hardly ever had dates, and most of the time, when she did, she canceled them. She worked nights and weekends, smoked a lot, and had no life except work. Eugenia wanted so much more for her than the narrow life she led, but it was hard to pry Eloise out of her office and away from her drawing board and desk. "Are you hungry?" She knew the answer before she said the words. Eloise was never hungry, she was too nervous to eat, and her image of the ideal female body was based on the models she saw every day, who all looked like they were starving. Eloise was as thin and undernourished as they were.

"I ate on the plane," she said, which Eugenia knew was a lie to get her mother off her back. "Who's here?"

"You're the first."

Eloise and Daphne were the closest of the sisters and Eloise couldn't wait to see her next younger sister. "No babies yet?" she asked, smiling.

"Not for another five weeks, unless the twins come early. The poor thing is enormous. She can't wait to see you, she's coming over tonight. The others should all be here by dinnertime."

After she settled in, they went to sit by the pool, with Eloise in a black bikini that showed off her remarkable body. She went to the gym at five in the morning before work every day, and as thin as she was, every inch of her was toned and sleek. She was thirty, and had the body of a twenty-year-old. They were chatting about the current trends, and her mother's experimental line of daywear in the next show, when another SUV pulled up, and a tall, very handsome Black man with broad shoulders and an athlete's build got out. He was strikingly attractive, and Eugenia's youngest daughter, Sofia, got out right behind him. She looked tiny next to him and they were talking and laughing. Sofia was the smallest of the sisters with very dark brown hair, porcelain white skin, and green eyes. She was wearing an army surplus camouflage vest with cutoff jeans and military boots she'd gotten at Goodwill. Her hair was in a braid down her back, as Daphne wore hers. All Eugenia knew about Sofia's date was that he was a doctor where she worked, and he looked far more respectable than she did. He looked like a Ralph Lauren ad.

Eloise and Eugenia walked toward them with welcoming smiles. Sofia's companion was wearing black jeans and a black T-shirt, with loafers. Sofia looked like a runaway teenager he had picked up as a hitchhiker. She was twenty-six years old, and a licensed nurse practitioner and midwife. They both worked at a medical center in Tennessee, which sent teams of personnel into the poorest areas of Appalachia, and Sofia loved her work. Eugenia was impressed that she had brought a man home to her family, knowing he would be the object of the intense scrutiny of her sisters. She had never brought anyone home before, or even said who she was dating. This was a first.

The man turned a wide dazzling smile on Eugenia and Eloise, shook hands with them, and introduced himself as Brad Jackson. Sofia hugged her mother and Eugenia invited them to have a cold drink on the porch before she took them to their house. The two sisters chatted while Brad thanked their mother for the invitation.

"Did everything go all right on the trip?" Eugenia asked them, as they all sat down for a few minutes.

"It was fine, except we had a tornado in the mountains last week, and I wasn't sure we could come. It flattened a lot of the shacks people are living in and caused a bunch of babies to come early, and there were a lot of people injured. We both haven't stopped for a week," Sofia said, and Brad nodded. "Brad is a trauma surgeon and he operates in a first responders' truck sometimes." She clearly admired him, and they exchanged a warm look that touched Eugenia when she saw it. They chatted for a few minutes, discovered that he had trained at NYU, was originally from Chicago, and his father was a cardiac surgeon. Sofia had said that he was thirty-five years old. Eugenia wondered what Brad's family would have thought of Sofia's ragtag outfit and combat boots. But Brad didn't seem to mind.

They were ecstatic when they saw the guesthouse she'd assigned them, and she left them to unpack and settle in. Brad handed Eugenia a large box of French chocolates he had bought at the airport, and she thanked him.

Eloise dropped into her mother's bedroom when she heard her come in.

"Wow, he's a good-looking guy, and more sophisticated than her usual men. He seems nice." Eloise smiled at her mother.

"I like him," Eugenia said quietly. "A hell of a lot more than Geoffrey," she said with a sigh. She hated Geoffrey's pretentiousness; she could never understand how Gloria could stand it.

"Of course, he's educated, intelligent, handsome, nice, and comes from an educated family. What's not to like? They're probably a lot more respectable than we are, even if his father isn't a lord," Eloise said with a grin. "We have to get Sofia some decent clothes to wear."

"Brad doesn't seem to care," her mother commented. And if he loved Sofia for who she was as a person, that was good enough for her.

"Is he coming to the wedding?" Eloise asked.

"I have no idea. I didn't ask her. And she hasn't said," Eugenia responded.

"Let's see how he survives this week," Eloise said with a mischievous expression. "He's brave to come for a vacation with a woman with three sisters."

"They'll be fine," Eugenia said optimistically, and Stefano and Liz arrived as she said it. They'd come in their own car and Liz had more luggage than Eloise, but Eugenia knew that everything she'd brought would be short and

50

tight, either in gold or with rhinestones on it, and cutouts in frightening places, worn with six-inch heels. Liz was a businesswoman and a smart one, but she dressed like a chorus girl. She tried to compensate for what she lacked in taste by overdressing for every occasion, which always made Eloise wince. She was the resident fashion police for all of them, even for her mother. The others didn't care as much. Eloise was a purist about fashion and style, and always said that Liz's wardrobe gave her anxiety. It all had glitter on it. They were going to see a lot of it for the next week.

Stef and Liz loved their little guesthouse.

Everyone gathered on the porch of the main house at the end of the day. Liz and Stef met Brad then, and the two men engaged in conversation immediately. Brad liked every member of the family he had met so far, and they liked him. He was knowledgeable about wines, sports, art, and music, and Sofia looked proud of the man she had brought home. Eugenia could see that she was crazy about him, which was why she had invited him.

They were enjoying a lively conversation when Gloria and Geoff arrived, looking tired and bedraggled from the trip. Geoff complained about the flight, the car service, and the driver before he even greeted anyone. Eugenia had flown them business class and hired a driver to get them to the Hamptons, and he didn't thank her. He had an aura of entitlement that made Eloise's skin crawl, and everyone tried to ignore it for Gloria's sake. Geoff had had to have a Covid test before leaving London and another one at the airport on arrival, and proof of vaccination, which annoyed him and he grumbled about that too.

Brad was very quiet as he listened to Geoff complain, and he watched the family's reaction with interest. Eugenia looked pained, Eloise looked furious, Stefano ignored him, and Sofia rolled her eyes, while Gloria tried to calm him down. Geoff paid no attention to them and Eugenia took him quickly to their guesthouse to drop off their bags and clean up before dinner. The driver carried their bags in and Geoff didn't lift a finger to help, or thank him as the driver set down their bags and left. Gloria always explained his frequent moodiness and outbursts by saying he was tired, like a child. He was incredibly spoiled. He firmly believed that being the son of an earl allowed him to be as rude as he wanted.

"Who was that?" he asked Gloria about Brad, as they changed for dinner.

"My sister Sofia's new boyfriend. He seems nice."

"Is he coming to the wedding?" Geoff asked her.

"I have no idea. Sofia hasn't asked me. Is that a problem?" she asked him directly.

"I don't care. But it might be for my parents. They're not as open-minded as your family."

"My mother won't like that. If he's dating Sofia, he'll be invited," Gloria said firmly. She sounded definite about it, and Geoff shrugged and went to take a shower.

After Geoff and Gloria went to change, Sofia groaned and sounded like a teenager when she asked her mother, "Do I *have* to change for dinner?" Eloise rolled her eyes when she asked the question. "I didn't bring anything fancy."

"You don't need to wear anything fancy," her mother reassured her, "just clean jeans, and maybe something a little less military," she said gently, referring to the knee-high combat boots.

"Come upstairs with me and I'll lend you something," Eloise volunteered.

"I'll look like I'm going to a funeral," Sofia grumbled. "Everything you own is black."

"At least you won't look like you enlisted in the Marines," Eloise shot back at her.

"Never mind. I'll figure it out," Sofia said, and left with Brad. He put an arm around her and gave her a hug and a kiss as they walked back to their cottage. Eugenia smiled as she watched them. They made a nice couple, he was intelligent and pleasant, and Sofia said he was an exceptional doctor.

"I like him so *much more* than Geoff," Eugenia said to Eloise when they were dressing for dinner, and Eloise wandered into her room as her mother was doing her makeup.

"Is Geoff going to be a problem?" Eloise asked her mother.

"I'm not sure. He's a problem about everything."

"I hope Gloria can calm him down and shut him up, or I will. He's so damn rude and so entitled. He doesn't appreciate anything you do for them," Eloise said. They went downstairs to join the others then.

Sofia had miraculously produced a pair of white jeans with torn-out knees from her suitcase, an oversized man's bowling shirt she'd bought at a vintage shop in Nashville, and high-top pink sneakers, which were an improvement over the combat boots. Eloise rolled her eyes again. She was wearing a very pretty black cotton Alaia sundress and black high-heeled sandals that laced up her legs. Eugenia was wearing white jeans herself, with a pink patterned silk Hermès shirt and gold sandals. Gloria was wearing a white skirt and white T-shirt, and Liz was wearing a backless white dress with rhinestone trim and silver high heels. The men all wore white or normal jeans, Stefano with a collared blue shirt, Geoff a blue-striped T-shirt, and Brad a crisp white collared shirt with normal jeans. He didn't seem to mind Sofia's eccentric vintage wardrobe and looked totally besotted with her. They were constantly talking or whispering to each other, smiling and laughing.

They seated themselves at dinner, and everyone seemed relaxed, until Eugenia realized halfway through dinner that Geoff never spoke to anyone. He avoided conversation and appeared to be sulking for some unknown reason. Brad didn't seem to notice, and spoke to Stef and Liz and Eloise all through dinner. No one seemed eager to talk to Geoff.

The meal was delicious. They had local lobster and crab, with a very decent French white wine, and they were all in high spirits and having fun by the time Phillip and Daphne showed up in time for coffee and dessert. Daphne looked enormous in a pretty pale blue cotton dress that somehow made her look even bigger, but lovely, and Phillip was wearing white jeans, a white Hermès shirt, and a blazer, and looked like a grown-up. Everyone was happy to see them. Stefano and the sisters all kissed each other, and no one could ignore the size of the twins.

"Oh my God, you look like you're having triplets, or quadruplets," Eloise said to her favorite sister. Sofia introduced Phillip and Daphne to Brad, and Daphne gave him a warm welcome, as did Phillip. Only Geoff had not spoken to anyone all evening, but the conversation was lively enough to cover it. Eugenia was annoyed by Geoff's lack of effort and communication. He acted as though no one at the table was quite good enough for him, as if they were all beneath him. Gloria made an effort to compensate and spoke to Brad through most of dinner, since she was sitting next to him.

Eloise made a comment to Gloria when they left the dinner table. Of all the siblings, they were the two who got along the least well, and sparks between them were not uncommon. The others were used to it.

"You should tell your fiancé to make a little more effort to be congenial with everyone, for Mom's sake. We're all guests here," she said under her breath. "Brad is a great guy, and it's not fair to Mom or Sofia to ignore him or make him uncomfortable. Geoff needs to act like an adult and talk to all of us. You may be willing to put up with his moods, but that's not how we do things on Mom's time. We're all here to have fun together." She didn't say that Brad was ten times the man Geoff was, and that they all already liked Brad a lot better. At the end of the meal, Geoff had regaled them with boring stories of his family history, how blue his blood was, and how important his grandfather had been, which no one cared about. Brad was a great deal funnier, far more modest, a lot smarter, and nicer to be around. And Sofia had blossomed since she'd been with him. Everyone liked Brad, which Geoff couldn't stand. Geoff hated it when anyone else got the attention or was in the limelight. He acted like a spoiled child, and Gloria indulged him, which Eugenia thought was a grave mistake and gave him bad habits for the future. And it annoyed Eloise that they were about to get stuck with Geoff forever. She couldn't understand how her sister could stand him, and he was a bore on top of it.

Geoff and Gloria went to their guesthouse immediately after dinner, and the others sat around, drinking and talking and laughing until well after midnight, as Eugenia watched them with pleasure. No matter what it cost her to pay for the vacation, this was what life was all about, and worth every penny.

Chapter 3

S tefano and Brad left to play tennis the next morning, and were getting along like old friends after the relaxed evening before. Daphne had gotten them a guest membership at her tennis and golf club. The women hung around after breakfast, making plans. Geoff and Gloria hadn't come to breakfast, still tired and jet-lagged from the trip. Geoff liked to sleep late and liked Gloria to stay with him.

Stefano commented to Brad as they drove to the tennis courts, "I'm sorry my sister's fiancé is such a bore. We're all trying to get used to him. It changes things when one's siblings get married. We've always been very close and we've been lucky with Daphne's husband, Phillip. My sisters have taken a while to get used to Liz, and Geoff is going to be tough, with his bragging and sense of entitlement."

Brad smiled at Stefano and looked relaxed. He liked Stefano, and all the rest of Sofia's family. And the undercurrent of Geoff's snobbishness and subtle racism didn't bother him. "Don't worry, I'm used to it. You can imagine what it was like doing my residency in Tennessee, and now practicing there. But most of the time, the patients I see are really great, and eventually they figure out that whatever color I am, I'm a decent guy and a good doctor and I take good care of them. That's all that matters. There is always going to be a Geoff in every group. It's something you learn to deal with when you're very young."

"You must get tired of it."

Brad shrugged it off, thinking of Sofia.

"Sofia is such a sweet person," he commented. "It's one of the things I love about her, among a lot of others. She's so pure and such a good human being, and she's a fantastic nurse practitioner and midwife. I don't think she has the prejudices that are so common in your world, and even mine. It's too soon to say anything, but we've been dating for a year, and I'm very serious about her. She's so innocent, I want to protect her. I just want you to know that our relationship is a very big deal to me. I want to tell your mother that before we leave."

"Thank you," Stefano said, and smiled at him. "That's good to know. My mother will be happy to hear it. You can't ask for more than that. Phillip is a good guy too. He is wonderful to my sister, which is all a parent can ask. How will your family feel about Sofia?" he asked Brad.

"They'll be shocked," Brad said sincerely. "Your family has been a lot cooler than mine will be. They're very traditional. They expect me to marry one of the Black women I know and have always dated. I always thought I would too, and then Sofia came along. I don't care what color she is, I love her. And I want to marry her one day. I'd rather it be with both families' blessing. I think mine will be okay once they meet her."

"For God's sake, have someone dress her decently before she does. She looks like a homeless person, or like she raided my closet when I was fourteen."

Brad laughed. "I don't care about that. I love her just the way she is. And the people she takes care of don't care either. She's the best midwife at our medical center, and everyone respects her."

Stefano looked pleased to hear it and then smiled at his new friend and possible brother-in-law, one day. He had been far more accepting than his sisters had expected him to be. He wasn't as uptight and conservative as they thought.

"I just want to make one thing clear," Stef said to Brad. "When I get you on the tennis court, I intend to beat the shit out of you. Just because you're new and a guest doesn't

Danielle Steel

mean there's a courtesy pass, when it comes to tennis. So you've been warned." He grinned confidently.

"And I don't care if you are Sofia's brother, I'm going to beat you until you squeal like a little girl. There's no mercy for rich white boys. I'm bigger, taller, stronger, and older than you are, and I'm going to beat the crap out of you." They pulled up at the club then, and they were both smiling. "Is this going to be a war on the courts?" Brad asked Stefano.

"No, a family feud, which is much more savage and more dangerous and a lot more fun. Prepare to die, Dr. Jackson. I intend to win."

They got out of the car, walked into the club, laughing, and headed for the courts, ready to have some fun.

Eloise, Gloria, Geoff, and Sofia drove into the village of East Hampton to go shopping. Eugenia had stayed at the house to talk to the cook and the staff and thought it would be more fun for the young people to be on their own. She was glad that Brad had gone off with Stef, so Stef could get to know him one-on-one. He seemed very serious about Sofia when Eugenia watched them together. Since there was no father around, Eugenia liked the idea of Stefano getting to know him. Sofia was happy with the warm reception Brad had gotten, and didn't seem bothered by Geoff's supercilious attitude. She was more tolerant than her sisters.

Gloria was talking about her wedding all the way into town, and everyone else looked bored. They parked the car, and walked past all the shops of luxury brands, as Gloria continued to talk about the reception, and finally Eloise turned to her, exasperated.

"I am so sick and tired of hearing about your wedding. We haven't seen each other in ages, is that all you can talk about?"

"It's a very important time in our lives," Geoff snapped at Eloise haughtily. "This isn't just any wedding. My father is an earl, or had you forgotten?" Eloise had to force herself not to respond that he never let anyone forget it. Sofia looked like she wanted to crawl under a rock. He was spoiling for a fight, and Eloise was ready to give him one. Geoff had clearly thought he and Gloria were going to arrive and be the stars because of their wedding, and instead Brad had stolen the show, because everyone liked him better. Geoff couldn't stand it. And Gloria seemed torn between soothing her future husband's bruised ego and allying with her family. It was a hard spot to be in, especially with someone as pompous as Geoff.

"Why don't we just all relax for now, and do some shopping?" Sofia said, trying to calm them all down, when Geoff turned to her with an angry look.

"I hope you haven't invited Brad to the wedding. Gloria and I don't even know him, and my parents might be upset."

"My mother is hosting the wedding," Sofia reminded

him. "And there's no reason for your family to be upset. Brad will be my date, which isn't up to them."

"As I recall, your family hasn't contributed a penny," Eloise shot back at him, furious at his intimidating Sofia, who was the meekest and the least aggressive of them all.

"That's none of your business." Geoff snapped at Eloise. "Your sister is lucky to be marrying into a family like ours. People pay for that honor these days. She'll have a title one day thanks to me and my family."

"Our father is a prince, Geoff," Eloise said haughtily, "and he's not much, but he's ten times the man you are. Your family are nothing more than pauper aristocracy with your crumbling estates. They call that white trash here," she said, and walked away and into the Balenciaga store. She wanted to see what merchandise they carried here, and Geoff was left on the sidewalk, speechless with fury, as he turned to Gloria and took it out on her.

"Your family are a bunch of rude savages," he said to his future wife when they were alone. "I'm the groom and I have a say in who comes to our wedding. The final say. I warn you, if that man comes to our wedding, I'll walk out." Gloria knew she couldn't do that to her mother, and Sofia was such a gentle soul that no one ever picked on her. It was an unspoken family rule, which Geoff had just violated by threatening her.

"My mother has the final say about the wedding. Can't you

just let it go?" Gloria asked him. "Sofia is right. Brad is a good guy and he's Sofia's date. Just back off, Geoff." She was tired of the tension and comments, and defending him to her sisters.

"He doesn't belong on our family vacation, none of us know him."

"This is *our* family vacation. You don't get to make the rules." It was as far as Gloria was willing to go, and he wasn't pleased. He expected his future wife to back him unconditionally, and she wasn't.

"This isn't about your parents, it's about you," Gloria said and walked into a bookstore, while he stood fuming outside. He was no match for any of them, but that didn't stop him. Gloria was shaking while she pretended to look at the books. She joined her sisters then to walk into the other high-end stores, and she spoke softly to her younger sister. Geoff was walking around town alone.

"I'm sorry, Sofia. It's just a very different culture in England," Gloria said, making excuses for him.

"No, it's not," Sofia answered. "There are racists everywhere. Geoff has an incredibly narrow point of view. And are you really going to marry a man who thinks like that?" Gloria didn't answer her, and was quiet for the rest of their foray into the village. The shops were terrific, and eventually Eloise and Sofia relaxed, and Sofia found a pair of vintage cowboy boots with graffiti on them that she fell in love with, and they were her size. She bought them, took off her high-top Converse, and put them on, and she was delighted with how they looked with her ragged denim shorts. Eloise smiled when she looked at her. She still dressed like a fourteen-year-old, but their battle with Geoff had brought them closer together. They both felt sorry for Gloria and thought she was making a terrible mistake marrying Geoff, and it seemed sometimes that she was more in love with her wedding than with the groom.

They drove back to the house and sat down to lunch together, except for Geoff, who said he had a headache, went to their cottage, and did not emerge for the rest of the afternoon. Gloria stayed with her sisters for a while and then went to check on Geoff.

Eugenia looked at Eloise and Sofia. "Did something happen in town?" she asked, concerned.

"Just Geoff being Geoff," Eloise said, helping herself to a fabulous-looking salad prepared by the chef. "Gloria is crazy to marry him. He's pompous, arrogant, entitled, and a racist."

"But she's going to marry him," her mother said in a neutral tone, to mask her disappointment. "We have to make our peace with it." She agreed with Eloise and couldn't understand what Gloria saw in Geoff. He was insufferable, and she'd end up supporting him, or her mother would. He didn't have a job, except an occasional freelance editing assignment. Eugenia didn't believe he could write. She knew that Gloria was paying for everything on her meager salary. Eugenia was paying the rest, and she couldn't afford to do that forever. They would have to support themselves if her business failed. She was planning to explain that to Gloria before they went back to London. Her theory had always been that if you were old enough to marry, you should be old enough to support yourself, and your spouse should contribute, not your mother. If they had a baby, they wouldn't be able to support it either, since they couldn't support themselves without her help. Gloria was twenty-seven and Geoff was thirty-three, and had never had a job he could live on. He had been living with his parents when he met Gloria, and had quickly moved in with her.

Gloria had a long history of poor choices in the men she went out with, which worried Eugenia considerably. This time was no different. Eugenia had somehow gotten maneuvered into the big wedding that Geoff and Gloria wanted, and it had grown exponentially into an unmanageable beast. His father being a penniless earl didn't warrant it, in Eugenia's opinion. Geoff was incredibly entitled and so was Gloria on his behalf. But it would all be over in four weeks and the deed would be done. Eugenia wasn't looking forward to it and neither were Gloria's siblings.

When Brad and Stefano appeared in time for lunch, each one was claiming moral victory, but the actual score had been a tie, twice, and they were planning to go back to the club the next day for the final match. They were in great spirits and ate a hearty lunch, and then everyone lay by the pool all afternoon. The weather was gorgeous. They swam and dozed in the sun. Geoff never reappeared but Gloria joined them halfway through the afternoon and said he was asleep. Daphne showed up for a visit with Tucker. Stef took him in the pool and helped him paddle around. Eugenia was in heaven, with all five of her children and her only grandchild around her, which was the whole point of the vacation. Brad was a welcome addition, and he managed to convey his message to Eugenia that his intentions were honorable toward her daughter. They had a few minutes alone after lunch when he told her, and she said she was pleased to hear it and thanked him. She asked him the same question Stef had, about how his parents would feel about it, and he said that they would adjust in time, because Sofia was so wonderful no one could resist her, which touched Eugenia's heart. He seemed like a very direct, honest guy.

Everyone was relaxed and happy by the end of the afternoon. It was the night of Daphne and Phillip's dinner party with some of their friends and neighbors, who were a pretty important group of hard hitters and well-known, successful people. Eugenia was touched that Phillip and Daphne had planned the evening for them. Eloise asked her mother what she was going to wear, and Eugenia said a simple white Hermès summer dress she'd bought before the pandemic and never had a chance to wear.

Eloise looked at Sofia then. "Let me lend you a dress," she said, pleading with her, and Sofia grinned.

"I was going to wear cutoffs and combat boots. That should be okay, don't you think?" Eloise groaned, and Sofia laughed, teasing her. "Okay, you can lend me a dress, but nothing too fancy."

"I promise," Eloise said, relieved. Sofia was a beautiful girl, she just didn't care what she wore. She had better things to do, and Eloise respected that. But she wanted to see her looking really pretty and well dressed, just once. The dress would be black of course, since it was all Eloise had with her, and all she owned. Whatever Liz wore would inevitably have gold or rhinestones or glitter on it, but Eloise was feeling benevolent about her. She was smart, and a decent person, and she loved Eloise's brother, so her flashy taste and penchant for stilettos and rhinestones could be forgiven. The one who couldn't be forgiven was Geoff, who had managed to alienate the entire group with his high-handed attitude. But they all promised Eugenia that they would behave at Daphne's party that night, no matter what Geoff said or did. They didn't want to upset Daphne or Phillip, and they were all curious about what the party would be like. Daphne had gone to check the last details with the caterer, and they were invited for eight o'clock.

They went to the party in two cars and arrived punctually. Eugenia saw to it that Geoff and Brad did not go in the same car, which suited them both and kept tension to a minimum. The difference in their manners and personalities was even more of a problem than a question of race. When they got to Daphne's house, they were amazed by the trouble she had gone to. There were four tables for eight on the patio, with a view of the pool all lit up, and extensive grounds and flowerbeds around them. There were lanterns strung up which shed a soft light on the tables, candles and flowers on all the tables, and candles floating on the pool like lilies. And everyone was relaxed and happy as the evening began.

The guests arrived promptly, handsomely dressed men in blazers and white pants, and women in cocktail dresses. Daphne was wearing a white and gold brocade tent which encompassed her enormous girth, and her husband looked proud of her. And Sofia looked lovely in the dress Eloise had loaned her. It was a simple black strapless column that showed off her flawless figure and bare shoulders, and Sofia admitted she liked it a lot. Eloise told her she could keep it, if she promised not to wear combat boots with it when Eloise wasn't around.

The group mingled until nine o'clock, and Eugenia

noticed that a number of women were wearing her cocktail dresses. She enjoyed talking to Daphne's friends, and before they sat down to dinner, a very attractive man came over to compliment her.

"You have a lovely family," he said kindly. She guessed him to be a little older than she was. In fact, he was sixty, and his name was Patrick Hughes, which rang a bell but she couldn't remember why. He was very soft-spoken and understated, in white jeans, a white shirt, and a well-cut blazer. He had short gray hair, and an air of quiet confidence about him. She could tell from experience that he was an important man. They talked about the fashion business for a few minutes, and he said he knew very little about it. He said he was in commercial real estate, which sounded innocuous to her. The only guests Eugenia hadn't met and didn't want to were a flashy couple that someone had brought as their houseguests. They looked pure Vegas. He was wearing a white western-style shirt and white jeans with white alligator boots, a Stetson, and a diamond rope around his neck. His wife was Russian, in her very early twenties. She was covered in expensive jewelry and wearing a skintight minidress that barely covered her, and carried a white mink wrap she didn't need but wanted to show off. She was wearing silver platform sandals with six-inch heels that Liz would have worn in a minute. She was a strikingly beautiful girl who looked like he had rented her for the evening, but she was his wife. All the other women looked at her with thinly veiled disapproval, and stood closer to their husbands. As it turned out, she was twenty-two and he was sixty-five.

Eugenia and Patrick were amused by her. "I don't know who he is, but I can tell you she's not one of my clients. I've never made a skirt that short," she said, and he laughed.

"I can tell you who he is. Austin Wylie, a very big-deal Texas oilman, whose multibillion-dollar fortune supposedly comes entirely from oil, but I have my doubts about that."

"Really? That sounds intriguing," Eugenia said with a smile.

"He's made some very big deals," and as he said it, the oilman himself approached Eugenia and asked to speak to her alone. Patrick Hughes looked amused and slipped away discreetly. Eugenia was shocked that Austin Wylie wanted to speak to her, and she noticed that Geoffrey, her future son-in-law, was deep in conversation with Wylie's wife, and standing very close to her. She seemed to be enjoying his company, more than anyone else would have.

"This isn't the place to talk," Austin Wylie said to Eugenia in a low voice. "My wife is looking for a company to invest in. She was very excited to meet you tonight. She loves your clothes. I'm wondering if you would be open to having a conversation with me about it, at another time. Just to hear what I have in mind. We have to keep our women happy," he said with a dazzling smile, as she tried not to stare at the diamond rope around his neck. He was a good-looking man with a masculine craggy face, but his accessories reminded her of Liberace. "Would you be willing to give me your number? I'd like to call you and have a serious conversation. Just the two of us, not Natasha of course." Eugenia didn't know what to say, but it suddenly occurred to her that he might be the answer to her prayers, if he was looking for an investment to amuse his wife. Eugenia couldn't imagine a collaboration with her, given how she was dressed. But as a silent partner in her business, anything was possible right now. She was desperate, and Austin Wylie's money was as good as anyone else's, maybe better. They weren't distinguished or elegant, but he obviously was worth a fortune, which Patrick Hughes had confirmed.

"Of course," she said, still taken aback by his interest and direct inquiry. He handed her two of his business cards then and a gold pen, and asked her to put her number on the back of the second one.

"I'll call you," he assured her, as she handed him the card back with her number on it. "Soon," he said, and walked across the patio to rescue his wife from Geoff. He was practically salivating standing next to her as she thrust her breasts toward him, and they were almost touching. She saw that Gloria had noticed it too and didn't look pleased. The couple left the party a few minutes later, having only come for cocktails with their weekend hosts, since Daphne hadn't had room for two more guests at dinner, when they asked her. She rushed over to her mother then.

"I'm sorry, Mom, was that man hitting on you? We don't know them. They're houseguests of people we hardly know."

"He wasn't hitting on me, it was just business. Apparently his wife loves my clothes."

"What does she do, cut them off to make them crotch-length?" Daphne commented.

"The dress she's wearing is actually Chanel couture," her mother informed her. "I recognize it. It's a tunic meant to be worn with see-through pants. She forgot the pants, though," Eugenia said, looking amused.

"She's young enough to be his granddaughter, and she looks cheap," Daphne said with disapproval.

"True," Eugenia agreed with her, but beggars couldn't be choosers, and she was rapidly becoming a beggar. If Austin Wylie wanted to invest in Eugenia Ward, or Princess Eugenie, or both, she wanted to hear what he had to say, if he called her. She wondered if he would.

"I sat you next to one of Phillip's good friends tonight. He's an incredibly nice man. He's had some tough times in the pandemic," Daphne said, and then hurried off to speak to the caterers and tell them it was time to sit down. It was nine-thirty, and a few minutes later Eugenia found herself seated next to Patrick Hughes, who seemed happy to see her. The man on her other side was a neighbor of Daphne and Phillip's whom Eugenia had met before, so she guessed that Phillip's good friend who had had a hard time in the pandemic was Patrick, and they had that in common, although she didn't say so.

"What did Wylie want, if it's not indiscreet to ask? I saw him hand you his card."

"He says he's looking for an investment for his wife, and she loves my clothes," Eugenia said simply, and Patrick nodded.

"I don't know if you're looking for investors, and there's certainly plenty of money there. I'd just be very careful. I've always had an odd feeling about where his money comes from. I don't know him well, but his name comes up from time to time on proposals I see. He tried to buy a commercial building from me a few years ago, and the deal fell through when we wanted more detailed information from him, as part of our due diligence. He vanished, which seemed smoky to me. It was a prime piece of real estate and he didn't care about the price, he agreed to it immediately. He's certainly in the big leagues," Patrick commented.

They talked about other things then, art and travel, and

Europe. He seemed like a very straightforward, low-key person and she enjoyed talking to him. They were both sorry when the dinner ended and they got up from the table.

"I don't want to interfere with your plans, but I wonder if you and your family would like to spend a day sailing with me. I have a boat here, and I'd love to have you all on board. We've got all the water toys to keep everyone happy for a day sail." The invitation seemed warm and genuine.

"We're a big group, there are ten of us."

"The more the merrier. I'm very fond of Daphne and Phillip, and the others seem just as much fun and just as charming." It was a very appealing invitation, and she cautiously agreed. "How would tomorrow be, if the weather cooperates? It's supposed to be a nice day, with a light wind, and if not we can motor, throw anchor for lunch in a cove somewhere, and swim, water-ski, whatever they want to do."

"That sounds irresistible," she said with a smile, and he looked delighted.

"I'll work out the details with Daphne. I'll send a van for you with one of my crew. The yacht club is very near here," he said, and a few minutes later he left, and Daphne mentioned the plan to her before they went back to their house.

"That was sweet of Patrick to invite us on the boat," she said.

"Is it safe for you?" her mother asked her.

"As long as I don't fall overboard." Daphne laughed, and the family left in the two cars they had come in, Eugenia and Eloise with Gloria and Geoff in one, and Sofia and Brad, Stefano and Liz in the other. Eugenia told her group about the invitation on the way home.

"I can't go, I get seasick looking at boats," Geoff said immediately.

"I thought the British were first-class sailors," Eugenia teased him a little.

"My ancestors were generals, not admirals. There is some belief that the Duke of Wellington is a distant relative. I'd rather stay home and read by the pool," he said coolly.

"I'll stay home with you," Gloria volunteered immediately.

"You don't need to. I can fend for myself for a day. I can go to the beach and take a walk, or stay here. Have fun with your family. It will be a nice change for you," and a relief for them if he didn't go.

Eugenia was just as happy he wasn't coming, but she would be sorry if Gloria wasn't there to enjoy it. They were still debating it when they got out of the car and headed to their house.

"I hope he doesn't come," Eloise whispered to her mother as they walked into the main house.

"Me too," she whispered back. "It's too bad for Gloria if she doesn't come."

"It's her choice, Mom," Eloise reminded her.

"It was a lovely evening, wasn't it? Daphne did a beautiful job putting it together."

"Who was that weird guy I saw you talking to, with the diamond necklace and the white croc boots and cowboy hat, with the woman who looked like a hooker? She had an accent."

"He's a Texan named Austin Wylie. The woman is his wife, she's Russian."

"They stood out like overdecorated Christmas trees," Eloise said wryly. "And who's the guy with the boat? He looked nice, if he was the man sitting next to you at dinner."

"He's a friend of Phillip's. It was kind of him to invite us." Eugenia had enjoyed talking to Patrick, he was very personable and easy.

"I hope the boat is big enough for all of us," Eloise said, kissing her mother, and headed to her room to watch a movie in bed. It helped her fall asleep at night.

"We'll see tomorrow," Eugenia said, thinking of Austin Wylie, and wondering if he would call her about the investment. If he did, it was really the answer to her prayers. She was still thinking about it when she fell asleep. She didn't care how weird the couple looked, she needed his money.

Chapter 4

They were all at breakfast the next morning when Austin Wylie called Eugenia on her cell, and she left the table to speak to him. She walked out to the porch and sat down in the swing.

"Good morning, I'm sorry to call you so early, but I wanted to catch you before you got busy. As I said last night, I'd like to meet with you. Would you have any free time today?" He was certainly eager, which was encouraging. For an instant, she thought about not going on the boat, but decided to stick with the plan. Austin Wylie could wait another day, if his interest was real.

"I'm sorry, we're going out for a day sail, and I don't know when we'll get back. Does tomorrow work for you?"

"Of course. What time is best for you?" he asked her, and

they agreed to meet in the morning at eleven. The house was big enough for her to have a meeting without being disturbed by the others, and having him wait a day wouldn't do any harm. "Enjoy your sail. See you tomorrow," he said, sounding cheerful. It really did appear that he was seriously looking for an investment for his wife. But he wanted to discuss the business end with Eugenia first. She wondered how big an investment he wanted to make and what he wanted in exchange, how big a percentage of her business. She didn't want to give up majority ownership, and hoped that wasn't what he was after.

When she got back to the breakfast table, the others had finished, and were chatting over coffee. Geoff preferred breakfast in bed and Gloria had taken it to him.

"Are you coming with us?" Eloise asked her, when Gloria came back from delivering Geoff's breakfast to him.

"Geoff says I should go without him," she said hesitantly.

"You should do what you want to do, not what he tells you to do. That's a bad habit to get into," Eloise said, and Gloria gave her an evil look. Geoff was making things hard enough without Eloise adding to it by criticizing him. Geoff could never tolerate criticism.

"Says the woman who hasn't had a relationship since college," Gloria responded, while Eloise rolled her eyes and picked up *The New York Times*.

"What's the name of the guy hosting us today?" Stefano asked his mother, and she told him, and Stef looked pensive.

"Oh my God!" Liz said and stared at them both. "That's whose boat we're going on? I read an article about him in *The Wall Street Journal* a week ago." Liz was the CFO of a very successful startup that had just gone public, and she had equity in the company. She didn't know how to dress but she was smart about money, respected in business, and well-informed. "He's the biggest commercial real estate developer in New York. He owns seventeen of the biggest, most prestigious commercial buildings in the city." She listed a few, and they had heard of them. "He owns them, but with all the big corporations working remotely and not ready to go back yet, his buildings are standing empty. He's worth billions, and his whole net worth is going down the tubes. His seventeen fancy buildings are ghost towns."

"Daphne said he'd had a tough time in the pandemic," Eugenia commented.

"We'd better enjoy his boat today. He won't have it for much longer. He's going to start selling some of the buildings soon, at a significant loss, but he can't hang on to them any longer. Someone will buy them for next to nothing. He's got a plane, a boat, and houses all over the place. But those seventeen empty commercial buildings are killing him." Eugenia felt sorry for him as she listened to her daughter-in-law. She was in the same situation he was, on a smaller scale, and he must have been even more worried than she was. She needed a lot less money than he did to get her out of the hole. "Actually this isn't the right time to sell, but it will be a great time to buy when the market hits rock bottom. I don't think we're quite there yet."

"I won't mention that to him today," Eugenia said with a pained look.

They got their things together shortly after that, and Gloria decided to go with them. Geoff had given her permission. He said he was going to lie by the pool all day and didn't want to deprive Gloria of a fun outing, which Gloria thought was generous of him.

They were all ready when Patrick's crew member arrived in a van. He was wearing a crisp white uniform, and they piled in, feeling like kids going on a picnic.

He drove them to Gurney's Star Island Resort and Marina in Montauk and stopped at the end of the pier. There was no boat moored there, just a speedboat big enough for all of them, with two crew members waiting to assist them. Patrick Hughes's yacht was too big to dock, and was at anchor just outside the port. The boat looked huge from where they stood.

"I'm sorry," the chief purser apologized to them. "They don't have a berth deep enough for us, so we anchor out.

It'll only take a minute to get there." They glanced in the direction he had indicated vaguely with a wave and if they had understood him correctly, it looked like a cruise ship sitting just outside the port. It was a three-hundred-and-fifty-foot motor sailer. The biggest boat the marina could accommodate was two hundred and twenty feet.

"Oh my God, is that the boat?" Liz asked, shocked. She had never seen a yacht of similar size before. Eugenia had been on a few in Umberto's days of glory when he was connecting people and earning commissions from them. But this was undoubtedly the largest. "No wonder he's going broke," Liz said under her breath to her mother-in-law as they left the dock and headed to the yacht on the horizon. The crew members on it looked tiny in the distance, and grew to normal size as the speedboat approached. There were six decks and an elaborate sail system. The chief purser had just told Brad that there were sixty crew members on board, in answer to his question. It was one of the largest sailboats in the world. It looked like a floating city to Eugenia, or an ocean liner. But as they came up alongside it, she could see its beautiful sleek lines. They pulled up behind, and entered an area below decks where all the toys were kept: jet skis, a one-man sailboat, even a small submarine, and every kind of water toy you could imagine. It made her sad to think that Patrick Hughes might have to sell all of it, if what Liz said was true. He must have loved the boat to have such a splendid one. And he had seemed so unassuming when they spoke the night before, and his invitation had sounded so genuine and simple. This was going to be the highlight of their vacation. They stepped out of the motorboat with the crew helping, walked into an elevator, and rode to the upper deck, where Patrick was waiting for them in white shorts and a T-shirt. He looked very fit, with a full mane of salt-and-pepper hair and electric blue eyes, and he smiled at Eugenia when he saw her.

"Welcome aboard," he said to her, and then to all of them. "We're going to pull up anchor in a minute. You're welcome to watch from the wheelhouse when we set the sails, or you can just relax on deck with a mimosa or a margarita." A stewardess was taking their drink orders.

They had all left their shoes on the lower deck when they came aboard, and despite the luxurious boat, the atmosphere Patrick created was easy and informal. They followed him into the wheelhouse as they left the port and headed out to sea so they could catch enough wind to sail.

Eugenia joined the others in the wheelhouse, which looked like the cockpit of an airplane, with dials and meters and state-of-the-art digital equipment. He introduced them all to the captain, who was from New Zealand. Most of the crew were British or Australian. It was an incredible experience just being there and watching the proceedings. Patrick came to stand next to Eugenia when they were well on their way. There was a good breeze and the captain said it was a fine day for sailing. They went back to the outer deck then and sat on the comfortable cushioned benches, enjoying the sea air, while uniformed stewards and stewardesses served their drinks.

"Would you like a tour?" Patrick offered Eugenia, and she nodded. It was a unique experience as he led her down to the next deck with two enormous living rooms and a movie theater. There was a piano, which he said he played occasionally. The dining rooms were on the next deck down. There was an indoor one and an outdoor one, an enormous galley, and the crew dining room.

Just below that was Patrick's master suite, which was informal and inviting, with big leather chairs and couches. The entire boat was equipped with an amazing sound system and contemporary art from Patrick's collection. He had an office, a dressing room, his own gym. Everything about the décor was personal and told you something about him. Eugenia noticed several photographs of him with a young man who looked strikingly like him.

"My son, Quinn," he said proudly when he saw her looking at one of them. "He has his own startup, engaged in food delivery in eleven cities. He's a bright boy. He doesn't want advice from me, and he's doing fine on his own." It touched her to see how proud he was of his son. He said Quinn was his only child when Eugenia asked if he had others.

"I'm not as lucky as you, with five." He smiled at her.

On the deck below were five spectacular guest suites, each with its own marble bathroom. Below that were things like massage rooms for the guests, a hair salon, and the movie theater. The designers had thought of everything, and so had Patrick, including an area for a helicopter to land on the top deck. Being there was like a dream. They walked back up the stairs and in every hallway and on every landing was the art he loved, much of it by famous artists. He lived in a rarefied world, and Eugenia couldn't help wondering how much he would lose if he lost everything. Her heart went out to him, knowing the pain he must be in, if he felt anything like she did about her business. And he had so much more to lose. He didn't look panicked or depressed, though. He seemed relaxed as he took her around the boat, and everywhere she looked, she was struck by how beautiful it was. They stopped at the deck where his stateroom was, and stood at the rail, looking out over the water, as the yacht continued to slice through the small waves, heading toward their destination.

"The pandemic has taught me a lot," he said softly. "You

learn a lot of lessons when things are difficult. I was always looking ahead to the future, and never thinking about today. Now I enjoy every minute that I have. And I've stopped worrying so much about tomorrow. I love this boat, but if I lose it, I will have been lucky to have had it at all. And one day, I'll have another one, if it's meant to be. I always had to have the biggest and the best, but I could probably be happy with a sailboat I could sail myself. I don't want to waste today, worrying about tomorrow. The future takes care of itself somehow. Better than you think it will. You've probably heard that I have seventeen big office buildings standing empty in New York. I'm probably the poorest rich man in the world, or the richest pauper. One way or another I'll figure it out. Maybe I'll have ten buildings when it's over, or two or five. Whatever happens, I know I'll get through it." There was a wonderful sense of calm about him. He wasn't frightened or frantic or panicked, as he might have been. He had a quiet self-confidence that reassured her. She liked just being there and talking to him.

"The pandemic hit me hard too," she said just as softly. "I design evening gowns. I was proud of the business I built for fourteen years. And then, from one day to the next, no one was wearing evening gowns, and everything stopped. My ship has been sinking for two years. I'm not sure if I'm going to hit bottom, or if I can pull it up again, or do something completely different. That's why I wanted to talk to Austin Wylie. If he can give me enough money to hang on, maybe I'll make it and I won't lose my business."

"The theory is good," Patrick said, frowning. He looked deep into her eyes and liked what he saw there. "Just be careful with him. I don't trust him, and my instincts are pretty good. Except about commercial office buildings. I guessed wrong on that one." He smiled at her, not hiding the truth from her. "I overstocked. Who knew that offices would become obsolete? Maybe they'll come back, or maybe they won't, or they'll change. I've got nearly fifteen hundred floors of empty office space. I have to figure out what to do with it. That's a lot of vacant space." She loved how calm he was, and how peaceful, even in the midst of what was a crisis for him.

"Me too. I have to figure out what to do now. I don't think evening gowns are going to make a comeback for a while. I need to broaden my horizons and figure out what to do in the meantime. Maybe evening gowns are obsolete too. Maybe forever."

"You can design anything, Eugenia. I've heard of your brand. You've got the talent and the taste, the experience and the training. You can apply it to anything you want. They have buildings in Chicago that are combined office buildings and hotels, apartment complexes and stores, all piled on top of each other, so people don't have to go out in bad weather. They don't do that in New York. Maybe that's what I need to start. I'm thinking about it." The idea sounded fascinating to Eugenia, and what he had said about her business did too. He made it sound as though it wasn't dead, it was just sleeping. And she had to figure out how to wake it up.

"I've designed a line of easy daywear that I'm going to show at Fashion Week in New York. That might be a new direction for me. We'll see how it goes." She still didn't know if it would be profitable or not.

"You'll figure out what to do," he said confidently. "And if you want any advice from a guy with seventeen empty office buildings, give me a call. Maybe we can help each other." He liked that idea and so did she, although she didn't see how he could help, and he was in trouble too.

"I'm meeting Austin Wylie tomorrow," she said.

"Two words. Be careful. Don't be greedy and don't panic. He's not the last train out of the station. That's when we make mistakes. There's always another train, or a boat, or a truck, or a scooter. You won't get left behind. Neither will I. We just aren't that kind of people. We're winners, both of us. Don't forget that. I have faith in you," he said, and she believed him, and he didn't even know her. "I have good instincts. I'll bet you do too. You built a big business for yourself. Your talent didn't go away in the pandemic. Things are dormant right now. They won't be forever. And when it's time to wake up, you'll be there on the ground, ready and waiting to get moving again, with the right idea at the right time. I'd stake my life on it. You just have to be brave enough to try something new." He thought of something else then. "Do your kids know you're struggling?" She shook her head with a rueful look. "I figured. You seem like a courageous woman, Eugenia."

"I don't want to scare them."

"What about how scared you are? Who's there for you?"

"Me. I've found that that's usually the right answer. I've never had anyone I could rely on except myself."

"That's a tough place to be. Call me if you need me, if I can help, or even if you just want to talk," Patrick said gently, and she could see he meant it.

"Thank you." Eugenia had tears in her eyes when she said it.

"My son does know, by the way, because there's no way you can hide the seventeen biggest empty office buildings in New York." He smiled ruefully.

"And who do you rely on?" she asked him.

"Me. Just like you do. That's a lonely place. Maybe we can help each other out. If you want to. You're doing fine on your own, but I'm happy to help if I can."

"Thank you," she whispered, and he took her hand and they walked up the stairs to find the others. She wondered now if the answer to her prayers wasn't Austin Wylie. Maybe it was Patrick.

"Where've you been?" Stefano asked her when they came back on deck.

"I gave your mom my personal tour. The purser will give all of you a tour, if you'd like." They said they would, and ten minutes later, they took off to explore the boat and left Patrick and Eugenia alone on deck. The yacht was slowly headed back toward shore to a protected cove where they would have lunch. Patrick had planned the route and the day for them. He wanted them to have fun, especially now that he knew Eugenia better. She needed some fun and good times to balance the bad ones. He could guess what a strain the last year and a half had been while she struggled with her business, with no one to help or advise her. He could at least do that for her now, even if they were only friends. He could sense that she was a brave woman and he wanted to help her.

They reached the cove he had chosen for lunch, just as the others returned from their tour. The chef had set out a sumptuous buffet on the dining deck, and it looked delicious as Patrick led them to their seats. They sat down at a table immaculately set with linens, crystal, and china with the boat's name on it, *My Dream*. It said everything about how he felt about the boat. And it was quite a dream for any man to have.

"I dream big," he said to Eugenia in a whisper as he leaned over to talk to her.

"I noticed," she whispered back, and he laughed. He was a big man with a big life and a massive business, and his problems were commensurate. Her own problems seemed like nothing compared to his, but they were big to her and had nearly drowned her.

Patrick had spoken to all of them by the end of the day, and the crew took out the water toys for everyone after lunch. The young men took off on the jet skis, including Phillip, and Eugenia's daughters and Liz floated around on the inflatable rafts and swam with each other. Daphne was in a big pink inner tube and loved it. They all had a fantastic time, and it was a day they wouldn't soon forget. Patrick had enjoyed it too. He liked Eugenia and her family even more than he had expected to. They were lovely young people with good values and bright minds, and he could see how much they all loved each other.

"You make me wish I'd had more children," he said to her as they motored close to the port in the late afternoon. They were all sorry to see the day end. "I wasn't married to Quinn's mother for very long," he said to Eugenia as they stood at the rail a little distance from the others. "Five years, which felt like a lifetime then. I was ambitious and all I cared about was building my business. My father was like that too. He took a small fortune he'd inherited and turned it into a large one. Business was all he cared about. And I was even better at it than he was, I took bigger risks. I grew up in Chicago, went to Northwestern, then business school at Berkeley, and I never stopped after that. I hardly knew my father. It was the only way I knew. Quinn's mother got pregnant so I married her, but I never opened my heart to her. I resented having married her. I was twenty-five, in business school at Berkeley, when we married and Quinn was born. He's thirty-five now. I was thirty when we got divorced. At his age, I was divorced with a ten-year-old I rarely saw. I was too 'busy.' I was pretty wild for a while, a long while. I had a lot of fun, and I didn't want to get tied down again. I hated our marriage, I felt trapped. I was too immature to be married and she was the wrong person for me. I'm not sure when I settled down. Maybe ten years ago when I turned fifty. Men are immature for a lot longer than women. I really only got to know Quinn when he was about twenty-five. We took some trips together, to Africa, India, and we did some Atlantic crossings on the boat, to Europe. And suddenly we had time to talk, and we had things to say to each other. I was a lousy father until then, but he gave me another chance, and it paid off, for both of us. We're close now, but he's like I was at his age. He doesn't want to get tied down, he wants to nail down his success first. That's a dangerous game. You can stay at the party for too long, and then you wind up alone. He can't imagine it at his age, but that's what happens. Business is a fickle mistress and it's not enough for the long haul. That's what I figured out at sixty, and here I am, with all of this and no one to share it with, and I may lose it all." Patrick was matter-of-fact and realistic. He wasn't sorry for himself, but he was aware of what he had done, and the mistakes he had made, and willing to admit it.

"I filled the void with my kids," Eugenia admitted to him. "And then they grew up, and I discovered the same thing you did. I'm alone. Kids are fickle too, and once they have partners, there's very little room for you in their lives, and you don't belong there anyway. You need your own life, but I never had time to make a life for myself. I was always working. And what happens now, if the business goes down the drain?" she asked, looking at him. There was no artifice about either of them. They were honest with each other and themselves, they were brave people and the time was right for both of them. They had been stripped of all the distractions and the accessories, and they had bared their souls to each other.

"If you lose the business, Eugenia, you'll start another one. That's what people like us do. I'm not going to retire, and neither are you. Would you go sailing with me again?" he asked her.

"I'd love to."

"Maybe alone next time. I loved getting to know your kids today. And I love talking to you. How does Wednesday sound to you? Is that too soon? I have to go into the city tomorrow for a meeting, and on Wednesday you could tell me how the meeting went with Wylie."

"That sounds great to me," she said. She liked the idea of being alone with him too, if sixty crew members didn't count, but they were discreet, and disappeared after they served him.

"I'll have one of the boys pick you up at ten again. Maybe you'd like to stay for dinner on Wednesday?" he said cautiously. He didn't want to scare her off, but he didn't want to waste time either. He had a powerful feeling about her.

"I'd like that," she said, and they left the boat a few minutes later and she thanked him profusely for a fantastic day. They were all pleasantly tired after the sun and air, and all the physical activity, and as they got into the boat to take them to the shore, Eugenia looked up and saw Patrick watching her from an upper deck. He waved and she waved back with a smile. She had something to look forward to now. Separate from her business. And she had the meeting with Austin Wylie the next day. She was on her guard after what Patrick had said about him.

They were all quiet and relaxed on the way back to the house. And just as their van turned into the driveway, a red sports car raced past them, coming from the house at full speed. A woman was driving, wearing a big sun hat and dark glasses. She sped by, nearly scraping the side of the van, turned onto the road, and took off. Geoff was standing in the driveway when the van pulled in and they got out, and Eugenia thanked the purser for driving them home.

"Who was that?" Eugenia asked Geoff, puzzled about the red car that had just passed them.

"I have no idea," he said innocently. "She drove in, took one look at me, turned around and left. She either made a mistake on the address or was looking for the owners. She never stopped to talk to me. I must not have been her type," he said, and laughed as he put an arm around Gloria's shoulders and kissed her. "Did you have fun?" he asked her, ignoring the others, and they walked back to their cottage so Gloria could change for dinner. Eugenia watched them go, and then walked back to the main house, thinking about the day on the boat, and Patrick. He seemed like a very special person, and she was happy to have met him, thanks to Daphne. But she had something else on her mind and it was gnawing at her.

Eugenia waited until Eloise went upstairs to shower and change, then walked out to the kitchen where the two maids were helping the chef with dinner and setting the table. She took one of them aside, the chattier of the two, and asked her a question out of earshot of the others. She was curious more than suspicious, but she wanted to know.

"Was there a woman here today, visiting our guest?" The maid hesitated, avoiding Eugenia's gaze, and then looked at her, not sure what to say. Eugenia was paying her for the week they were there and the worker seemed like a nice woman. She liked the family and hoped they would come back again. "I won't tell anyone what you tell me, but I'd like to know," Eugenia said seriously, and the woman nodded.

"He paid us each fifty dollars not to tell anyone. But yes, there was a woman here. She had an accent, Russian or French or German or something. She was here all day, she just left two minutes before you got home." It was obviously the woman driving the red sports car, in the hat and dark glasses, and with the comment about her accent, Eugenia had a powerful feeling that it was Natasha Wylie, which created a whole new dilemma for her of whether or not to tell Gloria about it. She deserved to know before she married Geoff that he was cheating on her, if he was. Eugenia couldn't believe that they had spent the day together and hadn't had sex. Geoff was a whole lot closer to Natasha's age than Austin Wylie, and better looking. But Austin was richer, which counted for a lot for a girl off the streets of Moscow, looking for rich men in America. Geoff would only have been a bit of fun for her.

Eugenia thanked the woman who had told her, promised again that she wouldn't give her away, and walked slowly upstairs to her bedroom. She had no idea how or when she would tell Gloria, or if Gloria would even believe her or would think Eugenia was lying so she wouldn't marry him. But whether Gloria believed it or not, she had to know. And Eugenia had to tell her. The burdens of motherhood weighed heavily on her shoulders. In a way, her daughter's future was in her hands. It was an awesome responsibility and the hardest job in the world.

Chapter 5

The next morning, after their fabulous day sailing on Patrick's extraordinary boat, Austin Wylie appeared at the house, driving a black Ferrari. He stepped out of the car wearing white leather pants, a black shirt open to the waist, and black alligator cowboy boots, and put a black Stetson on his head as he got out.

"Who on earth is that, Mom?" Eloise asked Eugenia, watching from the kitchen window, and then she recognized him. "Oh my God, it's the Texan from Daphne's dinner party, the guy with the Russian wife. What's he doing here?" He looked out of place but supremely confident as he walked up the front steps onto the porch and rang the bell.

"I have a meeting with him," was all Eugenia said as she grabbed her phone from the kitchen table and hurried to the front door, while the others continued eating breakfast and paid no attention.

Eugenia greeted Austin Wylie and invited him into the smaller living room. She noticed that he was wearing a different diamond chain around his neck and a pavé diamond belt buckle, which she assumed correctly was real, and when he took off his Stetson, he had a shaved head. It somehow looked right with the rest of his image. He looked like the caricature of a man with a multibillion-dollar fortune who was proud of it and wanted everyone to know. He was sending a very clear message.

"Thank you for meeting with me this morning, Eugenie," he said politely, and she didn't correct him on her name. She could guess that his wife had given him the name that was on the label of her haute couture gowns, a modification of her actual name, and slightly different from her eponymous ready-to-wear line, Eugenia Ward.

"I was interested to hear what you're thinking," she said calmly, with a businesslike smile, remembering Patrick's warnings about him the day before.

"I've done a little research," he said with steely eyes and a cold smile, and his heavy Texas accent. "It looks like you've been having some trouble in the pandemic."

"That's true." She didn't attempt to deny it, and remained unruffled by his comment. "No one has been going to big black-tie parties and wearing evening gowns for the past eighteen months, but hopefully we'll get back to that soon."

"What have you done about it?" he asked directly.

"At first, I just waited it out, assuming it would be over quickly, but I'm showing a new line of casual daywear at Fashion Week in New York next month. I haven't been out of jeans and sweatshirts myself in eighteen months." She smiled at him. "We'll be doing a lot with denim, and some handmade one-of-a-kind pieces."

"That's smart of you, if you can shore up your sales until times get better. From what I can tell, the fashion industry has taken a hard hit, you're not the only one," he said, his eyes locked into hers, and she didn't waver or flinch when he said he'd done some research. It was no secret that evening gowns weren't selling at the moment, let alone handmade haute couture gowns for astronomical amounts of money, or even wedding gowns. Large gatherings had not been allowed for over a year. Weddings had been canceled or postponed, or held with four to six people present. And wedding gowns had been a big part of her business. The last gowns she had delivered to her clients had never been worn. "It'll come back. Fashion always does. Women can't stay away from it, which is why I'm here. I've been looking for a project for my wife, and she's addicted to fashion, high-priced fashion. That was Chanel haute couture she was wearing the other night," he said proudly, and Eugenia nodded.

"Yes, I know, I recognized it." He looked satisfied and impressed for a minute. She didn't ask him if Natasha had lost the pants to the outfit or just forgotten to put them on.

"She's taught me a lot about fashion. My last wife was all about jewelry. Natasha likes diamonds and I give her plenty of them, but she's all about clothes. She introduced me to haute couture." He made it sound like "hot" couture, which in Natasha's case seemed appropriate, as Eugenia waited to hear the rest. "She's a bright girl and she needs a project, something to keep her busy. She's young. She can't follow me around all day. I've got four grown kids, and I don't want to start over with another one. The ones I have are enough trouble. They're always in some kind of mess that costs me a fortune. I could set her up in her own business, but she has no experience. She needs to learn the ropes before she can do that. And she *loves* what you do."

"Thank you," she said politely, and her smile was no more sincere than his. And then she remembered something she wanted to ask him, for her own peace of mind. "By the way, I thought I saw Natasha yesterday, driving a red sports car, but I wasn't sure it was her."

"Was I with her?" He smiled at Eugenia.

"No, she was alone," Eugenia answered pleasantly.

"Then it wasn't her. She doesn't have a license and she doesn't drive. I have a red Ferrari too, as well as the black one, but I like this one better. Natasha had a car accident in Moscow before she came to America. She was so traumatized that she refuses to drive. I've tried to get her to relax about it, but she's just too scared, so it must have been someone else, and she was at her favorite spa all day yesterday." All of which meant to Eugenia that he didn't know that his wife drove when she wanted to even without a license, since she was certain that Natasha had been Geoff's visitor the day before. She wasn't surprised Natasha had had an accident previously, given the way she pulled out of the driveway and nearly hit the van they were in. She'd been in a big hurry to get out. The hat and dark glasses had almost concealed her face but not quite.

"I'll cut to the chase, Eugenie." Austin went back to the subject at hand. "I want to invest in your business, so that Natasha can be as involved as she wants to be. Maybe she can work with you on some designs, that's up to you. We live in Dallas, so she won't be underfoot every day, but maybe you could play her up in the press at your shows, and she could be a part owner in the business, something for her to be proud of and keep her busy." What he was suggesting made Eugenia uncomfortable. She was not going to let anyone interfere with her designs, and having

Natasha as an ambassador of her line made her shudder. But she needed money, and Austin Wylie knew it.

"I can't let anyone collaborate on the designs," she said firmly, "but she could certainly appear as a star client at the shows during Fashion Week. I'm sure you have PR people who could place press items of her wearing the gowns, and she'd be welcome to visit us anytime. And of course if you invest in Eugenia Ward or Princess Eugenie, she'd be entitled to a healthy discount."

"I want her to feel some ownership, some pride in sharing the limelight with you. I wanted to put her on some of the boards I'm on, but she's not interested in hospitals or charity boards, and she has no experience in business. All she cares about is fashion. I was thinking that maybe ten million would buy her a nice chunk of your business, maybe even a majority participation." He was trying to get a bargain, and had tipped his hand while testing the waters. Now Eugenia knew where he was headed. She looked at him coldly and dug her heels in.

"Mr. Wylie, Austin, my business is worth a great deal more than that. When women start wearing evening gowns again, and it won't be long, my label will be worth a fortune again, just as it was before. Ten million won't even come close to buying you or her a majority interest." At her last calculation, twenty million would have made her more comfortable while she waited for the tides to turn. Ten million wasn't enough, and she wasn't selling a majority interest in her company for anything close to that. She wanted to keep control of it herself.

"I'm sorry to hear that, and I'm sure you will bounce back, but right now, today, a company that only sells evening gowns and wedding gowns isn't worth a damn. You have no income to speak of and a very heavy overhead, with stores in New York and Paris, a buying office, salaries, high-priced rent, expensive fabrics. You've got plenty going out, and not a damn thing coming in." Eugenia was well aware of it and went over the figures constantly, and her accountant had spelled it out for her. It was the terror she was living with every day, that she couldn't hold out until the good times returned. "You could also get some damn fine publicity if you put the spotlight on my wife as a co-owner, or even an investor." Eugenia cringed inwardly at the thought. "Maybe we could say a forty-five percent ownership for ten million," he suggested, and Eugenia shook her head.

"My business is worth a lot more than that, even today. But thank you for your interest." She didn't counter his offer, and she could always go back to him, unless he bought something else. But ten million was nothing to him and they both knew it. She wanted his money, but not his wife as the figurehead, nor her interference in the business.

Eugenia stood up then, indicating that the meeting was over, and Wylie looked disappointed.

"I hope you give it some thought, unless you have other investors of course."

"I've thought about it, to get us over this dry spell, but we're managing for now, and if our new daywear takes off, it will keep us going until evening wear comes back." Austin nodded. He didn't really care, he just wanted to give Natasha a project to keep her busy. She complained constantly that she was bored. And if he could buy her a major participation in her favorite line, she would be thrilled, and he'd be a hero in her eyes. He stood up and put his hat on, and Eugenia walked him to the door.

"Thank you again for your interest." She smiled warmly this time. She was disappointed too, but there was no way she was going to sell him nearly half her business for ten million dollars. She knew she had done the right thing, turning him down, and she wanted to talk to Patrick about it. She hardly knew him, but she trusted him.

The Ferrari shot down the driveway with Austin's foot on the gas, and Eugenia wandered back to the kitchen, thinking about the meeting. It had lasted exactly twenty minutes and had been futile. She was just as broke as she'd been before. As she walked into the kitchen, there was a heated debate going on between Eloise and Sofia, and

Eugenia smiled when she saw Sofia's outfit. It looked home-made and essentially ridiculous, but it was cute on her. Eloise was outraged, her every sensibility offended by what her sister was wearing. She took it personally, as an affront to the art form she loved.

Sofia was wearing an overall dress. The top was well-worn denim that had seen better days. It had been cut off at the waist, and instead of the overall pants, someone had sewn a pink tutu skirt to it, with a pink lining so you couldn't see through it. A pink sequin heart had been pinned to the front pocket, and Sofia was wearing it with pink high-top Converse she or someone had glued pink sequins to. And she had her hair in pigtails.

"For God's sake, Sofia, you look thirteen years old. Where did you get that monstrosity? I'm not going out with you today. I wouldn't be seen dead with you."

"I got it at the county fair for ten dollars. It's handmade," Sofia said proudly. "Like haute couture," she added, and Eloise looked like she was going to have a seizure.

"Don't you dare call that 'haute couture,' it's not haute anything, it's about as low as it gets." Sofia had great legs, and a perfect body and pretty face. Eugenia thought she could actually get away with the dress. She was wearing it with a pink T-shirt. "That's *not* fashion," Eloise said in a rage.

"It makes me happy," Sofia said, unaffected by her sister's

comments. She had heard them all her life. Brad looked amused as he listened to them, and left in the middle of it to play the deciding match with Stef. Geoff and Gloria had retreated to their house. Liz was in hers and Stefano's, answering emails from her office, and Daphne was coming over that afternoon to swim with Tucker.

"I like your military surplus better, and I don't like that on you either. You could wear streetwear," Eloise said, which was what she designed for Balenciaga.

"Streetwear is too depressing. It looks better on guys," Sofia said dismissively, but always kind, she added a compliment to her sister. "I like the bags you designed with the graffiti on them, but I can't afford them."

"I'll send you one," Eloise conceded. "How can people take you seriously when you wear clothes like that?"

"I wear scrubs when I see patients or deliver babies. I'm on vacation, so I can wear what I want."

Eugenia glanced at Sofia again, as she poured herself another cup of coffee. She was still thinking of the meeting with Austin Wylie, and was distracted. She had heard the arguments between Eloise and Sofia before, and this was no different, except that Sofia's outfit was even more whimsical than what she usually wore, and Eloise was even more offended. The crazy overall tutu outfit was an assault on all her sensibilities.

"You dress like either a cupcake or a Marine." Eloise glowered at her, and Eugenia looked at the outfit more closely.

"It looks like cotton candy," she said, and sat down with them in the heat of the familiar battle.

"I love cotton candy," Sofia said with a smile at her mother, undaunted by her older sister. Eloise was wearing black shorts, a black eyelet blouse with balloon sleeves, and sexy black sandals that laced up her long, shapely legs. She was chic and beautiful, but Eugenia thought Sofia was right about her funny outfit. It was happy. "I thought that too when I bought it. I was eating cotton candy, and the tulle skirt looked just like it." As she said it, Eloise stopped complaining and stared at her. She got up from the table abruptly and started to walk out of the kitchen, as though she had forgotten something.

"Where are you going?" her mother asked her. "Don't go away mad. You're all entitled to wear whatever you want. Your sister works hard, she's having some fun on vacation."

"Yeah . . . whatever. I have to do something." Her mind was a million miles away as she left.

"Don't take it to heart. You know how she is." Eugenia smiled at her youngest daughter, but Sofia didn't seem upset. She was used to it. She went back to the guesthouse she was sharing with Brad, and said she'd see her mother later, while Eugenia sat alone in the kitchen lost in thought, wondering what to do now without Austin Wylie as an investor. For a minute she had thought there was a glimmer of hope to save her business, but the tiny glimmer she had seen briefly had gone out, and she was right back where she was before, panicked.

She called Patrick before lunch and told him she had met with Wylie, and he was instantly curious, and happy to hear from her.

"How did it go?" he asked her.

"It didn't. He suggested we collaborate on designs, his wife and I, which nearly gave me heart failure, and the bottom line is he wants forty-five percent of my business for ten million dollars. He originally wanted a majority share, which I said was a nonstarter, and so is the collaboration on design. He wants to buy a toy to keep her entertained, and have her be the ambassador for my haute couture line. I turned him down. He had done some research, though, and knows the well is running dry. It doesn't take a genius to figure out that evening gowns haven't sold in a year and a half, with the whole world in lockdown. And he wanted to take advantage of it for a fire sale."

"You turned him down on all of it?" he asked her.

"Yes. So I'm back to square one, with no investors."

"From what you've said, you haven't looked for any. He's

not the only fish in the sea, if you really think you need investors, and you were right to turn him down. He'll be back with a better offer."

"I don't think so," she said, sounding discouraged. "I was pretty definite and so was he."

"That doesn't mean squat with a guy like him. He's a businessman and a shrewd one. He didn't get where he is by being dumb or giving up when he wants something. He wanted the most he could get for the least he'd have to pay. You turned him down, so now he has to improve the offer. We'll talk about it tomorrow. But trust me, it's not over yet, not at all." She was cheered by what Patrick said and looking forward to her day on the boat with him. She felt faintly guilty for taking a day away from her children, but they could entertain themselves without her for a day, and she was excited about seeing him. He was the first man who had sparked her interest in years, and he seemed just as attracted and intrigued as she was. Her children had their own lives now, and she had a right to one too, although she hadn't tried to have a life of her own for years, and it never worked out before when the children were younger. They took up too much of her time and attention, and so did her business. There hadn't been a serious man in her life in a very long time, or even a minor interest. But Patrick seemed like a very special, unusual man, and worth a closer look.

"We'll talk about Wylie tomorrow," he reminded her. "I hate to say it, but I have to go now. I have a conference call in two minutes about my crumbling empire." He sounded good-natured about it.

"That makes two of us," she said, smiling.

"It's just temporary. We'll be back." She loved how confident he was that their business problems were just a passing phase and not the end of life as they knew it. She hoped he was right. She was skeptical, but he was very convincing. "See you tomorrow," he said, and a minute later they hung up. She was interested that he thought Wylie was just trying to see how little he could pay her, and would make another offer.

She went to find Eloise then, and found her sketching furiously at a makeshift drawing board in her room.

"Working?" Eugenia asked, not wanting to distract her. She looked intent on what she was doing.

"Maybe . . . yes . . . I don't know yet. I'll talk to you later."

Eugenia smiled as she quietly shut the door, put on her bathing suit, and went out to the pool with a book. Everyone seemed to have their own projects that morning. She found Sofia at the pool in a khaki-colored one-piece bathing suit. The color was awful, but her figure was so perfect, it didn't matter. She looked beautiful anyway, and the overall tutu had disappeared.

"Army surplus?" her mother asked as she sat down on a chaise longue next to her. She was fascinated by her youngest daughter's wardrobe, and the offbeat places where she found it.

"Goodwill," Sofia said with a smile. She was reading a book by an Indian philosopher Eugenia had never heard of, who promised peace in your soul, which seemed like a good thing to aspire to, especially these days. But Sofia had a very Zen attitude about life anyway. She saw a lot of hardship and tragedy in her work, people who didn't get treatment for conditions that could have been cured and died from them unnecessarily, women who had no prenatal care at all, who had a dozen children and were on welfare, a high infant and maternal mortality rate that could have been avoided with minimal prenatal care, and babies born in squalid conditions instead of modern hospitals that were too far away to help. It gave her a different perspective on life than that of her sisters, and although she was younger than all of them, and looked it, she was wiser in many ways. She got along best with Daphne, who was calm and sensible too. Gloria and Eloise were too volatile and had always picked on her. As a child, Sofia had learned to stay away from them as much as possible. As the oldest and the youngest, male and female, she and Stef had never had much in common, and weren't close.

It was interesting to see where their strongest attachments were, and Gloria had always been the neediest and most self-centered and difficult. She was desperate to be the center of attention, and often achieved it by being the most strident and critical, demanding what she wanted in an aggressive way, which was alienating. Her lavish, very expensive wedding, even at a hard time in the world and for her mother, was a prime example of that. It wasn't an endearing feature in her character.

Eugenia was more patient with her than her siblings, who were tired of Gloria's constant ploys for center stage. She came across as entitled and spoiled, and Geoff appeared to be equally so, with very little to back it up, and no charm to make his demands appealing. They were a tough pair. Eugenia was finding his bad behavior hard to tolerate. Brad, on the other hand, was another winner, like Phillip. They were both lovely men, and good to her daughters. Brad had already won her heart four days into the vacation. He was a keeper, and she hoped he'd stay, although she didn't think Sofia was ready to settle down yet. She loved her work in the challenging conditions of Appalachia, and Brad had mentioned in passing that ultimately his goal was to return to Chicago, to be with his family and work with the urban poor there. Eugenia had no idea how Sofia would feel about that. In their own way, several of her children made their careers a very high priority, as she had, and Sofia was one of them. In her case, selflessly for the good of humanity, not for profit. She was the noblest of all.

They all helped themselves to lunch at the ample buffet the chef set up, and Daphne came over with Tucker when he woke up from his nap. She looked even bigger than two days before, which Eugenia thought wasn't possible. Sofia asked her some questions about the pregnancy, and Daphne let her feel her belly.

"They're in good positions, they're getting ready," Sofia said with a professional air. "Does your doctor think they'll come early?"

"She doesn't know. We're five weeks out, and with twins she said anything is possible from now on. When all of you leave at the end of the week, we're moving back to the city. We'll be back out here for the wedding, but other than that, my doctor wants me in the city now, close to home." Daphne was getting increasingly nervous about the delivery, worried that it would be twice as long and twice as hard as Tucker's had been, and that she'd have to have a Caesarean if either baby was in distress, or it took too long, or their positions changed.

"That's smart," Sofia said. "They're pretty low, but that's normal, they don't have much room, and they're not small.

They both feel very close to normal size, which is why you're so big. That's a lot of baby you're carrying." She smiled at her older sister, and was very professional, as Eugenia listened.

"I hope you have them before or after the wedding. I don't want to be delivering babies while adjusting Gloria's veil," Eugenia said, and they all laughed.

"No, but Sofia could," Daphne said confidently with a smile at her little sister.

"I delivered triplets once in a log cabin with no heat, electricity, or running water. The mother and all three babies survived, but I nearly didn't. That was my trial by fire. Everything is easy compared to that."

"It sounds terrifying," Daphne confirmed.

She had brought the nanny with her to run after Tucker. "I can't keep up with him anymore. He runs too fast and I'm too slow. Angelica is on vacation right now, so she won't take time off when the babies come. This is a friend of hers. She's sweet, but not as careful. I can't wait for Angie to come back when we get to the city." The replacement nanny looked very young, and was very pretty. She talked a lot, and she let Tucker do more and get more adventurous than his mother or regular nanny would have. The relief nanny kept telling him he was a big boy now and was going to be a big brother. But he was only three years old. She was running around the lawn with him playing tag, while the whole family talked and sat around the pool. Brad and Stef came back, and Brad declared victory, while Stefano vowed vengeance. They were all laughing, and Eugenia noticed that Geoff had slipped away from the group and was chatting with the nanny, who was wearing a red bikini. No one had paid attention to Geoff walking away from the group and talking to the relief nanny, while Tucker continued to run around with no one watching him. Eugenia was about to say something to Daphne but didn't want to worry her, so she kept an eye on him. The nanny had her back to the pool and was laughing at something Geoff said to her, standing close to him and facing him, as Tucker stumbled and fell backward into the deep end. He disappeared without a sound, startled, and sank like a rock to the bottom of the pool, as Eugenia leapt to her feet and gave a scream. Neither Geoff nor the girl in the red bikini had seen what had happened and didn't realize it. Eugenia started running toward the pool, and Brad reacted immediately, got there first on longer legs, and dove in as the nanny and Geoff stared at him, frozen in place as the whole group fell silent. Daphne started to cry as she ran toward the pool as fast as she could.

Brad came to the surface within seconds with Tucker in one hand, the child already unconscious, and he laid him down next to the pool and pressed the water out of him. Within seconds Tucker was awake, coughing and spluttering, and Daphne pulled him into her arms and held him. Brad was the hero of the hour, and Sofia came to them immediately, took her nephew in her arms, told her sister to sit down, and looked at Brad gratefully.

"Good work, Dr. Jackson." They were all shaken by the realization of how easily Tucker could have drowned, with no one watching him, even though they were all at the pool.

Daphne was shaking as she spoke to the nanny in the red bathing suit, who was crying, aware of what she'd done. She'd been so engaged in flirting with Geoff that she had totally lost track of her charge. Daphne's voice was shaking and harsh. "Call an Uber, go back to my house and get your things, and leave before I get home. You're fired. You could have killed my son." It didn't bear thinking about, the image was so awful, and a distinct possibility.

"I'm sorry, I thought . . . I was watching him . . . I didn't think . . ." Geoff had mingled into the crowd by then and she was standing alone, fired, disgraced, and could easily have been responsible for the death of a child. Geoff paid no attention as she picked up her sandals, blouse, and purse and left the pool area to wait for the Uber. Eugenia wasn't sure if the others had seen him talking to the nanny, and she didn't say anything. But she looked very serious for the rest of the afternoon. That event, coupled with the mysterious woman's visit the day before, probably Natasha Wylie, demanded a conversation with Gloria that she was dreading. She had to take a good look at who she was marrying before it was too late. He was clearly a womanizer, and possibly cheating on her weeks before their wedding.

Sofia made Daphne lie down for a while after the emotions of what had happened. Gloria and Eloise took care of Tucker, and Stef, Brad, and Liz sat quietly talking. Eugenia kept Daphne company and tried to calm her, urging her to focus on the fact that the worst hadn't happened, Tucker was fine, and things like that happen with children, and all's well that ends well. She tried to put a positive spin on it and didn't show that she was furious with Geoff even more than with the irresponsible relief nanny. He had distracted her from her duties just to flirt with her. She didn't know if anyone had noticed, but she had and that was enough. Geoff had disappeared into his guesthouse very quickly, and no one missed him.

Eugenia was mulling over all of it and the inevitable conversation she would have to have with Gloria before they left. Stefano had driven Daphne and Tucker home in her car, and Liz followed them to drive him back. The mood was solemn and dampened after the near-drowning incident, and no one was in a festive mood that night. Eloise knocked softly on the door of her mother's room as she dressed for dinner.

"Can I come in?" Eloise asked her cautiously. She could see how upset her mother was.

"Of course," Eugenia said, smiling at her, trying to look more cheerful than she felt, as Eloise sat down, with a folder in her hand.

"Well, that was certainly a shit show today, wasn't it?" Eloise said bluntly. She looked upset too. None of them could bear thinking of what if the worst had happened, and they thanked God that Brad had seen it and moved quickly. "Did you see what I saw?" Eloise asked her.

"And what was that?" Eugenia asked noncommittally, not wanting to admit to her daughter how furious she was with Geoff.

"That my sister's shithead fiancé was hitting on the nanny and distracting her from her duties, so Tucker almost drowned." Eloise had summed it up accurately, in her mother's opinion. "If Brad hadn't moved fast, Tucker would be dead." It was an unbearable thought for them all, and the memory of how quickly Tucker had lost consciousness after he sank was horrifying.

"I can't disagree with you," Eugenia said sadly. "I saw it too. I don't think Gloria did. I'm not sure anyone saw Geoff move toward the nanny and engage her in conversation. She was flattered and all starry-eyed talking to him. He seemed like a big man to her, all puffed up with himself. She bought right into his act. I was watching them before Tucker fell into the pool. I saw it happen. She had her back to him, looking into Geoff's eyes."

"He is really a piece of shit," Eloise said angrily. "I don't know what Gloria sees in him, except his title one day, and who cares."

"Apparently, she does," Eugenia said unhappily.

"She can't marry him, Mom. If she wakes up, she'll be miserable in six months, and divorced in a year." Eugenia didn't disagree with her, but there was a long way to go before Gloria woke up. "On another subject, I had an idea today. Maybe I'm crazy, or Sofia's fashion sense is contagious. I know you've been struggling with your couture line and business has been lousy, but looking at her today, I listened to what you said and tried to see her through your eyes, and suddenly I realized something. You dress a certain kind of woman, your very elite clients, and slightly less lofty ones for your ready-to-wear line. But these are all very wealthy women, usually married to rich men, or sleeping with them, who don't care how much they spend, want to impress other men, and use the clothes as status symbols to show off to their friends. But there's a huge market out there of women who make less money, aren't married or a rich man's mistress, and are very young. The youth market is a gold mine these days. That's what Balenciaga and other brands are after, as well as lots of lesser brands you don't even know about. The daughters of your clients, or women a tad older than that who want to look like kids. I know it's not what you do, but right now, groping to expand your market, I suddenly had this crazy idea that you could do a line for those young girls, or even women in the next age group up. Say thirteen to twenty, or twenty-five, girls who want to have fun with what they wear. You called it cotton candy, and that would be a great name for it. It could be a really smart commercial decision, in a completely different price bracket." Eloise handed her mother the file, which was full of quick sketches she had worked on all afternoon. There was a small color chart showing the range of tones Eloise could see them in, and none of them were black. They weren't chic, but everything about them said "Fun." Eugenia smiled as she went through them, and was touched by the time Eloise had spent on it. "They're mostly tulle and sequins, and inexpensive fabrics, but with the patternmakers you have, they could be well cut and cheaply produced, and you might start a whole new craze, and who knows, some forty-year-olds might want to wear them too." What Eloise had done was financially brilliant, and creatively inspired.

"You could sell them at a pop-up store, and do a small first run as an experiment to try them out." Eugenia was smiling broadly when she closed the file and looked at her daughter.

"Eloise, you are a genius. I love the idea. Some of our factories are starting to open, and none of these would be expensive to make." They were mostly tulle skirts with lots of sequins, mermaid skirts, a couple of circle skirts, glittering tops, heart-shaped appliqués, pink denim Levi-style jackets in less expensive fabrics. There wasn't a single design Eugenia didn't like, and they sparked a few ideas of her own. "I want to play with this some more, and I'll check out resources for these fabrics. I could do a small run in limited sizes, and see what happens," she said, excited by Eloise's suggestion. It was the best idea anyone had had so far to bring some cash flow back into the business and keep it afloat.

"It makes you look modern and young to reach out to that age group. You're not cheapening your line, you're adding a whole new one, in tune with the times, if you do it."

"Thank you." Eugenia put her arms around her and hugged her. "I think you may have just started a whole explosion of new ideas I never thought of. My casual daywear is still aimed at my traditional client. This is all for their daughters and granddaughters, and young women with a modest income who want to look cute."

"We should dedicate it to Sofia. I got the idea from her

and that ridiculous outfit she was wearing today. I think you should copy it and make it your signature piece. Cotton Candy could wind up being more profitable than your main business, and there's no shame in that." Coming from Eloise, it was a major change of direction from the purist attitudes about fashion that she considered sacred. This was all fluff and fun and a whole new attitude about what really young women wanted to wear. It was pure fantasy, and young women and teenage girls were going to love it. They'd have to make it affordable, which would be new for Eugenia.

"I'll start checking it out right away, and really target the line to the client. This is going to be fun if we can make it happen. I want to try it out fast, with a few main pieces to test the market," Eugenia said.

They were still talking about it when they went down to dinner with the others. The whole group was subdued that night after the shock of what had happened to Tucker, and the emotional drain afterward.

Eugenia didn't tell them where she was going the next day, and said she was going into the city. She still felt guilty taking time away from them, but Gloria and Geoff were going to the beach, Sofia, Liz, and Eloise were going shopping in Southampton, Stef and Brad were playing their rematch, and Daphne was staying home with Tucker, since she didn't have a nanny.

"Will you be home for dinner, Mom?" Eloise asked her at dinner when she told them she was going to the city the next day.

"No, I won't. I've got meetings all day in town, and by the time I get back, with the traffic, it will be late." No one objected or seemed to care, and she felt strange lying to her children, but she wanted to spend the day with Patrick, and didn't want to tell them. They might make too much of it, and she didn't know where it was going. It was too soon to tell. It was none of their business. And it was fun having a secret. It had been a very long time since she'd had one. She could hardly wait to see Patrick the next day.

Chapter 6

Eugenia drove herself to the marina in Montauk the next day, and waited on the dock for the speedboat from *My Dream* to pick her up. She had told Patrick she would be there at nine and she was five minutes early. He was excited about spending the day with her, and having her stay for dinner at the end of it. It felt like a vacation to Eugenia. She didn't have to take care of anyone, plan a meal, worry about anything, or be responsible. She and Patrick had a whole day to talk and relax, sail and swim, and get to know each other.

She got into the speedboat, and as they motored toward the yacht, she looked up, and saw that Patrick was waiting for her on deck, standing at the rail.

She had worn white jeans, a plain white T-shirt, and

sneakers, with her hair in a ponytail down her back and very little makeup. She liked a clean, simple look, which was her style, unfussy, unpretentious, without distractions. He met her on the lower deck and gave her a hug.

"Thank you for coming. I know you must have your hands full with your kids. Thank you for spending the day with me."

"It's a treat for me." She smiled at him. "Like a day off." Over coffee and pastries at the outdoor dining table, she told him about the mishap with Tucker the day before, and about her feelings about Geoff, and the mystery visit on Monday from the woman who she was sure was Austin Wylie's wife.

"Wow, if you're right, that's ballsy of her. What are you going to do? Tell your daughter?"

"I've been agonizing over it. Whoever the woman was, he spent the day with her and didn't tell Gloria, and then lied about it and paid off the help to keep their mouths shut. That's a hell of a way to start a marriage. She at least has a right to know. And I have to be the one to tell her. It's up to her after that. But I hate to see her make a mistake. We've seen the movie, and we know how those stories end," Eugenia said with a sigh. "Whatever she decides, she won't thank me for telling her."

"Being the parent of adults is so much more complicated than people realize. I always thought that when they graduated from college, or by thirty at the outside, they'd be on their way and our job was over, and we could just enjoy them when we see them. But it's actually harder than when they're kids. Now the stakes are higher and the consequences can be disastrous if they take the wrong job or marry the wrong woman. I have one son, as you know, and he keeps me awake at night at thirty-five. I can't even imagine what it must be like with five, and situations like you just described with your daughter's fiancé. You have to tell her, but she may hate you for a while.

"My son fell in love with a girl when he was a senior in college," Patrick said quietly. "He was so innocent. She had the face of an angel, from a very religious, wholesome background. She was twenty-seven, and such a sweet girl. She said a few things that didn't add up, and I felt terrible and had her investigated. She'd been married twice and had a child out of wedlock that was living with her grandmother in Salt Lake. She told us her grandmother was dead, and never mentioned the boy, of course. She'd had him at fifteen. She was kicked out of college for cheating and had been arrested several times after that for dealing drugs. I had a hell of a time telling Quinn how I knew and why I checked her out. I just had some weird instinct that made me do it, and I hated being right. She disappeared the next day, after he talked to her about it, and he never heard from her again. I think she was a sociopath. I'm grateful he didn't marry her. He wanted to, and probably would have. But he's never gotten seriously attached to any woman since, and now I'm worried about that. He works hard, and he plays hard too, just as I did at his age, but I don't think he's ever opened his heart to any woman again. And how long can you do that?"

"Some people do it forever," she said gently, but she understood what he was saying. "I worried about the woman my son married. She's a little older too, and from a completely different world from ours, but I'm actually starting to like her, and I can see what he sees in her. She's solid and smart, and works as hard as he does. She has a weird family who make me cringe, but I think she's good for him, and it doesn't matter that she dresses like a chorus girl from Vegas. I worry about my daughter Eloise working too hard, having no life except her career, and being alone. I'm very worried about the guy my daughter Gloria is marrying in three weeks, and shouldn't. The only two I don't worry about are Daphne, whom you know, who has a dream life with Phillip, and my youngest daughter, Sofia, who has her head on her shoulders, loves her job, and is a midwife in Appalachia."

"I really like her guy too, he seems solid as a rock, and they seem good together."

Eugenia nodded agreement. "I worry like crazy about the others, and there isn't a damn thing I can do about it. They have to make their own mistakes, but it's hard to watch. Now I know how my parents felt when I married at almost twenty-two, to a man I'd met in Italy and scarcely knew. He'd never had a real job in his life, and was forty-five years old, living hand-to-mouth from commissions he made putting people and deals together. He was all dazzle and no substance, and my parents were ultraconservative, solid, traditional people, and they were horrified. And then I had five babies in five years because he liked the idea of that but not the reality, and he later walked off with a fortune and nearly all my savings when we divorced. My parents were right, but who listens to their parents? No one I know." She smiled at him and he nodded.

"I didn't listen to mine either. My grandfather made a fortune from a small inheritance, making careful investments. My father used what his father had made to buy real estate, and he turned it into a very sizable fortune. I took it another step further with some very high-risk investments that paid off. It was all based on hard work and good solid judgment, and in my case taking chances other people were afraid of, but they worked for me. My father was married to the same woman for fifty-two years and they died within months of each other. When I married Quinn's mother because she was pregnant, they were heartbroken at how foolish I'd been, and devastated when I got divorced. They were staunch Catholics. My father was horrified by every investment I made, and every building I bought, and the risks I took. He said it would all come tumbling down one day, and he wasn't wrong. But if it does now, I know I'll make it back again, by the same hard work and smart investments. Quinn is more conservative than I am, and he's done well, but what is any of that worth if you don't have a partner you love to share the joy and hard times, and don't have a family? I forgot to pay attention to that, and went out with women I didn't care about, and rarely loved. And when I did love them, I ran like hell so I wouldn't get tied down. That's what I see my son doing now. And the toys are great," he said, waving at the mega yacht around them, "but what my parents had was better. That's where you did things right, Eugenia. You managed to have the family and the business."

"That doesn't keep me from being in hot water now," she reminded him, "and my ex-husband was a joke. He was basically a charming professional gigolo. I can't say that to my kids. So I got the kids right, and the business, but I blew it on the man I chose to share it with. I'm beginning to think you can't have it all. I always thought I could."

"You'll choose more wisely next time," he said with a smile. "You're grown up now. You can't expect to pick the right partner at twenty-one. You don't even know who you are then. My parents got it right, but they lived in a different world. They didn't have the choices or the exposure or the temptations we do to make a mistake. They came from the same background, same small town in Illinois, and met when they were twelve, and grew up together. I think that's why so many people go back to their childhood sweethearts when they marry for a second time later in life. It's hard to know who people are in the world we live in today. And a lot of them are fakes and frauds and practiced liars, sociopaths like Quinn's college girlfriend. There are a lot of sharks in the waters we live in. I meet them every day and I'm sure you do too. All you can do is stay true to yourself, be who you really are, be honest and keep your eyes open. I think in the long run, it pays off. You can make honest mistakes, but I correct them a lot faster than I did when I was young. But what I don't like about what my son is doing is that he keeps everyone at a distance. He doesn't let anyone in and he doesn't trust anyone, ever since that girl when he was twenty-two. That's a sad way to live." His worry for his son was in his eyes and Eugenia could see it, and sympathized.

"Maybe one of these days, the right woman will show up, and come over his walls and get through to him. I don't believe he'll stay alone forever."

"I hope he doesn't. It's not a life. I hope he has kids, and more than just one, like you did. It was brave of you, and smart." Interestingly, Eugenia and Patrick were both only children.

"It wasn't planned," she admitted humbly. "I just followed my husband blindly and believed what he said. It turned out he was lying. But I'm happy I have the kids, no matter how much I worry about them."

"Well, today is your day off," he reminded her. "This is our day. What would you like to do first? Swim? A massage? Lie in the sun and do nothing? Take the little sailboat out? Name your pleasure."

"Being with you," she said shyly. "I love talking to you." Patrick was so smart, so kind, and so open with her. He felt more comfortable with her than he had with any woman in years. He hadn't expected to feel that way about her, when Daphne said she wanted to introduce him to her mother. He was just being polite when he agreed. "What about lying in the sun, and figuring the rest out later?" she said, and he liked the idea. He didn't have to impress her with toys and activities.

"That sounds perfect." And she followed him up to the sundeck. There were sunbeds all around them, and they looked inviting. "You can change in one of the guest cabins if you like," he offered, and she laughed.

"I came prepared." She took off her T-shirt and jeans, and

was wearing a powder pink bikini under her clothes. She lay down on a towel he spread out for her. He had swimming trunks on under his shorts, which he took off with his pale blue T-shirt before lying down next to her. He had a well-toned, athletic body, as a result of many trainers and coaches that he hired to stay in shape. He played tennis and squash twice a week, and swam every day. Eugenia wasn't as athletic, but she was long and lean with beautiful skin. He touched her arm gently and noticed how soft it was.

They chatted on and off in the morning sun and then they both dozed. She offered to put his sunblock on for him, and he noticed how gentle her hands were and how light her touch, and he put some on her back. They were lying close together, and he was holding her hand when they fell asleep. They felt as though they had known each other forever, after what they had shared in a short time. She liked knowing about his family and his youth, and he was intrigued by what he knew of her. He couldn't imagine her with a man like Umberto. She was so totally without artifice or pretense, and her ex-husband sounded like a shallow fraud to him. She deserved better than the life she had led with him, his venal motives, and leaving her to bring up their children alone. But Patrick was impressed that she had done a good job, having met them. He wished that his son had come home with a girl like one of her daughters, but he hadn't even come close. He was currently dating a young actress in L.A., who was spectacularly beautiful, but had just gotten out of rehab for a coke habit, and had a previous boyfriend she was still involved with. It sounded like a mess to Patrick because it was, like all of Quinn's romances. There was always a hitch somewhere, a trick, a trap door waiting to open, an excuse not to get serious, or a backstairs escape for him. Quinn was getting too old for that, at thirty-five. Patrick wondered when he'd wake up, or if marriage and children weren't among his goals. His successful startup of the moment was.

Patrick and Eugenia woke up at the same time, rolled onto their sides, facing each other, and smiled.

"This is heaven," she said in a sensual soft voice as she woke up.

"It's *My Dream,*" he said, and smiled. "I've had boats before, but never one as wonderful as this. It took them four years to build and was worth the wait. If I sell everything, this will be the last to go. I could live on it. I like it better than any of my homes. I can just pick up and go whenever I want to. I have a little sailboat I take out by myself when I need to think or just relax."

"Should we give it a try, or is it a one-man boat?"

"Are you a sailor?" He looked surprised. She was so elegant and sophisticated, he couldn't imagine her in a tiny boat.

"I went to sailing camp in Maine when I was a kid. My father was an avid sailor, so he made me learn how to sail, since he didn't have a son." She smiled at him. "I haven't been in a little boat since then. It sounds like fun."

"I'll tell them to get it out after lunch," he said happily. It was noon by then, and he had ordered lunch to be served at twelve-thirty.

They went for a swim in the pool before lunch, and then showered and put on dry bathing suits, and the chef had put out salads, cold meats, and lobster. It was a delicious meal, and they talked all through lunch, making each other laugh at stories from their youth and early work years. After lunch, they went down to the lowest deck with the huge yawning opening, big enough for his toys to be moved in and out, and the little sailboat was waiting for them in the water.

It was as small as he had said, a beautiful little wooden boat, and he handed her in, and made her put on a life vest. He knew the crew would be keeping an eye on them from the distance to make sure they didn't run into trouble or capsize, and she was surprised to find that she still remembered the basic principles of sailing a boat that size. She made a few mistakes and he corrected them. It was a glorious afternoon, with just enough wind to fill their sails, and he guided the little sailboat expertly a fair distance from the yacht.

"You're actually a pretty good sailor," he said, surprised.

"Thank you, at least I haven't capsized us yet," she said with a grin.

"I've done that a few times myself. I'm a lucky man. I have a golden life and I never forget it, and these are the best moments, sharing simple pleasures with people you care about. I never lose sight of that," he said, and she nodded.

"Neither do I, although lately I've been afraid I'll lose everything I've built," she admitted softly.

"If you do, you'll build it again, or something else," he said, and he believed it. She told him about Eloise's idea, Cotton Candy. "That's pure genius, and the best way to reinvent yourself. It sounds like fun."

"I think it could actually work," she said, excited about it, as they sailed back to the yacht. They both hated to leave the sailboat, and when they did, he guided her to the spa on the lower deck. "Do you hate massages?"

"No, I love them, but I never have time."

"Today is your day off, remember? I have the best masseuse on the East Coast. Would you like to try her?" He had thought of every possible way to pamper her and spoil her and make it a magical day.

"That sounds amazing." He left her in the healing hands of the masseuse for an hour and came back to get her. She looked dazed, and said she had never felt so relaxed, and then she turned to him with a question. She felt like a child at Christmas, and he was Santa Claus. "Can we swim off the boat before dinner? I love swimming in the sea," she said.

"I didn't want to suggest it, it makes some people uncomfortable. I do it every day when I'm on the boat, twice a day." They dove in together, and swam a good distance. It woke Eugenia up after the massage. It was the perfect ending to a perfect day and invigorated them. She was a strong swimmer, and she was barely out of breath when they got back to the boat. He had stayed close to her in case she got tired, but she was an even match for him. They climbed back up the ladder onto the boat, and he took her to a guestroom to dry off and change back into her clothes. She had brought a light silver sweater she had bought in Italy years before, and was wearing silver sandals with her jeans. Patrick was wearing white jeans and a white polo shirt with the logo of the boat when he came back to get her.

They drank champagne on the deck and watched the sunset, and the chef had prepared another buffet of seafood. They ate a hearty meal, and there was soft music in the background. It felt slightly like a seduction scene, but with him it wasn't. He was so natural and normal with Eugenia that it felt like they were best friends rather than lovers, which was more comfortable for her. Patrick was sharing his world with her, not trying to seduce her or take advantage of her. She liked this better. He wanted her to spend the night, but he knew better than to suggest it to her, he knew she wouldn't have stayed. They were building something that was even better and he wanted it to last, and to savor it. He hoped they would remember these days someday.

"I think today was one of the best days of my life," Eugenia said to him, as he poured her a last glass of champagne. The crew had served them efficiently, but not hovered, so they had privacy and could talk freely, which they had all day, interspersed with comfortable silences.

"The first of many days like this, I hope," he said to her. "I've had a wonderful time too." She had turned off her phone that morning, since she had said she would be in meetings all day. She hoped that her children had managed to survive without a crisis. She had been gone and out of touch for thirteen hours by then. It was ten o'clock, and she and Patrick had packed a lot into their day alone. Swimming and sailing, sunbathing, delicious meals, and even a massage, and the pleasure of his company. And Patrick felt the same way about her. He felt as though he had found a rare pearl and he didn't want to lose it. He treated her with caution, admiration, and respect, more than any man she'd met, and she appreciated him and all his confidence. They already trusted each other.

"Patrick, I can't begin to reciprocate for a day like this. I feel like I've had a month's vacation. But would you like to have dinner with me and the children on Friday night? Everyone is leaving on Sunday, and I'm going back to the city. We'll be back in the Hamptons again the week of the wedding, which is on the last weekend in August, the week before Labor Day. But everyone is more relaxed now than they will be the weekend of the wedding. If it goes forward, that will probably be insanely busy."

"Do you think it won't go forward?" he asked her.

"It depends how my daughter reacts to her fiancé's mystery guest two days ago and if she noticed him flirting with the nanny yesterday. She may marry him anyway, although I have to admit, I hope she won't."

"I hope not too," he confided to her. "As you said, we've seen the movie, and we know how it ends. I don't think her odds are great for a storybook ending, given what you've said. And who knows what you don't know, and weren't around to observe? It sounds like she has her head in the sand about him."

"I think so," Eugenia agreed.

"If she were my daughter, I wouldn't want her to marry a guy like him."

"Her father doesn't care. She'll have a title. That's all he cares about. And he hardly sees the children, once or twice a year. She thinks her father walks on water. I don't try to disabuse her. She's entitled to her illusions."

"You have a tough role with them, with all the responsibility on your shoulders," he said to her, thinking about it. "At least my son has a mother. We didn't get along, but she adores him. Being the *only* parent is a hell of a hard job. I can see that now," and he admired her all the more for it. She was father and mother to her children and had been for years, which sounded like a thankless job. "When can we do this again?" he asked her.

"Whenever you like, and have time to put up with me for a whole day. Thank you for a magnificent day. You must have a lot to do right now." Eugenia knew what that was like, and expected to find fifty or a hundred work emails on her computer when she went home that night. Patrick's empire was bigger, and she suspected he would have even more.

"This was a joy for me too," he said, comfortable with her.

"Will you come to dinner on Friday?" she asked him.

"With pleasure."

"Come for drinks at seven-thirty, dinner after. Casual, jeans are fine."

"Can I bring anything?"

"Just you. And body armor, in case they get out of hand," she said, and he laughed.

"I'll enjoy seeing them again," he said, and after a few

more minutes, they got up from the table. The crew had left the area by then, and would return to clean up when they left. Patrick looked down at her standing in front of him, and carefully pulled her toward him, into his arms, and ever so gently he kissed her on the lips, softly at first and then harder, wanting more of her, but willing to wait as long as he had to. "I love being with you," he whispered, and touched her face with a single finger, drawing her features, and then he kissed her again. "Thank you for today."

"Thank *you* for today," she said, hating to leave his magic kingdom where anything seemed possible, even dreams. They walked slowly toward the stairs and made their way down several decks and he stopped her and kissed her again. Eugenia loved the feel of his lips on hers and how he kissed her. She had forgotten how sensual kisses could be, and she loved the strength of his arms around her. She felt small and safe within them, which was a long-forgotten feeling.

Patrick walked her to where the motorboat was waiting for her, and the crew helped her in, as he watched and waved as they pulled away. She sat looking up at the boat where she had just spent an extraordinary day, and she saw him appear on the deck outside his suite. He waved at her and she waved back. They were staying at anchor outside the port, and the deckhands helped her out of the motorboat that had brought her back to earth. She felt like she had fallen from a cloud, or like Cinderella after the ball.

She walked to where she had parked the car and drove back to the rented house. It was eleven o'clock, and the main house and cottages were all dark and quiet when she got there. They had all gone to sleep early. No one was waiting for her to report a disaster. They hadn't killed each other, the house hadn't burned down. She turned her phone on and there were no messages, except one from her dentist to remind her of a cleaning appointment the following week. All was well in her tiny universe, compared to Patrick's much bigger one.

She slipped into bed a few minutes later, thinking about him, and the day they had spent together. She knew now about his son, his parents, their marriage, and his own. She had seen him in his rarefied world. She knew about his business problems and he knew about hers. They were aware of each other's successes and failures due to the pandemic, and he made her less fearful about her own. It seemed like a perfect beginning, and even if she never saw him again, she would remember it forever as one totally perfect day, and Patrick as the man who had given it to her.

Chapter 7

The morning after her miraculous day on Patrick's yacht, Eugenia felt as though she had had a month's vacation, and was full of energy and bright ideas. She spent the morning calling factories she knew, and others she had heard of, describing what she had in mind, the kind of garments, and the quantity she wanted for a first run. It was a small order, but most of the factories weren't up and running again yet, and she finally found one in New Jersey that was willing to take her project on and said they could produce the order in a week, which seemed amazing, but she wasn't making wedding gowns, just play clothes for teenagers. Once they agreed to make the order, she was planning to go to outlets for inexpensive fabrics and see what she could come up with. She needed miles of pink tulle, lace, ribbon, trimmings, and a truckload of sequins, mainly pink. She felt like she was making a giant birthday cake, and was having fun doing it.

Eloise was impressed by the progress she had made by late that morning. And she told them all at lunch that Patrick was coming to dinner on Friday, to thank him for the day they had all spent on his boat. Everyone was fine with it, and said how nice he'd been to them. They were sorry not to have a chance to visit him again before they left on Sunday. It amused Eugenia that they assumed he would be delighted to have guests for the day again, and that he had nothing else to do.

She had made a decision that morning that she was going to have a serious talk with Gloria that afternoon. She couldn't put it off, since they were leaving in three days, and if Gloria wanted to cancel the wedding, it would be best to decide that now, although Eugenia doubted that any of the suppliers would return her deposits at this late date. She was past the contract dates for refunds, and if they canceled now, she'd have to pay in full. But the issue was Gloria's future, not what it was costing her mother.

She didn't want to deal with it on the day that Patrick was coming to dinner, nor on the last day of their vacation, which left only today. She was anxious thinking about it.

Minutes before she went to look for Gloria in the late

afternoon, she got a call from Austin Wylie, who said that he had reconsidered his offer, in light of what she had said to him, and that he knew how important her business was in better times. She guessed that Natasha had pushed him to do it, since he had already discussed the project with her.

"I'm thinking that fifteen million should do it, for a forty-five percent ownership for my wife," he said grandly. The money was improving but the percentage was still way off base.

"That's kind of you, Austin," Eugenia said politely, "but the percentage is still too high, and the money too low. I need to speak to my financial people and get back to you. I can't make a decision like this without them, and you took me by surprise with your first offer. I wasn't planning on investors. I'm not opposed to it, but the offer has to make sense." He wondered if she was putting personal money into it, which he couldn't assess. And if so, he knew his offer wouldn't stand up. He had hoped that she was desperate, which clearly she wasn't. She had played her hand well. "I'll get back to you," she repeated, and called Patrick as soon as she hung up. She had already sent him a text to thank him that morning, and he had responded warmly that he couldn't wait to see her and the others on Friday. She sounded mildly panicked when he answered her call after she spoke to Austin.

"Austin Wylie just called me," she said, breathless.

"I knew he would. What did he say?"

"He offered me fifteen million for forty-five percent ownership," she said. "That sounds way off to me."

"It's garbage," he said, "and he knows it. You need twenty million, correct?"

"It would help us hold on until business picks up again and returns to normal. Less than that won't make much difference. We've had no significant income for eighteen months, and our overhead is still high. We've cut back, but not enough," she realized now. Patrick thought about it for a minute. This was small potatoes for him, but he didn't want to make a mistake that Eugenia would suffer from.

"What do you think your business is worth? A rough guess. Fifty million, a hundred, two hundred? I don't know your industry well enough to judge."

"Our accounts receivable are enormous when things are normal. Our price tags are high. I'm not sure, and have to ask my accountant. But I'd say conservatively, the business is worth a hundred million, ready-to-wear and couture."

"I was guessing around that, or maybe higher. In that case, assuming a hundred, ask him for thirty million for twenty percent ownership. He'll push you down to twenty or twenty-five million, which is where you want to be, and don't give an inch on the percentage," Patrick said smoothly.

This was child's play for him. He bought and sold in the billions, and he was happy to help her with her negotiation. "And if you make a deal with him, Eugenia, obviously you'll have your attorneys look at it, but I want you to get two crucial clauses in the contract. One, that you can give him back his money, at your sole discretion, at any time, with no penalty. Two, that you get a morals clause in it, so that if at any time he is involved in any form of prosecution or situation that you deem unseemly, distasteful, immoral, or damaging to your business, the deal is off and dissolves immediately. I may be wrong, but if my instincts about him are right, that's important. I don't trust him. Promise me you'll get those two clauses, or no deal."

"I promise," she said, grateful to him again.

"And don't call him back immediately. Let him sweat for a day or two. You can call him back on Monday. It's good for him, and for you."

"Thank you," she said gratefully, and got off the phone a few minutes later. She went to look for Gloria, and found her with Geoff in their guesthouse. They were avoiding the others most of the time, except for meals. Gloria's siblings were easily irritated by Geoff's arrogance. They had hardly seen Gloria for the past few days; sometimes she took her and Geoff's meals to their house, and she ate alone with him. At dinner, they joined the others for family meals. But Eugenia was observing increasingly that Geoff was not someone who did well in a family setting and he had trouble getting along with others. Given the closeness of their family, that did not bode well for the future. The others were so tired of Geoff's constant bragging, they had stopped paying attention to him and barely spoke to him at dinner, which didn't stop him from expounding on the many theories he had opinions about that no one wanted to hear. He was painful to listen to and share a meal with, and he did his best to isolate Gloria with him to gain control of her.

Gloria opened the door to her mother with a suspicious look, and Eugenia smiled warmly at her from the doorway.

"Why don't you come and have a cup of tea with me? I've been looking for you all afternoon."

"I was here," Gloria said primly. "Why were you looking for me?"

"I just wanted to chat. We haven't seen a lot of you for the past few days." Gloria didn't invite her in, and Eugenia was sure that Geoff was listening to them.

"You were in the city yesterday," Gloria accused her, as though it was a capital offense.

"True, but you two have been keeping to yourselves." They both knew he wasn't comfortable with them, but Eugenia didn't say it. She didn't want to start an argument before they got to the main issue. "Come on over to the house," she said breezily, and started to leave.

Gloria hesitated, looked back over her shoulder to check with Geoff and he nodded, out of sight, but approving Gloria's contact with her mother. He was controlling her, like a puppet. "I'll be there in a minute," she said, and closed the door. Eugenia waited for her on the porch of her house, and Gloria approached cautiously five minutes later and sat down in a chair across from her, and repeated her question. "Why do you want to talk to me? Is this about Geoff?"

"In part, but it's really about you," her mother said gently. "Some things have worried me and I want you to be aware of them."

"He feels that our family is hard on him." Gloria was instantly on the defensive.

"That's unfortunate. He's a guest here, and needs to be polite and pleasant to the other guests. He's being rude to me when he's rude to Brad or avoids the rest of us, and you're being unkind to your sisters. They've been nice to Geoff. But that's not the issue." Gloria's lips were pursed in a thin line while she listened. "When we went to Patrick Hughes's boat on Monday and Geoff stayed here, I have reliable information that a woman appeared minutes after we left, and she spent the day with him, until we came back. I think that is very concerning behavior. What was he doing with another woman all day behind your back? And there was a second incident on Tuesday that several people noticed and so did I. He was chatting up Daphne's relief nanny and keeping her from her duties, to the point that Tucker almost drowned while she had her back turned and Geoff was charming her. I think Geoff has a roving eye, and I want you to take a serious look at that. The way your relationship is right now, weeks before you marry, is the best it's ever going to be. It doesn't get better than this. And if he's flirting with other women and cheating on you now, you are in for a lifetime of it, and I don't want you to go through that."

"So what are you telling me?" Gloria said in a nasty tone. "You're withdrawing your approval and canceling the wedding?"

"This isn't about the wedding, it's about the *marriage*. I want you to take a good look at who you're marrying, so there are no bad surprises later."

"The only bad surprise is how badly you've treated him since he's been here. Brad is Sofia's boyfriend, he's not her fiancé or her husband, thank God. Geoff is British nobility, he'll be an earl one day, and I'll be a countess," Gloria said grandly.

"Without a penny," Eugenia couldn't resist pointing out to her. "And I don't give a damn about titles. I care about who he is as a human being, and how he treats my daughter."

"And you'd rather have Sofia married to Brad?" It was a statement of thinly veiled racism, which horrified Eugenia and she didn't approve of. And Brad was a hundred times the man Geoff was.

"Yes, I would. Brad is a lovely man, he's wonderful to Sofia, he's a doctor, he will be able to support her, and I don't care what color he is. Gloria, I want you to be happy, and I don't want Geoff cheating on you and breaking your heart." She went straight to the heart of the issue.

"You're the one breaking my heart, because you've been such a bitch to me and Geoff since we've been here."

Eugenia fought valiantly to control her temper, and succeeded. The issues she was concerned about were real, and she didn't want to lose focus on them.

"That's not true," Eugenia said calmly. "And if I have been, I apologize. What about the woman who spent the day here with Geoff? That was her leaving the property when we returned from the boat, the woman in the red sports car." She did not say how she knew, and protected her sources. She kept her promise to the woman he had paid fifty dollars to keep his secret.

"Geoff told me all about her. He was very upset about it."

"When I asked him about it when we got back, he said

he had no idea who she was, that she had just come onto the property, didn't speak to him, and turned around and left. When in fact she spent the day here, for eight hours. What was he doing with her? And why didn't he say so then?"

"He was embarrassed," Gloria said heatedly. "He said she just showed up, found him alone, and came on to him. He said she practically raped him. He tried to get her to leave and she refused. She wanted him to sleep with her, she begged him, and she threatened to accuse him of rape if he didn't have sex with her. He refused all day, and when he told her you were coming back any minute, she finally left." Eugenia was stunned by the story, which she didn't believe for a minute. Geoff had covered his ass nicely with Gloria, who wanted to believe him innocent, and Eugenia couldn't prove otherwise, but she was absolutely certain that he had had sex with Natasha, and that she didn't have to hold him hostage to get him to do it. "It was that Russian slut who's married to the oilman from Texas at Daphne's party," Gloria said. He had even revealed her identity to strengthen his story. And Eugenia had been right. It was Natasha Wylie, even though her husband thought she didn't drive a car. It was a tapestry of lies that Geoff had carefully woven in order to convince his future wife. But Eugenia wasn't an innocent, and she wasn't in love with him. She had no idea why her daughter was. He was pompous and entitled, full of himself, narrow-minded, narcissistic, and prejudiced, and he would live off Gloria as best he could, just as Umberto had with her. It made Eugenia sad thinking of it. Gloria deserved better than that.

"And what about the nanny?" Eugenia asked her in a calm voice, fighting for every bit of self-control she could muster. This was not a temper tantrum, it was about whether Geoff was going to be a suitable husband or not. "Did you see him with that girl? He was standing three inches from her, with her tits nearly touching him. What was he doing even talking to her, let alone from that distance? He had no reason to be in deep conversation with her, while she nearly let Tucker drown."

"She was hitting on him, he told me so, but he figured you wouldn't give him a fair shake. You like Phillip better than Geoff because he's rich, so you suck up to him. Maybe you think he'll support you when your business goes bust and you have nothing left," Gloria said. It was a viciously low blow that no child of hers should ever say to her. "You let my father starve when you divorced him," she said angrily. "If you lose your business, it's what you deserve. Papa is almost eighty years old, and he has nothing left."

Eugenia was in a white-hot rage, which she barely managed to control. "I gave your father more than half of

155

everything I had when he divorced me, and I had five children to support and get through college. He almost destroyed my business then. And if he has nothing left, it's because he spends money like water and has never worked an honest day in his life. He depends on everyone else to support him, which I did lavishly for twenty years. That's more than long enough, and what happened between me and your father is none of your business. But who you marry is mine, and I think Geoff is a cheater and you're a fool if you marry him with your eyes closed. Wake up for God's sake, look at what he's done, just in the few days he's been here, right under his mother-in-law's nose. He has no respect for anyone, and certainly not for you. I don't care how rich Phillip is. All I care about is that he's a wonderful husband and father. I hope I can say the same about Geoff one day, but it's not looking that way to me. He's going to break your heart, Gloria. And no, I'm not canceling the wedding. But maybe you should. Take a long, hard look at him, and ask yourself some questions. This can't be the first time he's done something like this. You are going to wind up supporting him, and I think he'll be unfaithful to you. If you don't care, that's up to you, but don't delude yourself about who he is." Eugenia was very serious as she said it, and Gloria answered her immediately, on the defensive.

"He's a wonderful person, and I love him. Don't count

on seeing a lot of us after the wedding, if you're going to treat us like this, accusing him of cheating, and if you're going to fill your house with Sofia's brats when she marries Brad."

"I'm ashamed of you, Gloria," Eugenia said to her, as Gloria stood up. "And thank you for giving me the opportunity to give you the most expensive wedding imaginable, and telling me not to plan on seeing you after that. Who do you think you are? Who are you? You have a lot of serious thinking to do, about your own values and Geoff's. This isn't how you grew up, small-minded and disrespectful, ungrateful and bigoted."

"I'm getting married in three weeks and I don't care what you think," Gloria spat at her, stomped down the stairs off the porch, and marched back to the guesthouse, where Geoff was waiting for her. They were two lone soldiers against the world, which brought them closer to each other. Gloria believed all of his lies. He was a practiced liar, and Eugenia felt sorry for her. She was going to have a miserable life until she opened her eyes to who he was.

Eugenia had a heavy heart as she went upstairs to change, thinking of everything Gloria had said. They were cruel words, the angry words of a nasty, spoiled child, each one designed to hurt, and each one felt like a spear to her heart. She was stunned by Gloria's accusations about her father. She had always favored him, and he must have told her that her mother had left him penniless, which was the biggest lie of all. He would have left Eugenia bleeding by the roadside if he could, and she had given him far too much, in order to be kind. He was older, and had never had a job, and she had felt sorry for him. She realized now that she shouldn't have bothered. He probably was out of money, as Gloria said. But that was his problem now, and no longer hers. She had no intention of bailing him out again. She couldn't anyway, and didn't want to.

She was sitting quietly in her room, when Eloise came to check on her a few minutes later.

"You had a fight with Gloria?" she asked cautiously.

"I did. I wanted to speak to her about Geoff, before she makes a mistake. I think he's lying to her, and she believes him. I had to say what I did. The rest is up to her."

"Gloria fought dirty, even as a kid. She always hits below the belt, and dredges up things from the past."

"She won't forgive me for questioning her about him, but I still had to do it," Eugenia said with a sigh. "That's my job. Motherhood isn't a popularity contest, and I can't win with her. She thinks I cheated your father in the divorce."

"Oh God, did she bring that up again?" Eloise groaned. "He whines to her whenever he's broke. That's why I don't want kids. No matter what you do, you wind up with some vicious fifteen-year-old screaming at you. I'd rather not go through it. And Gloria got stuck on that page. She's still immature and a bitch." She spoke seriously, and Eugenia smiled. It was a strong statement but she believed it and had experienced it herself. Eloise wasn't wrong, but Eugenia didn't want a war with any of her children, although she had a feeling Gloria meant what she said. Under Geoff's influence, they wouldn't be seeing much of her, once she got the wedding she wanted. Eugenia knew there was nothing she could do about it, but she couldn't stay silent. She owed it to Gloria to say what she believed, painful or not, and it had been for both of them. Gloria had an ally in Geoff, but Eugenia stood alone at the top of the mountain, with all the responsibility, and always had. Even at their ages now, she had an obligation to protect them as best she could. And she felt she had failed with Gloria. Her daughter was flying blind into a brick wall, refusing to open her eyes.

Patrick texted her as she walked down the stairs to dinner. "How did the talk go? Are you okay?" He remembered what she had said about being mother and father and how lonely it was at times. He knew the talk with Gloria wouldn't be easy, if her mother was challenging the marriage and expressing doubts about Geoff that sounded justified. He didn't envy her.

"It was tough. I'll live. I did my job," she texted back. "She hates me now, but I had to say it." It was nice having an adult ally, and she was touched to hear from him, and that he was checking on her.

"You did the right thing. No other choice. She'll get over it," Patrick texted her.

"Maybe not. But it was still the right thing. I hate these ages, they're so hard."

"Enjoy the others. You're lucky you have more than one," he answered, and she smiled. "See you tomorrow. Can't wait."

She joined the others for dinner then. Gloria and Geoff did not show up, and Eugenia decided to let them be. There was no point forcing them to come to the table and sulk. Gloria and Geoff walked into the dining room in the middle of dinner. They were wearing identical gray hoodies and jeans, with backpacks on. The others were surprised to see them. Gloria looked at her family angrily, and Geoff said nothing.

"We're leaving," Gloria said to her mother in a cold voice.

"Now? For where?" They had startled her and the others.

"London, of course," Gloria said. "If you're all going to treat us like shit, there's no point our being here. We're going home." It was three days before they were due to leave and halfway through the week's holiday their mother had gone to great pains to arrange, which didn't matter to them. She looked straight at her mother then, as the dinner on their plates got cold. "It cost us two thousand dollars to change our tickets. I put it on your credit card," which she had use of for wedding expenses. Eugenia had paid for their tickets to the States, and was going to do so again for the wedding. "This is your fault anyway, that we're leaving early. So you have to pay for it."

"Nice of you to ask me," Eugenia said calmly. "Running away is never the answer. Why don't you stay and try to work it out?"

"Geoff doesn't want to stay in a house where he's not welcome, and neither do I."

"You're both welcome, as long as you behave," Eugenia said firmly, and the others watched, pained for her.

"That goes both ways. We don't like the way you treat us," Gloria threw back at her, in front of all the others.

"I'm very sorry to hear it." They heard a car pull up, their Uber had arrived.

"See you at the wedding," Gloria said cavalierly, and no one said a word. "In three weeks." She and Geoff didn't say goodbye to any of them, and didn't thank her mother for the trip, the vacation, the tickets, none of it. No thank-you and no goodbye, except Gloria's speech. Geoff had not said a single word. They left the house, got in the car waiting for them, and the group heard it drive away a minute later. Eugenia looked shaken, and glanced at all of them.

"I'm sorry you had to hear that," she addressed them all.

"What brought that on?" Stef asked her, mystified.

"We had a talk this afternoon. She didn't like what I said, so they left."

"She's the same as she always was, spoiled and entitled. I'm sorry, Mom," Stefano said to her. He was disappointed in his sister, but not surprised.

"Our talk today was about an incident that happened at the house when we were on the boat on Monday, and Geoff chatting up Daphne's relief nanny on Tuesday, which almost caused Tucker to drown. I couldn't let that pass without saying something to Gloria. Geoff convinced her he wasn't to blame, it's them against the world. Anyway, I'm sorry to drag you into it, and that they left early." She felt terrible about it, but it was the price to pay for doing her job as a mother, and she didn't shirk her duty, no matter how unpopular it made her.

There was a chorus of "I'm sorry, Mom"s around the table, and they slowly got the conversation back on track, but the atmosphere was subdued, and they all felt sorry for their mother. Eloise had shot off a text to her sister and called her a bitch and a spoiled brat. The opinion around the table appeared to be that, and Eugenia didn't comment. Gloria had responded with a slew of insults to her sister.

"Boy, the wedding is going to be really fun," Eloise commented. "I can hardly wait. Should we throw rocks or rotten tomatoes instead of rice? Do we all stand up in unison and object when they get to that part?" Sofia laughed, and Daphne followed, and Liz stepped in to try and repair the evening.

"I think we should play charades after dinner, or Cards Against Humanity, or go for a midnight swim. Let's do something fun. We can't let them spoil our fabulous vacation. Fuck them," she said, and for once the rough side of her seemed appropriate and everyone laughed and relaxed after the startling departure.

In the end, they did play parlor games and laughed a lot. Stef drank tequila shots and got a little drunk, and Brad joined him. Daphne and Phillip left early. She was exhausted at the end of her pregnancy, and she was taking care of Tucker without a nanny and running after him all day. Their housekeeper was babysitting for them that night.

"I'll say one thing, this family is never dull," Liz said, "but you guys are too polite. In my family, one of my brothers would have called Geoff an asshole, punched him in the face and given him a black eye, and in the morning everyone would be friends." Everyone laughed. She had been a good sport on the vacation and nice to all of them. She and Stefano had been married for two years, and everyone was finally getting used to her. She had a big mouth and a good heart, and Eugenia liked her better than before, after this vacation. She was even beginning to enjoy the sparkling outfits. They added life to ordinary occasions, and Stef loved them.

After dinner, they all went to their guesthouses and bedrooms, and Eugenia lay on her bed thinking about Gloria and the things she had said. She had meant them to be hurtful and they were. She was just sorry it had to end that way.

She guessed that they had caught a midnight flight to London. They'd be back in time for the wedding, and Geoff's parents were due to arrive shortly before that, via quarantine in Mexico, since they weren't vaccinated for Covid and they would be tested at the airport when they entered the U.S. Eugenia wondered if the wedding would be a disaster or if they'd all get through it. She felt as though Gloria had set dynamite traps for all of them, and she wondered who would light the first match to the fuse. It was almost inevitable.

Chapter 8

Austin Wylie called Eugenia four times on Friday morning, and she finally decided to take the call. He didn't wait for her to turn down his offer, he was calling her to improve it, which showed how anxious he was to invest in her business. "I want to make you the best offer I can. Natasha is driving me crazy. She wants part ownership in your business. Name your terms and let's see if we can make a deal." His Texas drawl was more pronounced than ever.

"I'm sure you've guessed that your last offer was not acceptable." She decided to follow Patrick's advice, and go for broke, literally. "I'm prepared to give you ten percent of my business for a thirty-million-dollar investment from you," she said, with her stomach in a knot. There was a long pause and he came back at her.

"Twenty percent of the business for twenty million, and that's my best and final offer." She wasn't sure it was, but she had gotten him exactly where she wanted him, with Patrick's help. She was giving up twenty percent of her business for the twenty million dollars she needed to stay afloat for a very healthy amount of time. He was going to save her from losing the company she had worked so hard for. She almost screamed with delight, and then she followed the rest of Patrick's advice.

"In addition," she said, "I want to be able to pay you back at any time, without a penalty. And because I run a very high-end business with demanding, very elite clients, some of whom have very important positions, I need a morals clause in the contract to protect the business. I'm sure we'll never have to implement it, but I can't take the chance." There was silence for an agonizingly long moment, while he digested it, and then his voice boomed into the phone.

"Done, you've got it, whatever you want, Eugenie. I'll have my lawyers draw up the papers. It's Natasha's birthday next week and I want to give her this as a surprise. You've got yourself a new partner, and you'll have the money in your account next week. Consider this call my handshake on the deal. You won't regret it. Natasha is a great gal and she's got great fashion sense. She's taught me a lot about what women want to wear." Eugenia shuddered at the thought, but with Eugenia owning eighty percent of her business, Natasha would have no influence and little chance to interfere. And she was getting the impression that Natasha was more interested in taking her clothes off than putting them on. She almost felt sorry for Austin Wylie and his naïveté about his wife.

She called Patrick as soon as she hung up with Austin.

"We did it! *You* did it!" she chortled into the phone. "We got exactly what we wanted. He called me four times and I finally picked up. I followed your template to the letter. He got twenty percent of the business, and I get twenty million dollars, which is exactly what I need to get off the rocks and get afloat again."

"Well done!" Patrick congratulated her and took no credit for the result. He was a very modest man and happy to help her. She needed it, and it had been easy for him to advise her. "Did you tell him about the no-penalty payback and the morals clause?"

"Of course. He hesitated for a fraction of a second on the last one, and then he said whatever I want and it was done. I'll have the papers and the money by next week."

"Make sure your lawyer looks at them closely. I still don't trust him."

"Hopefully, I'll be able to pay him back soon. I'm so relieved, Patrick."

"So am I, for you. You'll see, things will turn around now, you can relax."

"I was almost out of time." Daphne had certainly given a lucky dinner party for her, the investor she needed and a man she was crazy about for the first time in years. It was a double-header.

"How did it go with Gloria last night? Did she calm down?"

"They left," Eugenia said quietly. She had won with Austin Wylie, but not with her daughter. "I don't know if it was Gloria's idea or Geoff's, but they walked in on us during dinner, with their backpacks on, basically told us all to go to hell, and said 'See ya at the wedding,' no thank-you, no goodbye. Sometimes one's children can be so disappointing. And the worst thing is she's going to pay the price for it if she marries him. I'm not. And she's determined to do it. It's them against the world."

"It's her decision," he said gently. "You did everything you could. You can pull the plug on the wedding, but she'd probably marry him anyway. You can't stop someone when they're as determined as you say she is. You just have to grit your teeth and get through it."

"We will."

"See you tonight, and congratulations again on the Wylie deal. I don't like the guy, but you need the money, and he showed up at the right time. And you'll be protected with the conditions you asked for," thanks to him.

"He sure did. See you tonight," she confirmed.

Patrick arrived punctually at the house in his blazer and jeans, and with four bottles of fancy French wine. The chef was grilling steaks on the barbecue, and Patrick had brought Château Margaux. They opened it immediately to let it breathe, while they drank martinis on the porch. They were all happy to see him, and Phillip was pleased to see that his friend and his mother-in-law got along so well. He had noticed it on the boat too. He could tell that there was a warm connection between them, and he was happy for them both. Phillip was very fond of his mother-in-law.

Daphne had come to dinner and was being a good sport, but Eugenia could see that she was more and more uncomfortable. The twins were weighing on her heavily, and she couldn't wait to have it over with. The end was hard. There was no position where she was comfortable anymore.

"I feel like I've been possessed by aliens," she said to Sofia at dinner, and she laughed.

"You have. It won't be long now. If you sneeze, they'll fall out."

"I wish," Daphne said, anxious about the delivery ahead of her.

No one mentioned Geoff and Gloria at dinner, but

Eugenia was upset by the way they'd left the night before. It was such a cowardly way to deal with it, to just run away, and all Gloria cared about was her wedding, not who she was marrying, and they all agreed he wasn't a good guy. Gloria was totally under his influence, and believed everything he said. Eugenia was sure that he was lying about Natasha and had more than willingly slept with her. No one had had to twist his arm. And she didn't believe for a minute that she had held him hostage.

When the others went to bed, Patrick stayed for a little while to talk to Eugenia. They sat in the porch swing, swaying gently back and forth, and he kissed her in the moonlight, with the crickets chirping and the fireflies dancing, and a falling star overhead. It wasn't as romantic as being on his yacht, but it was warm and comfortable, and he had enjoyed talking to her children. He wanted to introduce her to his son, but Quinn was on a ranch in Montana where he went every year, riding and fishing with a group of friends. "He's not a sailor like his father, he's a mountain man," Patrick said, and kissed her again. "I'm sorry I can't have you on the boat tomorrow for your last day. I'm hoping to sell two of my buildings and the buyer is coming to discuss the deal with me. He's flying back to L.A. tomorrow night, so I can't put him off."

"I don't expect you to," she said with her head on his

shoulder, enjoying the moment. "You've already been wonderful to us. And you helped me make that deal today. We'll be fine here. The house worked out well for us. These vacations always go so quickly. Normally, we wouldn't all be together again until Christmas, but this time we have the wedding in a few weeks. And I have a feeling it's going to be a mess. I've only met Geoff's parents once and they're as pompous as he is, possibly worse. I'm not a big fan of threadbare aristocracy, they have a lot more to prove. We're not off to a great start," she said, and then looked at him. "Will you come to the wedding?"

"Do you want me there?"

"Weddings are usually a terrible bore if you don't know the people, but I suspect there will be fireworks at this one, so it will be more interesting," she said, and he laughed.

"I'm happy to be there to support you," he said.

"I'll send you an invitation. I'd love you to come as my date."

"I'd be honored," he said, and pulled her a little closer on the swing. "Let's have dinner in the city this week."

"I'd love it," she said. They kissed for a while, enjoying the end of the evening together, and then he left.

On Saturday, the last day of their vacation, the family spent their time together at their rented house and then had dinner at Daphne and Phillip's. This time no one mentioned Geoff and Gloria. She hadn't texted her mother when they arrived nor thanked her for the trip or the extra expense for the switched tickets in order to leave three days early. Eugenia enjoyed the others for the last day, and they had a lovely dinner at Daphne's house and then went back to their own. They laughed and talked late into the evening and drank a lot of wine, and after Eugenia went to bed the others went for a midnight swim. They all agreed that it had been a great vacation and they were sorry to see it end. Their day on Patrick's boat had been an added adventure, and they were curious to see what would happen between Patrick and their mother. It looked like something was starting, but they were discreet enough that no one was sure if it was romantic or if they were just becoming friends, but they seemed to enjoy each other's company.

"Maybe your mother will marry him and we can all go on vacation on his boat next year," Liz suggested, and Stef gave her a look.

"Slow down, they haven't been on a date yet. They met a week ago." They didn't know about the day Eugenia and Patrick had spent in seclusion on his boat.

"He's a cool guy and I like his boat," Liz said simply, and Stef shook his head. Eloise was nervous about going back to Paris, perennially worried about her job, and they were all going back to work on Monday. It was always hard to go back to real life after the vacations Eugenia provided them, where she took care of everything. It was all planned to perfection and she spoiled them like the children they had been and no longer were. Only Gloria was still trying to cash in on everything she could, like her wedding, with total disregard for the massive expense for her mother. It annoyed Stef and Eloise, but Sofia assumed that their mother knew what she was doing and could afford the vacation if she did it every year. It never occurred to her that the pandemic had impacted her mother's business. Sofia had no experience in business and financial affairs.

"I think that the investor's money she accepted yesterday is a big deal for her," Stefano said, sitting by the pool with his sisters at one in the morning. "She doesn't say a lot about it, but I think she's been really worried for the last six months. I hope that helps." He was concerned about her.

"Your mother is a smart businesswoman, she knows what she's doing," Liz said with total confidence.

They hated to see the night end, and their vacation, always a bittersweet moment, but this time they knew they'd be together again soon, at the wedding. Eugenia had made a point of inviting Brad and had handed him an invitation, which touched both him and Sofia, and he had promised to be there.

They were all packed when they went to bed that night at two A.M., and Eugenia's bags were standing in the hall outside her suite.

She set her alarm and got up with each of them when they left. Eloise was the first to go. With a ten A.M. flight to Paris out of Newark, she had to leave the Hamptons at five in the morning, and Eugenia gave her a big hug.

"Try to relax and stop worrying," she reminded her daughter. She stood on the porch and waved as the car drove away. Brad and Sofia were next, with a flight to Memphis at eleven. They left at seven, and Eugenia had breakfast with Stef and Liz before they drove back to the city. He said he thought it was one of their best vacations ever and Eugenia was pleased. She had worked hard to achieve it.

She checked the houses after they left, closed and locked everything up and left the keys where she'd found them, and drove to Daphne and Phillip's house to say goodbye. Daphne promised to call her if anything happened with the twins. She and Phillip were driving back to the city that night. They'd already stayed a week longer than the obstetrician wanted, just in case she went into labor and things moved quickly. Eugenia doubted she'd make it till the wedding, it looked like she was going to pop any minute, and Phillip was eager to get her home. Eugenia thanked them for the times they had entertained all of them, and they stood in the driveway and waved as Eugenia drove away.

It was strange getting back to her empty apartment. It seemed so quiet and lonely now that the children were gone. Eugenia was used to it, but their vacations always reminded her of how much she loved being with them, and how sweet it had been when they were all still at home. It was an adjustment being on her own again with no one to talk to.

After she unpacked, she took out the folder with her drawings and Eloise's, and did some more sketches for Cotton Candy. She smiled every time she looked at them. They were going to be so much fun to produce and she couldn't wait to see how they'd sell, and to whom.

Patrick called her that night to make sure she got home safely. She asked him how his meeting had gone the day before.

"Pretty well," he said, sounding pleased. "I wanted to sell him two buildings but he might buy three or even four. That would give me what I need to make some major changes on the ones I have left. It's all a chess game, with a little bit of poker thrown in. I might come out ahead in the end. It's not over yet," he said. "How about Tuesday for dinner? I have a lot going on tomorrow."

"So do I." She wanted to speak to the factory again about Cotton Candy, go to the wholesale market for the right fabrics, and rehire one of her patternmakers and two sewers to work on the new line. This was a whole new world for her, and for a completely different client. She was already set for her show during Fashion Week. All she had to do was hire models and do fittings, starting in two weeks. The runway samples were already made. She was showing a very reduced line to test the market for her daywear. She was making big changes to salvage her business, and she was praying it would work. And now she was going to have fun with Cotton Candy, put the clothes in a pop-up store she hadn't chosen yet, and see what would happen. "It's crazy that we're both rebuilding our businesses, isn't it?" she said to Patrick on the phone.

"That's what life is all about, reinventing yourself when everything goes to shit. And if it all fails, we sell everything. I'll keep the boat, and sail around the world." He made light of it. She loved his strength and his humor, his determination and optimism, and his perseverance. He gave her the feeling that he wouldn't let the ship go down. He hadn't yet, and neither had she. They had that in common, although her business was so much smaller than his, but it wasn't negligible either, and he had given her valuable advice.

"Tuesday would be great for dinner," she responded to

his invitation. When they hung up, she went back to her Cotton Candy sketches, and started making lists of everything she needed to do. She still had her assistant in New York, Pamela Atkins, but Pamela had been on vacation for a month with nothing to do until the weeks right before Fashion Week. Eugenia had reduced the staff dramatically in the last year as their business slowed down to a trickle, and finally dried up entirely. She was hoping to hire many of them back when they got started again, but for the moment, she couldn't afford them, and had no work to offer them. Most of her employees had been on unemployment. She tried to pick and choose among them, and decide who would be best suited to working on an inexpensive youthful line. But she wanted to do it with quality too. All the people in her atelier, which was dormant now, had been trained in Paris and were overqualified for what she had in mind.

She explained it all to Pamela on Monday morning. Eugenia knew she was an early riser and went to the gym every day, so she called her at seven. Pamela was thrilled to hear about the new project. It had been incredibly sad, watching the business stall in the last eight months, and it had taken a toll on Eugenia's spirits. She'd been anxious and nervous for a long time, and there had been nothing Pam could do to help. Their customers just weren't buying, with everyone locked down. They were going to put on a beautiful show for Fashion Week, but the new daywear was an experiment and by no means a sure thing. It was expensive, made with the best high-quality fabrics available, although getting the fabrics and trimmings in from Europe wasn't easy, and Pam wasn't sure their clients would adjust to the change.

But Cotton Candy was a concept she could wrap her mind around. She had a fourteen-year-old daughter herself, and it sounded right up her alley, at the right price point for even Pam to afford. She was forty-four and a single mom. She had decided to have a baby on her own at thirty, and hadn't regretted it, although she was finding the early teenage years harder than she'd expected. She and her daughter, Isabelle, had been so close, and now Isabelle disapproved of everything her mother did, and was vocal about it. But Pam knew she was going to love Eugenia's new line.

"This is a whole new market for us," Pam said, excited. "How did you come up with it?" She wondered if Eugenia had been seeking advice from consultants. The new line didn't sound like her at all and it was hard to imagine her doing it, or even coming up with the concept.

"Sofia wore one of her crazy outfits. Distressed denim overalls, with a pink tulle skirt and sequin heart appliqués. After Eloise stopped complaining about it, she got inspired, and the next thing I knew she handed me a folder full of sketches, and I knew it was the right way to go." It was one of the things Pam loved about Eugenia, how open she was to new ideas, always reaching and stretching. The new high-end daywear line was the evidence of it, and it was beautiful. But this was a leap of faith off the high diving board, and a real tour de force, with a great chance to be a commercial success. It was a brilliant idea and just what they needed to expand.

"Where are we going to sell it? Department stores?" It was better suited to that market, but they needed orders to do it for next season, and Eugenia wanted to move a lot faster than that to test the market.

"Eventually, but that would be for next spring. We can take orders at the Seventh Avenue showroom and do some kind of presentation during Fashion Week if I can get the pieces made fast enough. I want to get it out there quickly. I'm thinking of a pop-up, maybe in SoHo, or maybe we just turn the Madison Avenue store around for a couple of weeks, and see how we do uptown. Or we could do both. We don't have anything new in the store right now anyway." They had made one sale on Madison in the last month, which was disastrous, and she had practically given a gown away on sale to a good customer.

"This is going to be so new and fresh," Pam said. She

had a teenager's body herself and looked young for her age, and she and her daughter often traded clothes when she wasn't working. She could easily see herself and Izzie in matching outfits from what Eugenia was describing. Pam was gutsy enough to wear it, even at forty-four. She loved variety and fun clothes.

"I'm calling the factory this morning, and I want to look at fabrics this afternoon. No high-priced denim, maybe we put together some one-of-a-kind combined vintage pieces, but mostly I want to make items we can mass-produce in bulk, so we make some real profit with it. Do you want to help me pick fabrics this afternoon?" she asked her, and Pam jumped at it, but she had no one to leave her daughter with. Izzie was off for another two weeks, until she started school.

"Can I bring Izzie?" Eugenia thought about it, and then realized it was a great idea.

"Definitely, she can be our market advisor. That's perfect."

"I warn you everything she picks will be pink or purple."

"That's exactly what we want, and a lot of sparkle, ruffles, and bows. Girly. Nearly kitsch, but not quite. We can catch the wave on that, there's a big market out there we've never explored."

Pam smiled. "I don't think your couture clients are ready for that."

"My couture clients are hibernating, but don't kid your-self, they're buying mass market items online. I want their daughters and granddaughters now, and Izzie can point us in the right direction on that."

"And Sofia. It sounds like she is the inspiration for the whole line."

"Exactly." They made a date to meet after lunch at a huge wholesale fabric market at the lower end of the garment district. Eugenia had never been there but she knew where it was. Eventually they could buy in volume, but she wanted to see what their bestsellers were first.

They met that afternoon and Pam's daughter was the poster child for who Eugenia wanted their youngest clients to be, with a little more sophistication for customers in their twenties. It was a hot day in New York and Izzie had on pink denim shorts and a crop top with sparkly hearts on it. She had on the latest trendy sneakers, which looked used and cost eight hundred dollars, which Eugenia thought sinful for a child her age but Pam said she *had* to have them to keep up with her friends. Izzie was carrying a sparkly heart-shaped purse and had braces on her teeth, and long straight blonde hair like her mother's. Pam was wearing white shorts and a pink T-shirt with a silver heart, pink Manolo flats, and a white Chanel bag she'd bought second-hand. It was a modified youthful look suitable for her age.

"Okay, Izzie, tell us what you love," Eugenia told her. They looked at bolts and bolts of fabric, at least half of it pink, some lavender, pale blue, a little white, lots of metallics, fabrics with silver threads, a great red. Every fabric they picked popped, and Izzie had a great eye for color and for what her peers would love. Eugenia was fascinated by some of her choices, and trusted her advice. They picked some great patterns and stripes. They bought the fabric on the spot, got a good deal on it, and took it to the store in three cabs, with Izzie in one. She was having a ball. They put it all in the haute couture fitting rooms, which were big enough to use as temporary stockrooms. Their pattern-maker was coming in the next day, delighted to have work again. The designs were going to be simple at first, with variations on the theme. This collection wasn't about chic, it was about young and fun, and Eugenia wanted the fit to be right. She wanted to play with some of the fabrics and see how they draped and held up. They had work to do, and the factory had promised that if she got the fabric and the patterns to them by the end of the week, they could produce a modest first run very quickly. Eugenia was moving fast with Pam's help. Pam was used to multitasking, and following her boss at full speed. It had been a very productive day, and Eugenia thanked Izzie for her help, and asked Pam to get her a pair of her most coveted trendy sneakers to thank her. Izzie was thrilled and said she knew just the ones she wanted.

"What are we doing about a pop-up?" Pam asked her before she left, and Eugenia looked pensive.

"I have a crazy idea. I want to empty the store and fill it with the Cotton Candy line for a couple of weeks." Pam wasn't sure about the store, but they weren't selling any gowns at the moment. As long as it was temporary, she approved.

Eugenia had another idea too. The next day, she searched the internet and found a company in the Bronx that rented carnival and vending machines. They had a great vintage-looking cotton candy machine and she rented it and hired the operator to go with it, to make cotton candy and hand it out on Madison Avenue for two weeks. She assigned Pam to get the permit, which the vendor said was easy. It was all falling into place. The fabric hadn't been expensive, and the factory was giving her a good deal, as they wanted her business if she went into mass production with it. The factory owner was desperate, and people were grateful now to have a job and get work.

By the time Patrick picked Eugenia up at her apartment for dinner, she had been working on the project for two days, and the patternmaker and an assistant were busy in her couture atelier. Austin Wylie had emailed her the contract and she'd sent it to her attorney to check.

She told Patrick all about it, as she poured him a glass of wine and he admired the view from her apartment. It was modern and airy, the décor mostly white with colorful contemporary art. She had some of the same artists he did on the boat, although his collection was more impressive, but he liked what she had too. He sat down with a smile, admiring her. She was wearing a pink silk summer dress and high heels. He had come from the office, and wore a light beige cotton summer suit with a blue shirt. He had showered at the office, and was freshly shaved for their date. She loved his looks with his thick salt-and-pepper hair.

"You didn't waste any time," he said, impressed by what she told him. The Cotton Candy project, and the influx of money from Austin Wylie, which gave her some security, had energized her.

"It's a long way from what I usually do, but I'm loving it. My assistant's fourteen-year-old daughter was my market consultant on the fabrics. If you'd told me two years ago I'd be designing for fourteen-year-olds, I'd have laughed at you."

"You may wind up with an even bigger success than you had before. Volume is a big deal with the internet now. Fashion was a huge moneymaker before the pandemic, and it will be again."

184

"We'll see where it goes," she said, open to anything, which she hadn't been before. She'd had very definite ideas about how far she would go and what real fashion was, not unlike Eloise, but not quite as rigid. "How were your meetings?" she asked him.

"Encouraging," he said. "It's interesting how people react when you hit a rough spot. There used to be people calling day and night, begging to talk to me. The minute they smell trouble, they run like hell, and it's surprising who won't take your calls. I'm getting used to it, but it startled me. It's short-sighted of them. The tables turn fast in business, especially at this level. I found it humiliating at first. Now, after a year, I don't care. The minute it hit Page Six that I had seventeen empty buildings, the dogcatcher didn't want to know me, but now the brave ones are coming back, and they figure I may have some winning cards up my sleeve. I hope they're right." Eugenia was touched by how open Patrick was about his fall from grace and how painful it had been. She had experienced the same thing in the world of fashion. People weren't as nice to her or as respectful as they had been before, and it hurt her feelings too. Like him, she had gotten used to it, but she noticed, and she would remember.

She had just decided not to show at the next haute couture show in Paris in January, to skip a season and show again in July, to give the haute couture market time to recover. She thought it would be the last to come back to normal, and didn't want to show to an empty hall, which would be expensive and embarrassing. With her Eugenia Ward brand, she was going to focus on high-end ready-to-wear for the next year, and Cotton Candy at the low end, if it looked promising. She was about to find out.

He took her to Elio's on Second Avenue, which was doing a booming business with a sidewalk terrace. It wasn't romantic, but it was fun and noisy and crowded, and they both loved it. The food was good and it was easy, and they walked back slowly to her apartment, which was a long enough walk for them to continue their conversation. He had a town house on Seventieth Street, not far from her. As they approached her building, he stopped and kissed her and asked the question he had wanted to ask her all night, and hoped it wasn't too soon. He wanted to spend time with her, and they were both busy in the city, and worked late. He never left his office early, in good times or bad. Particularly now that he was networking to find buyers for some of his buildings.

"I'd love you to come to the boat this weekend," he said cautiously. "Maybe it's too soon to ask, and you can have one of the guest staterooms if you like. It's the only place I really disconnect from real life and all the problems, and you seem to love it as much as I do."

186

"Who wouldn't?" she said with a smile, thinking about the invitation. The offer of the guest stateroom didn't make it seem shocking or premature. By normal standards, it was early in the relationship to go away with him for a weekend, but she loved the idea too, and he wasn't forcing her to sleep with him. He wanted to share his world with her, and he had been a perfect gentleman with her so far, and nothing but kind on the day she'd spent on the boat with him.

"I'd love it," she responded to his invitation, and he kissed her again.

"I promise to behave myself," he said earnestly, and she believed him. She had no reason not to, and it sounded like a fabulous weekend. She could hardly wait, and again she had no intention of telling her kids. Her private adult life was her business and not theirs. She had met the first man she'd been attracted to and really liked in a long time, and he seemed to like her. Where it would go no one could predict. They were both struggling with overwhelmingly complicated business situations and had almost lost everything they'd built. It was a common bond between them, and he was helping her with good advice and she was grateful for it. They were working twice as hard now to salvage what they could. And at their ages, she didn't feel she owed her children any explanations. She walked into her apartment thinking about him. Having met Patrick seemed like a gift, and spending the weekend on his yacht, nothing short of a miracle. Maybe the tides were finally turning. She enjoyed his company more than she'd expected to. She trusted him, and was willing to take a risk.

Chapter 9

The weekend on *My Dream* was everything Eugenia had imagined it would be and more. They sailed north, after he picked her up in New York. He had a berth on the Hudson River, next to a cruise ship. He only used it a few times a year when he had the boat in the States. Most of the time she was in Europe, but this year he had brought her to the Hamptons, while he used his house there. He had told Eugenia that he usually spent the month of August in the south of France, but this year, with Covid still lurking, he had wanted to stay closer to home, and he hadn't been sure until July if Americans would be allowed in Europe. As it turned out, they were, but he hadn't known that would be the case when he made his summer plans. They sailed around Cape Cod, and then to Maine that night. Patrick had asked

189

Eugenia if she could stay until Monday morning and she said she could, if they got back early enough. The first shipment of Cotton Candy was due from the factory at midday, and she wanted to be there to look it over when they received it.

They stayed offshore most of the time, going into port in the evening for an exceptional lobster dinner on Friday night, and stayed at anchor outside the port and watched a movie in the theater. They took Patrick's little sailboat out in the morning, swam in the sea, and lay on the sundeck after lunch, and went for a sail after dinner on board that night. The boat provided endless opportunity for entertainment, sports, and just time to be together and talk. She stayed in the biggest guest cabin on Friday night and the stewardess brought her breakfast in bed in the morning, while Patrick answered emails in his office before they went sailing.

They sat talking on deck until late on Saturday night, and he walked her to her stateroom and kissed her.

"Thank you for another incredible day," she said as he held her.

"I had a wonderful time too," he said in a husky voice. "I don't want to press you, but you know I'd love it if you join me in my cabin. It's up to you," he said, with a hopeful almost boyish look, and she smiled. She felt so comfortable with him after all the time they were spending together that she felt as though she had known him for longer. She put her arms around his neck and he held her close and kissed her.

"I think that sounds like a nice idea," she said in a whisper, and when she did, he swept her up gently in his arms and walked her down the hall to his suite. The door was open, and he closed it with his foot, laid her gently on his bed, lay down next to her, and carefully undressed her, as she unbuttoned his shirt and he took off the rest. There was a soft light in the room, almost like candlelight, and the moon was shining into the room, as he made love to her. She didn't feel as though she was making love to a stranger, but with a beloved friend. He was a gentle, thoughtful lover, and he looked at her with such tenderness afterward as he held her.

"Thank you for staying with me tonight. I wanted you so badly, but I didn't want to rush you and scare you off," he said, and she kissed him.

"I wanted you too, but I was afraid it was too soon, and I didn't want to spoil anything, or rush it."

"You couldn't have spoiled anything," he said, running a gentle finger around her beautifully proportioned body. "I love being with you, and making love to you. We have such a good time together." He stretched out next to her then and put an arm around her, whispering in the dim light. He turned it off and the moonlight shone in on them.

"This is so perfect, it makes me feel like I'm dreaming,"

she said sleepily, and dozed off next to him. He tucked her in, and leaned on one elbow, looking at her, wondering how he got so lucky. She was an amazing woman. He loved her courage and her spirit, her bright creative mind, and her kindness.

They spent Sunday lazily on deck, after waking up late, as the yacht sailed slowly south again, toward New York. They were going to dock at the pier in the Hudson after staying offshore for the night, and entering the port in the morning.

They went to bed early and made love again. They only slept for a few hours, and he woke her up to see the Statue of Liberty as they motored into port early on Monday morning. It felt like a movie being with him. She had never felt so spoiled and pampered. He thought of everything to please her, and his lovemaking was slow and sensuous and passionate.

They had breakfast on deck, next to a cruise ship as people stared down at them, and he had the crew draw curtains around the outdoor dining area so they had privacy.

"I feel like royalty traveling with you," she said with a giggle, and he grinned at her. "I hate to go to work. Shades of Cinderella again, every time I leave you." He had a car and driver waiting on the dock for her. The port was busy at that hour, and the passengers on the cruise ship were disembarking at the same time. He walked her to the car, put his arms around her, and held her tight.

"I'll call you tonight," he promised. "Have a good day."

"Thank you for a fantastic weekend." He was becoming addictive, and she didn't want to sleep without him. "Do you want to stay at my place tonight?" she asked him, and he smiled broadly.

"I'd love that. I'll call you later and we'll figure out dinner." She nodded, gave him a quick kiss, and got into the car. The driver took her suitcase and put it in the trunk, and a minute later they drove away as Patrick rushed up the gangway for a Zoom call in five minutes.

She felt like a princess being driven to work, dropping off her bag with the doorman at her building on the way to the store, where Pam was already waiting for her. Eugenia was wearing sneakers and jeans, a navy-and-white-striped T-shirt, and a blazer, with her hair in a neat ponytail. They had work to do, clearing another of the couture fitting rooms for all the Cotton Candy merchandise coming in. They were going to put it on racks. The clothes for her runway show were already hanging in the third fitting room, with the accessories Eugenia had chosen, and the exquisite wedding gown that was the finale of her show.

Pam had gotten a cappuccino for Eugenia, and they got to work setting up the racks as soon as she arrived.

"Nice weekend?" Pam asked her pleasantly. She had no idea where Eugenia had been, or with whom. She assumed she had stayed home that weekend, or visited Daphne in the Hamptons.

"Very. How's my marketing consultant?"

"She's staying at a friend's house in Connecticut, so I can work late if we have to."

The clothes arrived from the factory promptly at noon, and Eugenia, Pam, and the salesclerk from the store opened all the cartons, put everything on hangers, and steamed them, after Eugenia examined each one and was satisfied with the quality of the work. She was grinning with delight as she looked at the result of Eloise's brilliant idea. They had a full line of clothes in three sizes and several colorways. More than enough to get started.

"Where are we putting it?" Marina, from the store, had no idea what Eugenia was doing, and was stunned by the merchandise they'd been unpacking. It was about as far one could get from Eugenia's other lines.

"I don't have the SoHo pop-up yet," Pam informed Eugenia. "I called three realtors. Two of them never called me back, and the third one said she had nothing decent available at the moment. A lot of lesser brands have grabbed them for Fashion Week."

"We don't need it. I have a better idea, for free," Eugenia

said, eyeing the merchandise closely. They'd done good work at the factory.

"You're going to put them out on the street?" Pam looked dubious. "They'll get stolen." Eugenia turned to Marina then.

"There are four bolts of pink tulle in the first fitting room. Grab my staple gun and my glue gun out of my desk, and leave the tulle in the store. We'll be down in a few minutes." Marina hurried off to the fitting room next door, and took the bolts to the store one by one. They were heavy to carry even though it was only tulle. There was one bolt of pale lavender tulle with sequins glued to it, and she took that too in case Eugenia wanted it.

Pam and Eugenia maneuvered the racks on wheels into the freight elevator behind the fitting rooms, got the racks out onto the sidewalk and into the store, and locked the door behind them. Eugenia took her jacket off and tossed it on a chair. The chair was sleek and modern, covered in nubby white wool to match the rest of the furniture in the store. There were two small antique chests, and Eugenia directed Pam and Marina to move them to a stockroom in the back of the store. They wouldn't work with the clothes.

They set up two more racks, put the stock on them that had been hanging, and moved those to the stockroom too. The selection was sparse, since they were doing so little business, and had had no new evening gowns to show for months.

Eugenia positioned the racks where she wanted them with the Cotton Candy line hanging on them, set up an empty rack, and began moving things around. As she did, she took out six dresses and two pink denim jackets and laid them on the white bouclé couch to deal with later. She started moving the Cotton Candy around on the racks at full speed, and shortly after there were jackets, shorts, skirts, and dresses all set out in progressive sizes with the colors of the clothes looking like a sparkling pastel rainbow, as her two employees watched her in admiration. She had an eye for display and merchandising, even with playful teenage merchandise.

"We need five more mannequins, and you need to undress the one in the window." The mannequin was wearing a sleek bun of dark hair. Eugenia told Pam, squinting at the clothes, "And we need to get two long blonde wigs, two red ones, and two with dark brown hair. Put away the blonde one in the window. The spare mannequins are in the upstairs storeroom."

They brought them down and assembled them, and Eugenia dressed them herself with the outfits she had laid on the couch. She put them in more playful poses than the staid one in the window. When she was through, they were still bald, but there was a perfect lineup that gave the tone and flavor of the style of the clothes. She grabbed the bolts of tulle then, unrolled them, created big balls of crushed tulle the size of beach balls, and put one in two of the mannequins' hands. By the time she finished bunching the fabric into balls and crushing them a little, and put them on the floor at the feet of the mannequins in the window, it really did look like cotton candy, and she didn't even have to use the staple gun or the glue gun. The window looked terrific. Eugenia was pleased, and asked Pam to take a picture of it and text it to Izzie and ask her what she thought of it.

"We need the wigs right away," Eugenia said to Marina, and sent her to a shop she knew on Lexington to get them. She was back twenty minutes later, with what Eugenia had ordered.

"They didn't have enough long ones. I got two with short dark hair, one with bangs and one with pigtails. I thought it might look right with our new look."

"Perfect, thank you." They all unwrapped the wigs and Eugenia put them where she wanted them, just as Izzie answered her mother's text.

"Sorry, I was in the pool. It looks fantastic, Mom. Tell Eugenia I love it." Pam relayed the message to her boss, as Eugenia stood back to look at what they'd done, then walked outside to view the window from the street and liked it even better. Now all they had to do was discover who their customer was. But the display work had been done in less than three hours from the time they opened the crates. Pam was standing shaking her head, and admiring the way it all looked.

"Eugenia, you're a genius."

"No, Eloise is." Eugenia took no credit for the concept. She just hoped she wasn't crazy with what she'd done. She had embraced it completely. No one would have recognized it as Eugenia Ward's store except for the name on the door and the address. They were standing around admiring how everything looked, when Eugenia's cell phone rang and she went to answer it, pulling it out of her purse. It was Eloise, calling from Paris, and ten o'clock in the morning there.

"You wouldn't believe what I'm looking at," she said with a wide smile. "The store is completely transformed. Welcome to Cotton Candy, and all thanks to you." As she said it, she heard a sob at the other end, and her smile faded instantly. "Eloise? What's wrong? Darling, are you okay?" The sobbing continued for a full minute while Eugenia tried not to panic. "Tell me. Are you hurt? Did something happen?"

"Yes, I was right. I got fired."

"Oh shit. Just like that? Why?" Eloise's design work was excellent, she couldn't believe it was about her designs, and she'd worked there for seven years.

"I told you, Mom. They're making huge cutbacks, everyone is, even the big brands."

"And they walked in and fired you just like that?" Eloise

had been worried for so long that her mother hadn't taken her concerns seriously.

"No, but the only markets that are doing well for anyone right now are in Asia. They told me that they have to make drastic cuts in Paris. A third of the staff was fired today. They offered me Bangkok or Hong Kong, but I don't want to live in Asia. I want to stay in Europe. And they said they had to let me go if I didn't want to move. I would do Italy or London, or even Germany, but not Bangkok or Hong Kong, and they're making the same cuts all over Europe. They're not offering anyone jobs here." She was still crying and sounded devastated. "They said they'll start rehiring when business picks up, but not for a while. Maybe in a year. But they can't promise anyone anything now. So I'm done. They just told me."

"You're sure about Hong Kong? You might like it."

"No! And I don't speak Chinese. Another girl on my marketing team is going to Hong Kong, but she's half French and half Chinese and speaks the language. I don't. What am I going to do? I don't want to live in New York, and I hate to give up my apartment here. I love it, and it took me three years to find it."

"First of all you're going to take a breath and calm down. You'll find another job in Paris eventually. You need to think about this calmly, and talk to a headhunter there," but they both knew that the fashion industry was suffering every-where, and had been for a year and a half.

"No one's hiring here."

"Now. That will all change in a few months. And your Cotton Candy line looks incredible. We turned the store around, and we're ready to roll." She had sheets of prices, but they hadn't had time to put price tags on the clothes yet. Eugenia knew that people would be shocked at how reasonable they were, especially at Eugenia Ward's. The numbers were laughable compared to their usual prices. Eloise didn't want to hear about it now. And Eugenia was trying to think about how to help her.

"When do you finish there?" Eugenia asked, assuming Eloise had to give them a few weeks.

"In three hours, at close of business. They gave us all severance. They were very nice about it, but I'm out of a job, and I was *fired,* Mom." It was a first for her. She had gone outside to call her mother, and had walked around the corner so no one would see her crying, but she had seen the others crying too. It was a hard blow for all of them.

"Wow," Eugenia said. "Well, don't worry about the apart-ment now. We can figure that out later. Why don't you just take a break and come home? You can help me with Fashion Week in a couple of weeks. We've got the show all organized except for fittings after we hire the models. We'll be taking orders in the showroom. And I'm going to open the doors to Cotton Candy tomorrow."

"That was fast." Eloise sounded surprised.

"The factory was hungry for business. I'll have Pam send you pictures. I've got six mannequins in the window, wearing our best looks. And I owe it all to you," she said gratefully. "Eloise, get a ticket, hop on a plane. We can figure it all out from here. I really could use your help, in a week or two I'll be swamped," she said sincerely. "And I still have a wedding to put on."

"Oh my God, Mom, if you ask me to help Gloria with her wedding, I'll shoot her or myself. She gives me anxiety. More than I already have," Eloise corrected. "And I'd like to help you, Mom, but I don't know anything about that kind of clothes."

"Neither do I, but you inspired them, and I think it's the best thing you've ever done for me."

"Don't make me sorry I did," Eloise said, smiling through her tears.

"You can't afford the luxury of feeling sorry for yourself," Eugenia said more harshly. "The race for jobs is going to be acute everywhere for a while. You just have to be patient and hang in. Come home. I'm going to Paris at the end of September, to present the ready-to-wear line in the show-room and take orders. I'm going to be juggling a lot, and I could really use a spare set of hands, and your genius for design."

"Those tutus I sketched for you don't need a design genius. If they were produced according to my sketches, all they need is a busload of screaming fourteen-year-old girls. I can't believe how fast you got them made."

"Neither can I, but they're all set up here and ready to rock 'n' roll."

"Maybe I'll come home in a couple of days." Eloise hesitated. "Thank you for the offer, Mom. I'll let you know. I need to think about it."

"Don't think about it, just come. You're coming for the wedding anyway. This just gets you home a week or two early."

"I know, Mom," Eloise sounded exasperated. "But it brings me back fired and in disgrace."

"You didn't hold them up at gunpoint. There is a global crisis, and people everywhere are getting laid off. You'll find another job, El. Now buy a ticket, pack a bag, and come home. It's admirable that you want to deal with it yourself, but there's not a lot you can do about it."

"I have a right to be upset. It just happened."

"Yes, you do," her mother confirmed. "But you're going to have to be a little patient."

"Okay. I have to go. I'll call you later and tell you what

I'm doing." Thirty suddenly seemed so young to Eugenia, and so unprepared to weather life's crises. She really was sorry for her.

They hung up. Eugenia had gone outside to talk to Eloise about getting fired. She walked back into the store and Pam and Marina stared at her.

"What happened?" Pam spoke first.

"Eloise got fired." Pam was shocked. "They are making huge cutbacks."

Eloise reported to Daphne by text. And five minutes later Daphne called her sister.

"What the hell happened?" she asked Eloise.

"Too many employees and bad sales figures. It's everywhere."

"What are you going to do now?"

"Mom wants me to come home, but I look like a total loser if I come home now."

"So what? Just come home," Daphne concluded. "See you soon," she said when they hung up.

Worrying about Eloise took some of the pleasure out of transforming the store. Eugenia walked home a little while later, still thinking about her.

She told Patrick about it, when he came to her apartment

for dinner and to stay with her that night. He was surprised to hear it and sad for Eloise. It was exactly what she'd been afraid of and she was right. She had felt it coming, like a tidal wave, and it had finally caught up with her.

Patrick staying at Eugenia's apartment was very different and less glamorous than her staying on his boat. He was at a loss to help her with her children. He hardly knew them. All he could do was be reassuring to their mother. Patrick was impressed by how supportive they all were of each other.

Her household was much simpler and quieter than his, but it gave them time to walk around as they chose, and to make love anywhere they wanted in the apartment. Her housekeeper went home at six-thirty, and they took full advantage of it. They played the stereo and listened to music, and sat on the terrace in the warm night air.

Eloise took her mother's advice and came home. She was nervous and on edge, and heartbroken over losing a job she loved. She was stunned by how fast Eugenia had waved a magic wand and the entire Cotton Candy collection had appeared. By the time Eloise came home three days after her call to her mother, they had sold more than half the collection, and it had taken off like a forest fire. Eugenia was stunned by the appetite people had for it. About half their customers were teenagers, shopping on their mothers' credit cards, with their full knowledge and permission, and the other half of their growing fan base were trendy young women with the bodies of even younger ones. They looked sexy and cute in the sequined denim jackets, the skirts, the dresses, the tulle confections, and the abundance of sequins on everything. Eloise couldn't believe how her mother had transformed the store. They had already caught the attention of the fashion press and Page Six in the *Post* to report the craze. Eugenia had tapped into her customers' desire to look like fairies and mermaids and little girls. They were devouring Cotton Candy, in the best sense of the word. And the vendor with the cotton candy truck in front of the store was handing out great cloud-like balls. Much to Eugenia's astonishment, they sold every single item within a week, and she had already ordered more.

She told Patrick about it and he came to see it before the last of it sold. And in the midst of the shopping frenzy, Natasha Wylie showed up and introduced herself to Eugenia. She was wearing a stretch leopard-print bodysuit and looked at her new partner's pink candy land in amazement. Eugenia hadn't expected to see her so soon. The deal had been cleared by her attorneys, signed within two days, the funds transferred within three, and Eugenia Ward was suddenly cash-rich again, with twenty million more in the bank. Natasha looked even more spectacular than she had at Daphne's dinner party.

She watched two teenage girls and their mothers carrying five shopping bags out of the store. Pam had ordered pink ones for them in record time. Everything had happened at breakneck speed.

The day Natasha showed up, Eloise was helping her mother set out new merchandise, and they had brought two of their salesclerks back to wrap everything in pink tissue with half a yard of pink tulle exploding out of the bags containing their customers' purchases.

"We are partners now," Natasha said proudly. She was wearing platform slides with seven-inch heels to go with the bodysuit, and her raven dark hair hung straight down her back. She looked more like sixteen than twenty-two. "I read about this on Page Six. It is very smart." She totally got what Eloise was trying to do and approved. "First we sell them Cotton Candy so they look like little girls, then we sell them evening gowns like real women. Where are the gowns?" She glanced around, but there were none in view.

"They're not on display at the moment. I wanted to test the strength of the new line," Eugenia explained. Natasha was interested in everything around her.

"Very smart. You and your employees work very hard." Everyone was moving at full speed. Eloise came to join them when she spotted Natasha. She remembered her immediately from Daphne's dinner party, with the man in the Stetson with the diamond necklace. They weren't easy to forget. And Eloise put her fashion purist aesthetic aside for now. It had been dormant since she got home and went to work helping her mother. It was actually in a deep coma. She was dazzled by the craze they had started, which Eugenia had turned into marketing genius. The money was rolling in faster than they could count it. It was a major coup, and they had no idea how long the craze would last, but for the moment it was increasing day by day.

"You need help at the store?" Natasha asked Eugenia, and was clearly ready to pitch in. It looked like fun to her. She tried on some of the clothes and they looked great on her. She had a flawless body, which she worked on daily with a trainer Austin had brought with him from Dallas. They were staying in the presidential suite at the Four Seasons, while Austin did business in New York.

"We're managing pretty well," Eugenia said, amused by her. She was so earnest, and friendly to everyone. She told all the girls trying on the clothes that they looked beautiful and hot. Eloise could hardly repress a laugh, and until then, she hadn't smiled since she got home. But the success of Cotton Candy was something to smile about, even crow.

Natasha stayed for another hour, bought two pairs of pink sequined very short shorts, and a denim jacket to match, with a giant pink sequin heart on the back. She promised to come back soon, and Eugenia was surprised to find she liked her.

Daphne came by after her weekly checkup and couldn't believe the scene either. She gave her sister an enormous hug in sympathy for her heartbreak at Balenciaga.

"Mom has started an avalanche. Everyone's talking about it," Daphne said, licking wisps of the candy floss the vendor with the bright pink cart had handed her outside the store.

"What did the doctor say?" Eugenia asked her when she joined them.

"That I'll go into labor any minute. She's surprised I haven't yet. And if I get any bigger it's a C-section for sure." She wasn't happy about it, but at this point getting them out without a C-section was terrifying too. Her face looked beautiful, but her body looked like she'd swallowed a balloon. "I can't even stand up without help, or get out of bed," she complained. "Anyone who tells you having twins is fun is lying." She lumbered over to a chair and sat down. She couldn't stand for long either. "How is it being back in New York?" she asked her sister.

"Sad," Eloise said with a mournful expression. "I miss Paris, but it's nice being with Mom, and you." She smiled at her younger sister.

Eugenia took her two daughters to lunch at The Grill while Pam and three salesclerks minded the store. Daphne didn't eat a thing. She said she didn't have room, she just drank iced tea. "Has Liz been to see it?" she asked, while her mother and sister ate their salads.

"Not yet," Eugenia answered. "She's working on a merger at the startup where she works. She's going to try to come this weekend. She sent us a magnum of pink champagne when we launched the line, to wish us luck."

"She's going to love this," Daphne said, and Eloise shook her head.

"She's not our customer. It's not jazzy enough for her. Our customers are more naïve, younger, and want to look more innocent. Liz favors femme fatale. She's more given to rhinestones than sequins."

They knew exactly who their client was now, and they had a lot of them.

After lunch, Eloise and Eugenia headed back to the store and Daphne went home to rest.

"I hope the next time I see you both is at the hospital," she said with a smile as she left them.

"The poor thing looks so uncomfortable," Eloise said sympathetically. "I couldn't do it."

"Yes, you could, if you had to," Eugenia said, as they walked back to the store to get some air.

"Thank God I don't have to."

"The reward is worth it," Eugenia responded.

"Aren't the bride and groom due back any minute?" Eloise asked her, and Eugenia shook her head.

"Not till next week. His parents are arriving tomorrow, however," she said to Eloise with a sigh. "I hate to say it, but I didn't like them when we met two years ago. Arrogant, pompous, impressed with themselves. No money but lots of pretensions. We just have to put up with them for Gloria's sake, and it's only for a week. They're organizing the rehearsal dinner, and I still don't have the details yet. I don't even know where they're giving it. I have enough on my hands with the wedding. I haven't received an invitation yet. I guess they'll just tell me when they get here. It's a little vague for my taste," she admitted.

"Gloria is making a terrible mistake," Eloise said, as they reached the store, with the Cotton Candy samples in the window, and a crowd of customers inside, which there hadn't been for a year and a half.

"I tried to tell her that when she was here. She doesn't want to hear it, and she defends him to the death. That's why they left," Eugenia said, unhappy about it.

"It's her choice, Mom," Eloise said.

"I just hope he doesn't break her heart."

They pushed open the door to the store then, and joined the crowd.

Chapter 10

Prudence and Henry Crawford, Lord and Lady Crawford, the Earl and Countess of Westingham, Geoffrey's parents, arrived in New York after a two-week quarantine in Mexico. They were initially appalled at the idea, but decided that a week in Cancún and a week in Mexico City would be pleasant, and they had friends who had retired in Cancún because of the low cost of living. In the end, they had a pleasant time, enjoyed the margaritas, the tequila, the weather, and the low prices, and arrived less than a week before Gloria and Geoff's wedding, two days before the bride and groom arrived themselves. They were holding the wedding at the Shinnecock Hills Golf Club in Southampton. Daphne had arranged it, since she and Phillip were members. It was the most exclusive hotel in the Hamptons. Eugenia rented the same compound that they'd had earlier in the month, since it had worked so well and housed all of them. As a courtesy, she had booked the Crawfords into the Maidstone Inn in East Hampton, which they found so shockingly expensive they switched to an Airbnb in Bridgehampton and said they would take Ubers to the various wedding events. Eugenia didn't offer to have them stay with her, since she figured she and they would need a breather from one another. Weddings were stressful, and Eugenia had found the Crawfords overbearing when she met them. Henry drank a lot and talked incessantly about every relative in his family tree and how closely they were related to the king or queen, and Prudence was strident and giddy and asked incessant questions about Gloria's bloodline. After a painful dinner two years before, Eugenia had been sorely tempted to invent axe murderers and criminals in her ancestry. The Crawfords were outspokenly dubious about the origins of Italian princes, and Henry said that most of them were illegitimate, which would be good dinner conversation with Umberto at the wedding or rehearsal dinner. Eugenia still had to get the details of that event from Prudence. She had asked her repeatedly in emails, which Prudence did not answer. Gloria said that her future mother-in-law did not use a computer, but Prudence didn't respond to Eugenia's handwritten letters either, on impeccable Cartier stationery with Umberto's crest on it. And

Eugenia's family had their own crest, having descended from minor British aristocrats who had left England centuries before. Eugenia had resisted the temptation at their first meeting to say that they were probably horse thieves.

The Crawfords had admitted to her that they weren't fond of Americans, but had even less regard for Australians, who were originally all convicts. They hated Catholics, which all of Eugenia's children were, because of Umberto. Eugenia had grown up Episcopalian herself, which was very close to the Roman church, but the Crawfords considered it closer to the Church of England, which worked for them. During the dinner, they said they took a dim view of the Irish, although Prudence's great-great-grandmother was an Irish baroness. They declared their total contempt for the French, and hatred for Germans since Henry's grandfather had been shot down over Germany during the war in a bombing raid, but fortunately had already sired Henry's father. Spaniards were just as worthless as Italians, only maybe just slightly worse. They talked about how large their manor house was, how many indentured servants they had once had, and mentioned a distant relative of Pru's grandmother who had fought with Wellington at Waterloo. They dismissed the novel Gloria was writing and were sure that Geoff's would be a bestseller, and they never mentioned the fact that Gloria was supporting him on her meager salary at a London publishing house. Eugenia had a migraine after the evening. She described it to Daphne and Phillip afterward. He laughed and said they couldn't wait to meet them.

Eugenia called the Crawfords at the British club in downtown Manhattan where they were staying before leaving for the Hamptons. She had never heard of it, and it was a correspondent of Henry's London club. She felt she had to call them to be polite, so she did, and invited them for a drink at her apartment that night. She asked Eloise to join her, but she was having dinner with friends, and had no desire to meet the parents of a man she couldn't stand, whether they were about to be related or not. So Eugenia was left to face the music alone. She put little French cheese biscuits, pretzels, nuts, and some other snacks in silver bowls, and quickly changed into a pale blue Chanel linen suit to greet them. They were half an hour late, and explained that they had gotten off at the wrong subway stop and wound up in Spanish Harlem.

Prudence was wearing three rows of large fake pearls and a polka-dotted red dress two sizes too tight that made her look like Minnie Mouse, and Henry was perspiring profusely in a gray wool suit in hundred-degree weather. Eugenia was amazed they hadn't been mugged on the subway. Everything about them screamed "foreign tourists." They were looking around the apartment with interest as Prudence handed Eugenia a tiny brown box with a pink ribbon on it, which she saw rapidly was a box with four chocolates in it, the kind hotel chambermaids left on your pillow at night when they turned down the beds, and must have been on their bed at the club when they checked in.

"Sweets for the sweet, my dear," she said grandly. Her hair was blonde mixed with white, and hung limply around her face after their subway adventure in the crushing heat. They walked into the living room as Prudence looked around, taking everything in. "My, isn't everything so white and modern. How American," she said, glancing at her husband, "isn't it, Henry?" He was admiring the view of Central Park and turned to smile at Eugenia. "Our park at the manor was about that size originally, of course it's a bit smaller now." His grandparents had sold off everything they could after the war, as many people had to. Eugenia didn't mind poverty, but she hated pretentiousness, especially with nothing to back it up. She knew that Henry had worked at a bank in the city, and Prudence had been a secretary before they married. Geoff had said it in passing one night when he was drunk.

They struggled through an hour of inane conversation about the club where they were staying, which was related to a minor yacht club in London, and then Eugenia finally brought up the rehearsal dinner.

"I still don't know where you're holding it," Eugenia said politely. "Is everything all set?"

Prudence looked uncomfortable for a minute and then recovered. "You know, it's so beastly complicated to do anything online these days. The club recommended a few places which were insanely expensive, and I don't do well on a computer, and Henry doesn't either. I thought I'd let you organize something. You know all the local places, and I didn't know if you'd prefer to do it in the Hamptons or in the city, so I thought it best to let you decide and organize it this week," and she'd never asked. Eugenia stared at her in disbelief. She and Pam had been going crazy, with the help of her florist and a wedding planner that had cost her a fortune, to go over every detail of the wedding for a hundred and eighty-two guests, with everything from welcome bags to hotel arrangements, two bands, and flowers flown in from all over the world, not to mention Gloria's dress, suitable for royalty, and Prudence Crawford had done nothing about the rehearsal dinner. Eugenia wanted to throw the pretzels at her, as Henry blithely sipped his gin on the rocks and Prudence looked her in the eye and didn't show a drop of remorse. Eugenia could also guess that they didn't want to pay for a dinner for a hundred and eighty guests when they heard the prices.

"I wish you had told me earlier," Eugenia said politely. "So what's your plan? No rehearsal dinner?"

"We don't know anyone here, so it really doesn't make sense for us to give it. You're welcome to organize something if you'd like, as they're all your family and friends. There are only three of us," Prudence said, "so it's only fair that you manage it." Eugenia fully understood that "manage" it meant pay for it. Geoff had bragged repeatedly about all the people his parents would invite, and they had vanished into thin air. The wedding was five days away and Eugenia had her hands full with hiring models and fitting the runway pieces of her new collection, and there would be no time for that after the wedding, or not enough. Fashion Week was starting a week after the wedding. She needed this week to take care of that too. And she doubted that even her wedding planner could find a venue and organize dinner for nearly two hundred people in four days, not to mention the fact that she was already spending double the original budget, and they were breaking the sound barrier on that, at a time when she needed every penny for her business and family to survive. She had gotten relief from disaster with Austin Wylie's investment, but she had to be careful with it, for the business, and not spend it on her daughter's wedding. She had no idea what to do, and Prudence and Henry effectively dodged the issue until they

217

left her apartment, after a brief and very tense visit with that piece of news.

Eugenia sat down in a chair in the living room after they left, wondering what the hell to do. She called Pam at home, who was arguing with Izzie about what she was wearing to go to a movie with friends, and there were boys involved. Eugenia didn't envy her that. She had been there five times and would have cut her liver out with an ice pick rather than do it again. Fourteen-year-old girls, and even boys, were not her favorite. Even the nice ones lied like dogs, and managed to get drunk to the point of alcohol poisoning at least once in their lives, even with her watching like a hawk in their youth. Hers did it too. They all did.

"I'm up shit creek," she said, sounding desperate as soon as Pam picked up the phone.

"What happened?" She knew that Eugenia was entertaining the Crawfords, and anything could have gone wrong. She could tell that something had, and she told Izzie to cool it for a minute, she was talking to her boss.

"The rehearsal dinner," Eugenia said cryptically.

"What about it? Where are they doing it?" Pam asked her.

"They're not. They just dropped it like a hot rock back in my lap, saying it's all my family and friends, so it's really up to me. There's no way I can do a dinner that size or find a venue four days out. What the hell am I going to do?"

"Is killing them an option?"

"I wish. Shit. I'm screwed. I'm sure they didn't want to pay for it, or can't. They should have said so. At least no invitations have gone out, so people must think there is none by now. I thought she was taking care of it and just hadn't bothered to clue me in."

"What about family only, and maybe the people who've come from far away?" That had been the original tradition, but nowadays anyone who could afford it invited all the guests to the rehearsal dinner. And in typical style, Gloria had invited all her old school friends to the wedding, everyone she knew in college, anyone Geoff knew in New York, and all their acquaintances. Gloria wanted as big a guest list as she could muster, at both events. "You don't need invitations," Pam said. "I can call them, or invite them by email. And I can call around and see who has a room that size that's open in spite of Covid. Things are opening up again," Pam offered, shocked at the news.

"I don't really want to do something indoors with all that going on." The whole wedding was being held outdoors at the club for that reason. It had been carefully planned with the Covid sanitary measures scrupulously taken into account.

"Maybe one of the restaurants has a big enough terrace space for thirty or forty people and would rent it out. I'll find something," Pam said confidently, and hoped she could.

219

"I can't believe they did this to me, and she wasn't even embarrassed. She gave me one of those mini boxes of chocolates hotels leave on your pillow, there are four chocolates in it and she acted like she was handing me the Hope Diamond."

"We'll figure it out," Pam reassured her.

"Thank you, Pam," Eugenia said earnestly, still flummoxed by the way the Crawfords had sidestepped the whole event and never told her. She had assumed it was all in order, and they were holding up their end of the deal on the only part of the wedding they were responsible for. She was fuming, and would have called Gloria in London to complain, but it was one in the morning for her, and probably smarter not to call when Eugenia was as angry as she was. Why was everything her responsibility, and she was the fount of all bounty at any price? She wanted to tell Gloria that her new in-laws were shits, but recognized it was better she didn't. If they couldn't afford it why didn't they just say so? She couldn't afford the wedding either, but wanted to keep her promise to her daughter.

Eugenia was still angry about it when she met Patrick for dinner at Fleming's, which had a lovely outdoor space and delicious food, and was in walking distance from both their homes.

He had seen as soon as he picked her up to walk to

dinner that she was annoyed. He kissed her, and she seemed stiff.

"Did something happen?" he asked her, hoping it was nothing he had done. He had never seen her angry before. She was polite but she looked upset.

"I'm sorry, Patrick. I just found out that the groom's parents bagged on doing the rehearsal dinner but kept it a secret. In the save-the-date, we said that there was one, location to be confirmed. They never planned it, no invitations went out, and I stupidly stopped asking and just assumed they had it under control since I never heard from them about it, and thought they had forgotten to send me the invitation."

"They don't sound like nice people," Patrick said sympathetically. He could see that she was genuinely troubled about it. Even though she didn't like Geoff, she wanted everything to be perfect for Gloria. She was her hardest child to please, nothing was ever enough, and she expected everyone to prove their love by how much they did for her, and in her mother's case, how much she paid for.

"Their son isn't nice either," Eugenia said, still annoyed, and sorry to burden Patrick with her displeasure. They sat down at the restaurant and ordered wine, and she started to relax in his company.

"What are you going to do?" he asked her.

"I don't know. My assistant is scrambling to find a venue,

preferably outdoors because of Covid, and I'll do it for family and out-of-towners who have come a long way. *If* we can find a place. Otherwise, no rehearsal dinner. I don't care, but Gloria will. I'll never hear the end of it."

"It wasn't your responsibility, it was theirs. They let her down, you didn't."

"She won't see it that way. I'm the magician who always has to pull the rabbit out of the hat to prove how much I love her. The others are all much more reasonable, but she isn't. She has used this whole wedding as a proving ground and a weapon."

"That doesn't sound like fun," he said gently, and she smiled.

"It isn't," she said, taking a sip of the excellent white wine he had ordered, Chassagne-Montrachet.

"I have an idea," he said, thinking of how he could help her and take some of the burden off her shoulders, with everything she had to do alone, which didn't seem fair to him.

"I don't think we could pull off dinner for two hundred people on short notice," he said.

"Of course not. I didn't expect you to. I just needed to vent." Men always thought they had to *do* something when you complained, when sometimes all women wanted was for someone to listen. Eugenia was used to solving her own problems, although Patrick had been very helpful so far, with his suggestions about the deal with Austin Wylie.

"But if you're only going to do a dinner for family and a few friends, we could easily handle a buffet for forty people, even fifty or sixty, on the boat, outdoors. That's no problem. My chef loves to show off, I have the staff and the location sitting right in the Hudson River. People like events on boats, it feels special. And I do meetings for that many people on the boat sometimes. What do you think?" She stared at him as he said it, and tears filled her eyes, she was so touched. "In fact, we can move the boat to the Hamptons and do it there, since most people will spend the whole weekend there."

"Are you serious?"

He nodded and patted her hand on the table. "It's not complicated. We're all set up for that, and your guests might love it."

"Are you kidding? They'd like it better than the wedding, and so would I. Oh my God, I hate to take advantage of you, Patrick. But that would be so perfect."

"Then that's it. You can talk to Jonathan, my chef, tomorrow, tell him what you want, and have your secretary email your guest list tomorrow." He was one man who suggested an action plan that really did solve her most pressing problems when she told him about them. Her daughter was the luckiest person in the world, and so was she. His plan was a thousand times better than some dusty old club, indoors on top of it.

"You are utterly amazing," she said, and leaned over and kissed him. "You don't even know these people, and you barely know my daughter." Patrick had only seen Gloria once, since she had already left in a huff when he met the others for a second time. "I don't know how to thank you. You are saving my life, and adding something wonderful to her wedding. And I want to pay for all the expenses, food, alcohol, whatever you spend on it."

"I'll take it out in other ways," he teased her. "Listen, we're both in a tough spot at the moment, or at least we have been. It's nice to be able to help each other, and blessings are meant to be shared," he said sincerely.

"From what I can see, you're the one helping me, I haven't done a damn thing for you, and now I'm bringing thirty or forty people to your boat for dinner. I don't want this to be a one-way street. That's abusive."

"Not if I volunteer it. And I just did. Now I want you to relax and have a lovely evening." He kissed her and she texted Pam and told her the plan. "We're saved. Rehearsal dinner on Patrick Hughes's boat, for family and inner circle. Details tomorrow. Love, E."

They had a leisurely dinner and walked slowly back on

Madison Avenue. Several stores that hadn't survived the pandemic were still vacant, but most stores were open again, some newcomers had appeared, and the city was alive again. Patrick stayed at Eugenia's apartment that night, and felt at home there. They were both surprised at how comfortable they felt so quickly with each other. They took a bath in her bathtub that night after they made love, and then made love again. She made him breakfast in the morning, and he left for his office from her home. She was going to speak to his chef that morning, about the menu for the rehearsal dinner.

She worked out all the details with Pam when she got to her own office, the guest list of twelve family members, including the Crawfords, plus eleven couples who were coming from the West Coast and the Midwest. None of their friends from London could come except via quarantine in Mexico, and none of them had the time to do that except Geoff's parents. That made a guest list of thirty-four people maximum, which Patrick had said was a piece of cake. She spoke to the chef, and they chose a varied menu for a buffet, and by noon Pam emailed the invitations. Three couples declined immediately, having made other plans for the night before the wedding, leaving twenty-eight guests as a possible maximum, which sounded intimate and perfect to Eugenia, and would to Gloria as well. Patrick had saved the day with his fabulous yacht. And the menu sounded delicious.

"And we can put up see-through plastic curtains if the weather turns bad. There are some storm warnings for this weekend. They'll probably change direction by then, but if not, we'll be prepared." Patrick had suggested that they move the boat to the Hamptons, since people would be staying there for the weekend with the wedding there on Saturday. The club had told her they could install a tent for the wedding, in case of bad weather, for a large additional amount. So they had a Plan B for all eventualities, and a rehearsal dinner in place in less than twenty-four hours after learning that the Crawfords hadn't held up their end and never bothered to tell her. Eugenia didn't call Prudence. She would find out from their son or the official email Pam was sending to the wedding party, the family, and long-distance out-of-towners. Gloria's sisters were her bridesmaids and Daphne her matron of honor, if she hadn't given birth by then.

With everything in order, Eugenia called Gloria in London. It was six P.M. there and she was still in the office. She had gotten the email too, and Eugenia was taken aback by her first comment.

"Why did you interfere and do it on a yacht so you could show off, when you know Geoff gets seasick?" Gloria accused her.

"Are you serious? You're complaining about having it on

a fabulous yacht when his parents completely dropped the ball on the rehearsal dinner and never told me? I found out at seven o'clock last night. What did you expect me to do? Rent Madison Square Garden? He saved my ass and Geoff's parents, and your rehearsal dinner. And he's renting a berth at the dock at a different yacht club that has a port big enough for his boat to come closer, so guests don't have as far to go in the tender if the sea is choppy. His boat has stabilizers so Geoff will be fine. The boat will never leave the dock, and no one will get sick."

"He says he gets sick even when a boat is tied up at the dock, he just called me when we got the email."

"Then tell him to take medicine, for God's sake," Eugenia said, exasperated.

"I thought that we agreed that the rehearsal dinner was for *all* the guests," Gloria continued to complain.

"Not with four days' notice when nothing has been done about it. It's a miracle we can have a rehearsal dinner at all, and that's the Crawfords' fault, not mine. Patrick just saved the day, and I can't believe you're complaining about it." Eugenia was furious at Gloria's reaction and lack of gratitude.

"It's such a small skimpy group, that isn't what I wanted and what we agreed on," Gloria persisted.

"Fine, tell Geoff's parents, don't tell me. I think this is outrageous, you're not grateful or even polite, all you do is want something else or something more. How did you get so entitled?"

"Oh, because I'm not as sweet as Daphne, or crawl up your ass like Eloise?" Gloria said nastily.

"I am paying a fortune for this wedding, which is costing twice the budget we agreed on, and you and Geoff keep adding new expensive elements every time I turn around, without even asking me. I am hosting the wedding, he's not. And now I'm stuck with the rehearsal dinner too. He and his family need to grow up and get some manners, with all that alleged blue blood of theirs. I've just about had it." She had raised her voice and didn't like to do that, but Gloria was pushing her too far, particularly with her complaints and entitled demands.

"And Geoff's parents will be upset about Brad," Gloria whined, and Eugenia clenched her teeth.

"Frankly, Brad is twice the man, or ten times the man, your future husband is, or his parents, and is much more polite. He won't cause a scene at the dinner or the wedding, and if Geoff or his parents do, I will personally escort them to the door."

"You see, this is why Geoff and I left the Hamptons early, because you don't respect us."

"Gloria, you and Geoff don't know the meaning of the word 'respect.' And his parents are no better, not giving me any warning that they decided not to give the rehearsal dinner, which is their responsibility not mine, and dumping it in my lap on four days' notice, and I assume they expect me to pay for it, or you do."

"Obviously, Mom," Gloria said scathingly. "They can't afford it, you can."

"Don't be so sure. You don't know what I can afford. I haven't sold an evening dress or a wedding gown in eighteen months, and I have not skimped on this royal wedding you want, and think is your due. I want to give you the wedding of your dreams, but you need to give some serious thought to how you behave, what you expect, and how you treat people."

"You're the one who treats people badly, Mom. You have no respect for Geoff's sensibilities. He's a very sensitive person. He feels it physically when he thinks people don't like him or respect him."

"I can't listen to this," Eugenia said. "I have to hang up now. I'll see you when you get to New York," and she hung up, with all of Gloria's words ringing in her ears, words of hate and ingratitude, racism and entitlement. On every level, she was completely out of control and off base with her ideas. Eugenia was shaking when she ended the call and for nearly an hour afterward. She couldn't even talk about it, and went to the casting meeting she had to attend to pick models for her show. It distracted her from thinking about her ungrateful daughter. They had all the models picked by the end of the day, and fittings were scheduled for the week after the wedding, which was cutting it close. And they had to work with the models' other bookings, because several of them were walking for more than one designer. They were young and beautiful, and had to be babied through all of their shows and bookings, since every season some of them had never walked the runway before and were fresh off the farm or from other smaller cities, and had no idea how rigorous and professional it was. Pam was good at shepherding them through the process. And then she remembered to tell Eugenia that Natasha had called.

"She said to tell you that your partner called," Pam said, smiling.

"I'm actually getting to like her. She is rough around all her edges, but she's honest and real," and Natasha had told Pam that before she met Austin in the south of France, she had been a factory worker in Moscow. And she didn't pretend to be anything more than she was. The honesty of it touched her.

"She wants two invitations to the show."

"Give them to her. She's right, she's my partner. She can have four if she wants."

"And she placed another Cotton Candy order. She wants a fifty percent discount on it," Pam said with a disapproving look.

"Give her that too," Eugenia said fairly.

"We can't put her and her friends in the front row," Pam said firmly.

"Really? Why not?" Eugenia was fed up with people's prejudices and lousy behavior and treatment of others, although Pam was only trying to protect the look of the show. "She's going to look like a girl off the streets of Moscow, while she was working in a factory. How she accomplished that, in a bed or on her feet, is absolutely none of our business. She'll look like she likes my clothes and is a fan, especially if she's wearing something of mine. She's good advertising, and she loves what we do," she tried to reassure Pam, but she could see that she hadn't succeeded.

Eugenia had just finished talking to Pam when her cell phone rang, and without looking to screen it, she picked it up and never bothered to look at the caller ID.

"Hello, darling." A deep sexy voice with a heavy accent was on the other end of the line. She knew the voice.

"Hello, Umberto," she said calmly. "Welcome to New York. How was your trip?"

"Fine. I did what most people from Europe are doing. I came through Mexico, with a two-week quarantine in

Mexico City. I have friends there. I need a favor," he said, cutting through his usual charming dialogue when he wanted something. "I have a friend with me for the wedding. She's lovely, you'll adore her." Umberto always brought a woman to anything, even events that involved his children. "She's a French viscountess," like every woman he knew. "She's a lovely girl. We traveled light from Mexico. She needs a dress for the wedding. I told her she could borrow a gown from you. Darling, please don't make a liar of me." He had been doing that himself for years.

"Umberto, I did that the last time you came to New York, with the German baroness who looked sixteen years old. The girl never gave the dress back. It was a fifteen-thousand-dollar dress. It looked great on her, but neither she nor you ever paid for it. I can't afford to give away dresses. I'm sorry, but the answer is no."

"You can afford anything you want," he said, irritated. "And she's twenty-two, the same age you were when you married me." His famous charm hadn't worked on Eugenia in years. She had had too much of it for too long and she knew all his tricks.

"I'm sure you can find her a pretty dress at Bergdorf's, which you can afford," Eugenia responded.

"You never change," he said accusingly.

"Sadly, neither do you." Once she had opened her eyes

to him, she had never been able to close them again. "Are you ready to walk your daughter down the aisle?"

"Of course. I did for Daphne." She didn't remind him that the girl he had brought had slept with one of the guests at the reception, and a security guard. She had never told Daphne, but she had discreetly asked Umberto to get her out immediately, which he had done, and then came back to the reception to dance with his daughter. She didn't mention it now. "How are the parents? I gather he's an earl."

"Apparently," Eugenia said, struggling not to lose her temper.

"I got the email about the rehearsal dinner. You're giving it?"

"They forgot to," was all she said. "Maybe you should have dinner with them. I don't have time."

"And it's on a boat?" He sounded skeptical. "Not a small one, I hope. I hate small boats. They make me seasick, big ones never do."

"I think you'll be all right on this one," she reassured him. "It has stabilizers, and we're not leaving the dock, so you'll be fine."

"Well, another one of our little chicks, taking flight into married life. I like Geoff. I had dinner with them a few months ago." She had no idea how he could say that about liking Geoff, but she didn't comment. He viewed all their children as though he were a benevolent uncle and not their father. He never asked the right questions or wanted to get too deeply involved. Gloria had never told Eugenia that she had seen him, which was typical of her. She was always on his side. To Eugenia there were no "sides," just what was good for the children, and she didn't think Geoff was.

At the end of the day, she was exhausted, after everything she'd done. Gloria and Geoff were arriving the next day and after that the pace would be stepped up. Gloria had to try her dress again to make sure it fit properly, in case she had gained or lost a pound or two. There were a million details for Eugenia to see to, even with Pam's help, and Eloise, who was willing to assist too, with work, the wedding, the rehearsal dinner, Fashion Week coming up with her new line, and Cotton Candy flying out of her store.

Eugenia had promised to call Patrick when she got home, and she was going to. He wanted to come over, and she lay down on her bed for just a minute, and fell sound asleep until morning. Patrick called her to find out where she was, and she didn't even hear the phone.

Chapter 11

Gloria and Geoff arrived on Wednesday, three days before their wedding, which was cutting it close. They stayed at Eugenia's apartment, which Gloria still considered home when they were in New York. They were all leaving for East Hampton on Friday morning, with the rehearsal dinner on Patrick's boat that night.

Everything was moving at high speed, and Eugenia greeted them warmly when they arrived, despite the unpleasantness between them earlier in the week. Geoff was on his best behavior, and had had a haircut. There was a thin veneer covering Gloria's underlying anger on every subject, which Eugenia chose to ignore. She didn't want to spoil her daughter's wedding week, and kept things light.

The bridal couple had dinner with Geoff's parents on

Wednesday night, and Gloria had a fitting for her wedding dress on Thursday morning with her mother and her best sewer. There were only a few minor alterations to be made to achieve perfection. Gloria looked exquisite in the spectacular gown. She was going to wear her auburn hair in a loose bun at the nape of her neck, with her veil over it. Everyone in the room, the sewers, her mother, and her older sisters, Eloise and hugely pregnant Daphne, stood watching her in awe. Eugenia said she was the most beautiful bride she had ever seen, and meant it, and the dress was magnificent. The sewers helped Gloria take off the gown carefully and carried it away, wrapped in white satin to protect it, to make the final adjustments. It had been very moving to see her at her final fitting. Gloria and Geoff had dinner with Umberto and his woman of the hour, Delphine, that night, Thursday, which gave Eugenia time to have an early dinner with Patrick on his boat. He was moving it to the Hamptons the next day, Friday morning, while the family drove to the rented house for the weekend, and on Friday night Patrick was hosting the rehearsal dinner. Thursday night was their last chance to have a quiet dinner alone, while Gloria and Geoff had dinner with her father and Delphine. It was a heavy schedule to keep up with and Patrick noticed that Eugenia looked tired when she came across the passerelle onto the boat. He called down to the gym for the head masseuse to come up and massage her feet while he poured her a glass of white wine.

"You spoil me," she said, smiling at him. "I don't know what I did to deserve this, but it's sheer heaven."

"I figure this is your last night of relative peace and sanity for the next few days. How is everyone behaving?" He knew that Eugenia had been nervous about additional battles with Gloria.

"They're all right. I've hardly seen them, I've been so busy, going in a thousand directions. Fashion Week will be a relief after this." She questioned now the wisdom of holding the wedding so close to Fashion Week, but it had seemed like a good idea at the time.

She nearly fell asleep over dinner, and he wished she could spend the night, but she needed to go home, pack the last details, and leave for the rented house in the Hamptons the next morning. She was more grateful than ever that Patrick was taking care of the rehearsal dinner. She didn't have to do a thing, except for the wedding on Saturday. Then she had to get to work on Monday to prepare for her fashion show a week later.

Patrick hated to bring it up over dinner, but he'd been studying the weather reports for the weekend before she came on board. There was a tropical storm heading toward Long Island, due to hit land on Friday night, which made him uneasy. It was moving through the Caribbean and heading for the mainland, gathering strength and speed. It might just miss them if it hit the mainland late on Friday night, but it didn't bode well for Saturday, the day of Gloria's wedding.

"Do you have an alternate plan for Saturday?" he asked Eugenia, concerned about the wedding. "In case of bad weather."

"The club said they can put up a tent if it rains." It would add another eighty thousand dollars to the bill, which she wasn't happy about. "But they said that tropical storms usually wear themselves out before they hit land." Unless they got stronger and turned into hurricanes, Patrick didn't say to her. She had enough on her plate without his worrying her more than she already was, while trying to keep track of everything. She had managed to avoid any arguments with Gloria, but she was handling her with kid gloves and they were keeping their distance from each other. The tension between them was always just below the surface. Gloria was still angry at her mother and her questions about Geoff. She was his fiercest defender, which added further tension to the wedding plans.

Eugenia left the boat early, as she still had a lot to do and needed to get to bed. Friday would be a busy day.

*

When she woke up on Friday, it was raining and there was a slight wind. It got stronger as she got to Long Island, to the rented house. Her car was full of details for the wedding: escort cards and place cards, the calligraphied menus, the party favors for each guest, silver frames with a photograph of Gloria and Geoff in each, which the guests could replace with their own photographs later.

It was raining harder by midday and the yacht crew put up the plastic curtains to keep the party area dry, hoping the rain would stop by dinnertime. The boat was so beautiful that the weather didn't matter, but it would make for a prettier party if they could see the sun setting. But the dark clouds showed no sign of disappearing, nor the wind of abating. The clouds got darker and bigger and the wind stronger throughout the day, while Eugenia organized everything she'd brought. Gloria was staying with her. Geoff was staying with his parents at the Airbnb they had rented in Bridgehampton that night. He couldn't see Gloria after the rehearsal dinner, until the wedding. He thought it was a stupid tradition, and tried to talk Gloria into letting him stay with her at the rented house, but she wouldn't let him and insisted it was bad luck.

When they all got to the dock for the rehearsal dinner, in the vans Patrick had sent for them at their various locations, the sea was choppy but the boat was secured at the dock. The boat rocked a little but not enough to make anyone sick. Geoff said he was already queasy when they got to the yacht, and it was only rolling slightly. The crew had done a beautiful job decorating the boat and the tables. There were white streamers flying from the masts in the wind and rain. There were white lace tablecloths on two long dining tables and the buffet, and white orchids and gardenias and candles everywhere. It looked incredibly romantic and Eugenia thanked Patrick, as a small band played romantic show tunes. He had consulted Daphne for Gloria's favorites. There was suckling pig and a full buffet, and a shellfish table decorated with beautiful shells. He had gone all out to make it festive and elegant. Geoff's parents were awestruck when they saw the size of the boat, and so was Umberto. He made a point of being nice to Patrick, and the bridal couple looked happy and proud. Geoff was feeling better by then. There were numerous toasts at dinner, and excellent champagne. The food was delicious, and the atmosphere was warm and relaxed, as the storm continued to worsen and the wind got stronger by the hour. They were protected by the curtains the crew had set up in the driving rain, and Eugenia noticed Patrick consulting quietly with the captain at frequent intervals. The captain looked concerned as the wind whipped around them and the crew added additional bumpers to prevent the yacht from slamming against the dock and getting damaged.

"It hasn't hit land yet, but they just upgraded it to a hurricane," the captain informed Patrick in an undertone no one else could hear. The wind was very strong, and the rain was coming down in sheets. The yacht was rolling more than at first, but no one was sick or complained. They were having too much fun to notice. "It's expected to hit land between one and two A.M. They're expecting flash floods on the roads, and they want to set a midnight curfew for the area. We need to send them home so we can tighten things down and put them away," the captain said, and Patrick looked chagrined. "I think the sea is going to get rougher soon."

"I hate to break up the party, everyone's having a good time."

"They won't if we get it full on when it hits land, and you don't want people getting hurt when they leave the boat. The ride back to wherever they're staying is going to be tougher and wetter than when they arrived." They had already removed some small objects that could fly away.

Patrick took it seriously, and a few minutes later he spoke to Eugenia quietly and told her what the captain had said. She was sorry too, but they didn't want anyone getting trapped in floods, or hit by falling trees on land if it was as

241

bad as they said on the weather reports. "I think we have to send them home," Patrick said regretfully. It was eleven-thirty, and they were all having a good time, drinking a lot and singing on the dining deck, with the plastic sheets all around the area to protect them. Most of them hadn't even noticed how bad the storm had gotten, and didn't care. The boat was rolling but her stabilizers kept her fairly steady. Even Geoff hadn't complained of seasickness. He had eaten heartily and was drinking heavily.

"If it stays like this, it's going to be a mess tomorrow at the wedding," Eugenia said, worried.

"It's either going to get a lot worse or a lot better when it hits land," Patrick said, concerned.

The captain joined them while Patrick and Eugenia were conferring. "I think we need to take them home now, sir," he said in a firm tone. "The wind is picking up." A few minutes later, Patrick stopped the band, and made a short announcement, and apologized for the sudden end to the evening.

"We want to get you all back to your houses and hotels safely before the storm gets any worse," Patrick said. "I'm so sorry, but if you gather up your things now, the vans are waiting for you on the dock." There were four vans waiting to drive them home. And the crew was waiting to tie everything down and put things away.

It only took them a few minutes to get their wraps and party favors, and some of the gardenias from the table, and once they left the yacht and went ashore, the guests realized how bad the storm was. The gusts nearly knocked them off their feet, as they fought the wind walking to the vans. Crew members on the dock helped to steady them. Most of them were very drunk, except for Patrick and Eugenia, who made sure that everyone got into the vans. Geoff tried to climb into the one Gloria got into and she stopped him with a firm hand and a smile.

"You can't go home with me, remember? It's bad luck, you have to go to the house with your parents. You can't see me again until the wedding." She said it gently but loud enough for him to hear her in the strong wind.

"Bloody hell," Geoff responded angrily, "who knows if there'll be a fucking wedding with a hurricane about? We might as well enjoy a good fuck tonight," he said as he stomped off to the next van, already soaked to the skin. She had heard what he said, but it didn't change her mind. She needed all the luck available if she was going to marry him. Her brother heard what Geoff said too. Stef didn't look pleased and didn't comment, but he and Liz exchanged a glance. Eloise had also heard. Brad and Sofia were in the van with them. The crew member who was driving took off for their rented house then. He wanted to get them home quickly and get back to the yacht to help. Patrick was already working with the crew to tie things down as fast as they could, and the sails had been bound tightly to the masts. But a gale like that could break one or several of the masts and kill people.

Phillip and Daphne had left a little earlier in their own car. She was exhausted and worried about Tucker being frightened in the storm. She wanted to get home to him quickly.

Eugenia was in a van with the Crawfords, Umberto, and his date, to drop them off at the Maidstone Inn for Umberto, and the Crawfords at their Airbnb. Geoff jumped in with them before they took off, still in a drunken rage that Gloria wouldn't let him go home with her.

"My bitch of a future wife wouldn't let me go home with her," he said by way of explanation, forgetting that his future mother-in-law was in the van with them, but he didn't care. "Does anyone have a bottle of Scotch?" he asked loudly, and no one answered, while the deckhand driving was trying to avoid growing rivers of water covering the road. The other two vans had taken some of the guests back to their hotels. It was a challenging drive getting to the inn, trying to avoid small floods that were starting, and it took them half an hour to get there. It was midnight by then, and the deckhand was anxious to get back to the boat.

Umberto and his date hurried into the inn and they proceeded to the Crawfords' Airbnb. Eugenia helped them get out, and Prudence was looking nervous and pale. "I don't like storms like this," she said to Eugenia. "My sister was killed in a typhoon when we were children." Geoff made no effort to help his parents and staggered into the house. Eugenia and the deckhand watched them fight the wind to get inside and once they were in, they took off to navigate the rivers flowing around them to get Eugenia home. She wasn't afraid, but she was worried about Daphne and the others. And if Daphne went into labor, she might not be able to get to the hospital, and certainly not to the city. Eugenia was glad that Geoff wasn't staying with them in the condition he was in. His parents could deal with him tonight.

The crew member got Eugenia home as quickly as he could, with the water swirling around them on the road. She ran into the house in the white satin evening pajamas she had worn, and they were soaked through by the time she got into the house and found the others in the kitchen, talking and lighting candles. The compound had just lost power and they were all in the main house looking for candles and flashlights.

"This was a little more excitement than we were expecting," Brad said, handing out flashlights to all of them.

"We have tornados in Tennessee." Stefano opened a bottle of wine, and handed a glass to those who wanted it.

"Well, it was a fun party," Stef said, and everyone laughed. They walked into the spacious living room, and sat watching the storm through the picture window. It looked like a hurricane now. Brad reminded them to stand well away from the picture windows in case one broke, so they wouldn't get hurt by flying glass.

Gloria left the living room to call Geoff on her cell phone, to apologize for not letting him come home with her. He answered quickly and shouted at her, "If you don't want to get laid tonight, I do, and that's exactly what I'm going to do, and there are plenty of women at the bar at the inn who would be happy to fuck me, so fuck you, Gloria," and hung up on her. She was sheet white when she walked into the living room and even in the light from the flashlights, her mother could see it.

"Everything okay?" she asked gently.

"Actually, no," Gloria said with an intent expression and left the room again. She had seen slickers and boots in the storeroom behind the kitchen, and went and put them on with the lace pants and top she had worn to the rehearsal dinner. The slicker had a hood and she put it over her head and, picking up a set of the keys to one of the rented SUVs they had, slipped out the back door with her cell phone in her pocket. And a minute later the others heard the wheels of the car spin on the gravel and then take off, and they looked out the window to see who was arriving, and all they could see were the red taillights of the SUV disappearing down the drive. Someone was leaving and it took them a minute to figure out who.

"Where's Gloria?" Eloise was the first to ask. She had seen the look on her face and could guess where she went and why. She had gone to comfort Geoff and calm him down. She headed to the Maidstone Inn, where he said he was going to pick up women.

"I'll go after her," Brad volunteered and got up to go, and Eugenia stopped him.

"You can't go. If anything happens, we might need a doctor, and if you leave in the only other car, we'll all be trapped here if we have to evacuate or need help." She was thinking of Daphne a few miles away, if she went into labor and couldn't get to the hospital. This was becoming serious and they all knew it, and Brad stopped.

"Gloria's a good driver and the car is solid. She knows where she's going and she'll be okay," Eloise said, and could guess easily that she was going to see Geoff. She was sure they had had some kind of an argument after the way he left her.

Stef lit a fire in the fireplace, and they all sat around talking quietly. Eloise got the latest news reports on her phone. The hurricane had unleashed its full fury on Long Island, and had made landfall only a few miles away, and there were floods building all around them. Eugenia didn't like the idea that Gloria was driving. But their Airbnb wasn't far away and she didn't have far to go. The Maidstone Inn was close too, but no one knew she had gone there to intercept Geoff and calm him down before he hurt himself, injured someone else, got arrested for being drunk and disorderly, or started a bar fight. He could be an aggressive drunk.

It was scary driving in the storm, and Gloria was as careful as she could be. She had been to the Hamptons often and knew the roads well, and the roads in town were full of water, but it wasn't as deep as it had been getting there, and the SUV was high and avoided some of it. It had four-wheel drive, and she pulled up in front of the inn fifteen minutes after she had left the house. She was sure he would be there.

She walked up the steps of the hotel in her slicker and boots and lace pants that were soaked from the knee down from the muddy water she had walked through. Her face was as white as her lace blouse. The bar was bulging with activity, and someone was playing the piano. People were singing and drunk, safe from the storm in the hotel, which sat considerably higher than the street. And they hadn't lost power. All the lights were on. She looked for Geoff in the bar, didn't see him, and decided to walk upstairs to make sure he wasn't staggering around the halls. There was no one at the desk to stop her and she ran quietly up the stairs, just in time to see him kiss an equally drunk woman and slip into a room with her. Gloria's heart was pounding as she walked to the end of the hall and knocked on the door. There was no answer and she pounded on it. The woman she had seen opened it, already stripped down to her bra and a black lace thong. Geoff already had his jeans off and was standing behind her unbuttoning his shirt. He was furious when he saw Gloria. The woman looked confused and very drunk.

"I told you what I was going to do, and I'm doing it," he said viciously, "you bitch. You should have let me come home with you." There was no remorse, no apology, no explanation. He was too drunk to care, and she realized now that what her mother had told her was probably true. He had probably cheated on her before, and this was the night before their wedding.

"I'm not as dumb as you think," she said, keeping a level gaze on him, as the girl he had picked up walked away and lay down on the bed and left them to their argument. She was too drunk to care and passed out while Geoff shouted at Gloria. She had seen enough and turned to leave, while Geoff called after her. "See you in church," he said, and laughed uproariously.

"The wedding's off," she said in a clear voice. "Don't come back to the house. I'll have your suitcase dropped off at your parents'. And don't come back to my apartment in London. I'll send you your shit."

"Oh, big fucking deal. You think I care? That girl I picked up is probably a better fuck than you are. You're so fucking uptight, you're just like your mother and sisters. You'd be a real pain in the ass to be married to, without a little jolly time on the side," he said, as she pulled off the small antique ring that he had given her as an engagement ring, because his parents had sold everything else to fix the roof. She threw it in his direction, and it landed somewhere near him on the floor. "I don't give a fuck what you do," he shouted after her as she left the room and hurried down the hall, "and you write like shit," he added, as her eyes filled with tears, but she had her back to him so he didn't see them, and she didn't stop or turn back. "I was just going to marry you for the money," he added insult to injury, calling down the hall. "You don't deserve to be a countess." He was still shouting as she ran down the stairs, and he didn't follow her. He was raging drunk, but there was a ring of truth to what he said and how he said it, about marrying her for the money. And even if he had apologized or crawled to her, she knew what he was now. She hadn't wanted to see it, even if everyone else had.

She ran to the car in the driving rain and wind, got in, and drove back to the house, sobbing all the way. It took her an hour to get there on the way back. The water on the roads was higher, and she had to drive around pools of water. The power was still off when she got to the house. She walked into the little room behind the kitchen and took off the boots and slicker. She was soaked in spite of them and the white lace pants were covered in mud. She walked into the living room, less than two hours after she had left, and they were all still there, talking in subdued voices, watching the storm by candlelight. It was two in the morning, and they were drinking wine by the fire. They all looked up when she came in, and no one said a word. Gloria's hair was matted to her head from the rain and wind, she looked ravaged, but she was fully sober.

"I just got a text from the Shinnecock Hills Golf Club. Several of the columns were blown down and fell into the kitchen and catering area. The wedding is canceled," Eugenia said, seriously.

"Yes, it is," Gloria said, looking at her. "You were right. Geoff was about to screw some woman he picked up at the bar at the Maidstone. He's drunk off his ass, but he said enough. I told him the wedding is off. Maybe if the club is damaged, you can get your deposit back," she said. "I'm sorry, Mom, for everything." She left the room and walked upstairs to one of the bedrooms she knew was empty and lay down on the bed. She didn't want to talk to anyone, or sit with them. What she had seen at the inn had been traumatic, and she needed time to absorb it, and who he was. She had only begun to realize in the last hour how cruel she had been to her mother, and why the others were so angry at her. She needed time to understand it, and her part in it. He had egged her on, but she had been willing to do it, to participate. Not only did she now know who Geoff was, she didn't know who she was anymore, and she needed time to figure it out. That was all she was sure of now.

In the firelit living room downstairs, Eugenia looked at Eloise. "Do you think I should go up to her?"

"No, I don't," Eloise said quietly. "She needs time to think, and to grow up, and maybe you do too. You can't fix everything for us all the time. She screwed it up, with you, and all of us, and she has to fix it. You can't do it for her." Eugenia sat thinking about what she said, as Stefano spoke up.

"She's right, Mom. She made a pretty big mess for herself, with everyone. She needs to think about it, or she'll never learn the lesson. It's a big lesson to learn. Thank God she didn't make the mistake and marry the guy. She'll be okay, when she figures it out."

Eugenia listened to him, and nodded. She knew he was right, and maybe she needed to grow up too. She couldn't protect them anymore. They didn't belong to her anymore. They belonged to themselves.

She sat quietly, thinking about all of it, as the storm seemed to get worse outside. They were just starting to get up to go to bed. It was after three, and the hurricane showed no sign of abating. According to the news on their phones, the flooding had gotten worse, roads were blocked, highways were closed. The highway patrol was telling people to stay in their homes unless they were dangerously flooded or were in areas being evacuated, which they weren't yet. But a map shown on the screen indicated that the evacuation area was coming closer to them. They were all slowly shuffling up to bed when the front door opened and Phillip and Daphne walked in. He was carrying Tucker, sound asleep. They looked like refugees, bundled up in slickers, Wellingtons, and rainwear. Everyone came alive again when they saw them.

"Our house is flooding," Daphne said. "Sheriff's deputies told us to evacuate. Angelica went home to her parents. I'm sorry to barge in." Phillip looked at her pointedly, and she bit her lip, fighting tears. "My water broke an hour ago. The road to the hospital is completely flooded. The patients got evacuated two hours ago and airlifted out. And the highway to the city is closed. I think I might be in labor, and I don't know what to do." She burst into tears, and Sofia stepped forward instantly to comfort her.

"You're going to be fine," she said calmly, and Brad called 911 on his cellphone. He spoke in codes that were familiar to him and Sofia but not the others. Eugenia had called Pam and asked her to send emails to all the guests to tell them the wedding was canceled due to the storm. They didn't need to know the rest yet.

"What about an airlift out?" Brad asked the dispatcher he was talking to. "We've got a big flat area where they can land. Right. Got that." He gave them the address. "Put us first on that list. We may be good for another hour, but we need out, fast. That's right, twins." He ended the call and summed it up for the others. "They can't airlift you out right now, Daphne, the winds are too high, the helicopter would flip, they're all grounded. They'll get here as soon as they can take off again. And the flooded areas are rising. They think they can come to you in a police boat, but that depends how far you are in the delivery. You don't want to deliver in a police boat in a flood. For now, let's sit tight, and see where your labor goes, if you're really in labor. You may just be feeling Braxton-Hicks contractions. Tonight has been pretty stressful. I'm here, and your sister is the best midwife in Tennessee. You're in good hands. Why don't you go upstairs and let Sofia check you? The first responders are going to stay in close touch. I'm not worried about you," Brad said, and Daphne wanted to believe him. Phillip looked somewhat reassured but not completely. His wife was about to have twins in a flood with no way to get to a hospital. And they were only a week early, which was considered full-term. They both knew that in a house far from a hospital there was going to be no pain relief for her, and one or both of the twins could be at risk. It wasn't a good situation, and Phillip hugged Daphne as she went upstairs with her sister, and Eugenia followed. The others waited downstairs.

Sofia seemed strikingly calm as she led the way to their mother's bedroom. She spoke in low, soothing tones, and reassured Daphne that everything was going to be great. Tucker was still sound asleep on the couch downstairs.

"Why do I have to be in labor now, with everything going wrong?" Daphne said, with tears in her eyes, as Sofia moved toward the door to get the medical bag she always traveled with. She had everything she needed in it to do a delivery, and so did Brad.

"Nothing is going wrong," Sofia corrected her. "You're healthy, the babies are healthy, they're term. They're a good size, and I deliver babies every day in worse conditions. My patients would be thrilled to deliver in a house like this. We have everything we need, like our very own hospital, with a doctor and a nurse practitioner. First class all the way." She smiled, disappeared for less than five minutes, and was back with the medical bag that she had brought in her suitcase.

She slipped off Daphne's jeans and underwear, covered her with a towel, asked their mother to bring some sheets and towels, and went to wash her hands. When she came back, she checked Daphne, still smiling and chatting softly, as though nothing untoward was happening. If she was concerned or worried, it didn't show for a second. Everything was cheerful and happy around them, as Sofia smiled at her sister.

"Great news, everything is moving just as we want it to. If you hang around and don't go into labor for a long time after your water breaks, you can get a nasty infection. That's not where we are, Daph. Things are progressing nicely. Your cervix is soft and dilated, you're at six centimeters, which is great. Things may start to move fast in a little while, but we're not there yet. You're at six without even knowing for sure you were in labor. I think this is going to be a piece of cake." She made it sound like it was exactly what she hoped to find, which wasn't the case. Daphne was far enough along in labor that there was no turning back, and no way to slow it down.

Daphne had a contraction right after Sofia examined her. Daphne had forgotten how bad labor could be, and was starting to remember.

"I don't want to have them now, like this. Can't we do anything to stop it?" she asked, and Sofia shook her head.

"These guys are ready, and you know how kids are, they do whatever they want." Sofia checked the fetal hearts with her stethoscope and said they both sounded strong. "I'm going to check you again in a minute, I want to see how fast we're making progress, how fast things are moving." But she could see that Daphne had moved into transition from the look on her face when she had a contraction. She was concentrated, focused, and oblivious to everything around her but the pain. She couldn't be distracted. Sofia waited a minute after the next contraction and checked again. It was going fast, Daphne was at eight. It was going too fast. Daphne was going to deliver long before help could reach them. Sofia had delivered babies in much worse circumstances than this, but the hurricane and the flood made it impossible for help to get to them if they had any kind of crisis. They were on their own, without even electricity.

"Do you want to sit up?" she asked Daphne. "Or lie on your side? What's your body telling you?"

"That I can't move, they're so heavy, they pin me down, and it's hard to breathe." Sofia had a portable canister of oxygen, put a mask on her sister's face, and turned it on. "Do you have anything for the pain?" Daphne asked, starting to look panicked as the pain got worse rapidly. Eugenia had gone to be with Tucker, and Phillip walked into the room to be with Daphne. Sofia filled him in, in an upbeat, calm, reassuring way, but he understood what the risks were, and how rough the delivery was going to be for Daphne. She could get no pain relief at all, and would have to do it twice. He felt terrible for her, and spoke soothingly to her. Daphne was crying, as much from fear as from the pain. She held tightly to Phillip's hand as another contraction hit and was so brutal it took her breath away.

The contractions started coming harder, faster and closer together, as Sofia timed them, and after ten more minutes she checked her again. Daphne was letting out a scream now when she had a contraction. Sofia looked at her and spoke in a stronger voice. "Daph, look at me, I want you to focus. You're at ten, we can do this together. On the next contraction, I want you to push as hard as you can." She told her how to do it, and as she did, Brad walked into the room and Sofia told him where they were in the process. She wanted him there to check the babies, if they had a problem when they came out. He stood on Daphne's other side and held her leg wide, and told Phillip to do the same, to help give the babies a wide berth. Brad's fear was that they could be too big to deliver vaginally. They looked like it to him, but Sofia was the better judge of that. And he couldn't ask her in front of Daphne. He guessed that she agreed with him, and suspected what she was thinking, and that she hoped they were both wrong. There was no way they could do a Caesarean here to get them out, and mother and both babies could die.

Daphne pushed for an hour and they made progress but not enough. The contractions were fierce and she was trying not to scream, but most of the time she couldn't stop it. Sofia moved her close to the edge of the bed, and Phillip supported her shoulders. She was sitting and pushing with all her might, and all of a sudden there was a gush of blood and water, and the first twin made a big move down the birth canal. "One more really big push, and your baby's head is going to be born. Come on, Daph, you can do this," Sofia said, concentrating on the first twin.

"I can't," Daphne said, sobbing.

"You *can*," Sofia said. "Push as hard as you can," she told her, as the next contraction hit, and Brad saw her unwrap a scalpel and make a small incision for an episiotomy. She kept telling Daphne to push, and all of a sudden there was a face looking at them, and a loud wail, as the baby slipped into Sofia's hands. "You did it!" Sofia said jubilantly. She cut the cord, wrapped the baby in a towel, and handed her to Brad. It was Daphne and Phillip's daughter. Their son would be next. Sofia spoke soothingly to Daphne while they waited, and Daphne and Phillip were both crying, as they gazed at their baby girl. Sofia let Daphne hold her for a minute, and then Brad took her again, and declared her perfect. She was beautiful and looked like Daphne.

And then the contractions started again with a vengeance. They were worse than the first ones and Daphne didn't stop screaming between the contractions. Sofia had to extend the episiotomy and their son was born ten minutes later, after six unbearably painful pushes, but it was over. They were born, and healthy. "I am guessing seven pounds on your daughter and eight or nine pounds on your son," Sofia told her sister, who was lying down holding one in each arm.

She delivered both placentas, and gave Daphne a shot of the morphine she was carrying but hadn't wanted to give her during the birth. She could take no risks with no hospital nearby. Daphne was dozing and groggy when Sofia sewed up the episiotomy, which had served Daphne well. Given the size of the babies, it could have taken many more hours and the babies could have gone into fetal distress. Brad complimented Sofia on what a good job she'd done, and Daphne and Phillip echoed his words.

"You were amazing!" Daphne said to her, and they held hands for a minute, and then Phillip went to get the rest of the family. Eugenia kissed Daphne and told her she was the bravest woman she knew, and Eloise looked totally rattled and was crying, and said the babies were beautiful. Stef watched his sister from the doorway, as she held both her babies and looked like a Madonna. She looked peaceful and happy, and Liz came closer to take a peek and said they were gorgeous. Eugenia went to get a scale they'd seen in the kitchen, and brought it up to the bedroom. Sofia weighed both of them. The baby girl weighed seven pounds, fourteen ounces, and the baby boy nine pounds, two ounces. Her guess had been close.

"You've been carrying around seventeen pounds of babies. No wonder you looked like that," Sofia said, impressed.

"And felt like it." Daphne smiled.

Eugenia gave up her room to Phillip and Daphne that night, and she slept with Eloise. Sofia checked Daphne every hour for hemorrhaging and any complications, and gave her enough pain meds to get her through the night after a rough delivery. The first responders called Brad at seven, and told him they could land on the property then, to take Daphne to the hospital in Southampton. "Do I have to go?" she asked Brad and Sofia. "I want to stay here."

"Phillip and the babies will go with you," Sofia explained.

"They won't keep you for more than a day or so, to make sure you didn't pick up an infection from delivering in a non-sterile environment, and then they'll send you home. Your babies don't need to be in an incubator. They're fine, and so are you." Her sister smiled at her, relieved that it had gone well.

"Thanks to you." Daphne gave Sofia full credit for getting her through it. Brad gave the helicopter clearance to land and went outside to wave them in. The hurricane had moved on, the winds had died down, and the rain had stopped. There were still floods in the area, but the worst was over. Daphne and the babies had come through it without a hitch. Tucker stayed with his grandmother and aunts after looking at his new brother and sister. When the helicopter landed, Gloria came out of her room squinting, awakened by all the noise.

"What happened? Are we being invaded by aliens?" She looked around at everyone.

"No, by paramedics," Phillip said, smiling. "Your sister had the twins last night. Sofia delivered them." He was beaming, and Gloria looked shocked.

"Oh God, I took a sleeping pill," and then she remembered everything that had happened, Geoff and the girl he was going to have sex with and the things he said. She knew nothing would ever erase the words or the memory.

The paramedics took Daphne out on a stretcher, with her babies in her arms. They strapped her securely into the helicopter and Phillip jumped in next to her, and they each held one of the babies. The doors closed and the helicopter went straight up, circled once, and took off toward the hospital in Southampton.

Geoff called Gloria half a dozen times on her cell that morning, and she didn't answer, and Prudence Crawford called Eugenia, sounding outraged.

"What happened to the wedding?" she demanded to know.

"My daughter canceled it," Eugenia said coolly. "Didn't your son tell you? The club was damaged anyway and they had to cancel. There isn't going to be a wedding."

"He said something about a misunderstanding," Prudence said, confused.

"There was no misunderstanding," Eugenia said in a hard voice. "She found him on his way to bed with another woman at the hotel. And I believe that's not the first time he cheated on her. It's over, Prudence. The wedding is canceled. The club was too damaged by the storm anyway. It would have been canceled in any case. Have a safe trip back to England, and give my regards to Henry," and with that, she hung up, and hoped never to hear from them again, or their son. Eloise had been listening to her and

263

cheered when she hung up. Gloria had heard it too, and spoke sadly.

"Thank you," was all she said, and went upstairs to pack. She had a lot of thinking to do about how she could have been so wrong about Geoff. She was sad and angry all at the same time, and in great part at herself, and she apologized to Brad when she saw him on the stairs. "I'm sorry. I'd like to say I was kidnapped by aliens who ate my brain. But I wasn't. I don't know what happened. I'm just sorry. I hope I can make up to you for how rude we were."

"I'm not going anywhere." Brad smiled at her. "We have plenty of time to get to know each other and be friends."

"Thank you," she said again. She was deeply ashamed of everything Geoff had said and that she had let him say, and the way they had behaved. She hugged Sofia when she saw her, who understood and had a forgiving nature. And living in the South, that kind of blind prejudice was not new to her, or to Brad.

Patrick called Eugenia at noon, from his captain's cell phone. His had fallen overboard while they were tying things down in the storm. "That was amazing last night, wasn't it?"

"It certainly was," she said and laughed. "Gloria canceled the wedding because Geoff was about to cheat on her last night and she caught him. Daphne had the twins and they're gorgeous. They just airlifted all of them to the hospital a few minutes ago, and they're fine. We're all packing up and going home. And I have an extra day to work on my show."

"Wow, and I thought I was busy last night. Can I drive you home in one of our vans?" he offered. "They just opened the highway. I was going to drive home anyway."

"I have a mountain of stuff to take back, including the party favors and the wedding dress."

"I've got plenty of room."

"And a column fell on the catering department at the club last night, so they canceled before we did, and I don't lose my deposits."

"Sounds like a win-win all around," Patrick said, laughing. "You can tell me all about it on the drive back."

Eugenia's children all left an hour later. Gloria and Eloise took Tucker home to the city to stay with them and their mother. Stef drove Liz back. And Patrick picked Eugenia up as soon as they left and helped her load the van. The cleaning staff were already at work disposing of the sheets and towels used during the delivery.

"You certainly live an interesting life," Patrick said to her.

"Is that an insult or a compliment?" she asked him.

"Definitely a compliment. My life seems very dull by comparison, and you take it all in stride."

"I have more children than you do," she said with a sigh.

"I'm sorry for Gloria, but I'm so relieved she didn't marry him."

"Me too. He wasn't a good guy."

"I know."

"I'm happy to see you." He leaned over to kiss her, and she was happy to see him. "Where shall I take you in the city?"

"To my office. Where else?"

"I could think of some other places, like my house."

"As soon as I finish the show," she promised, and he smiled, content with whatever time he could get with her.

Chapter 12

For the next nine days, Eugenia worked nonstop on her show. She worked all week and straight through Labor Day weekend, and Eloise helped her. This was familiar territory for Eugenia. By Labor Day every detail of the show was the way she wanted it, the music was perfect, the models had the look she wanted, the clothes fit them perfectly. She had decided on the hair and makeup for each model. Every detail for the runway show had been worked out, and they had a presentation of Cotton Candy set up in their Seventh Avenue showroom, and the orders were pouring in.

Eugenia had only seen Patrick twice in the last week, and only briefly. She was so tired, she nodded off and almost fell asleep at dinner. He teased her about it afterward.

"I've always known how boring I am, but most of my dates pretend they're fascinated and try to stay awake."

"I'm so sorry, Patrick." She hadn't had more than three hours of sleep a night all week. It was the nature of the business during Fashion Week.

Patrick was coming to the show, and had asked to bring his son. He said Quinn had been to Fashion Week before, probably to see the models he dated. But it amused Patrick to attend Eugenia's show with Quinn. He was eager to see more of Eugenia again once the show was behind her, but she was going to Paris in two weeks for Paris Fashion Week, to do a presentation of her new high-end daywear line and Cotton Candy, which was set up in their Paris office. Since Patrick was less busy than usual, he had told Eugenia he wanted to come to see her in Paris and take her out, and she said she thought it would be fun. He still had his plane so he could fly private to Paris, maybe with Quinn. He wanted to enjoy the luxuries he still had.

Things were starting to look up for him too. He'd made another deal and had sold three of his buildings now, at a loss but not too dramatic. He still had fourteen unoccupied buildings, but some of the larger corporations were moving back in and he had increased their rent. He still wanted to try to reconfigure some of his buildings on the successful Chicago model of a block of floors as a hotel, another block as office space, and the top twenty floors as luxury apartments with spectacular views of the city. It worked in Chicago, and he didn't see why it wouldn't work in New York. There were even department stores, shopping malls, supermarkets, and movie theaters as part of the buildings. He was excited by the concept and was determined to try, and from the three buildings he had sold he had the money he needed to experiment with it. He was working with an architect on the concept for the first one, and had already sparked some interest.

The day after Labor Day, on the morning of her show, Eugenia was backstage, checking the models before they walked out on the runway. Eloise was with her and had helped style the show. Gloria had flown to London the day after the canceled wedding, and Brad and Sofia were back at their medical center in Memphis. Daphne was home recovering from childbirth and enjoying visits from Eloise when she had time. Eloise was enjoying New York more than she had expected to, after seven years in Paris. Eugenia had invited Liz to the show, and given her a front-row seat, and Liz was excited to be in the front row, particularly for her mother-in-law's new concept of chic daywear. Natasha Wylie was in the front row too, with two friends, explaining to everyone near them that she and Eugenia were partners.

Every fashion editor and store buyer from around the world was present, as usual. And all of the fashion press. It was exciting just being in the audience, and Patrick was excited for Eugenia. Quinn was amused to see his father at the show, since it wasn't his usual style, but Quinn had noticed that in spite of the big business headaches Patrick had, he was happy these days, and Quinn wanted to meet the woman who was responsible for it. He noticed that his father was shy about talking about Eugenia, and was very protective of her. Quinn had a feeling that it might just be serious. He knew his father hadn't had a regular girlfriend in years, and had no interest in marrying again.

The show was as exciting as Eugenia had hoped it would be, and the critics loved it. She had hit just the right tone between chic and casual, with clothes that looked great and were easy to wear but were still high quality and looked it. Her denims were beautiful and had a slightly dressy feel to the way they were cut in trim suits and dresses. The other fabrics she had chosen were appealing, and the palette of colors she had chosen was flattering to women of all ages. Patrick was hugely impressed when he saw the show, and it brought everything she had explained to him to life.

Quinn enjoyed admiring the models. There were some exquisite girls in the show. The new trend was to use less attractive models, unlike the big stars of earlier decades, but Eugenia was more old-school about that, and there were at least three girls he would have liked to date, and two that he already had, out of thirty-five in the show. The final look was a less formal wedding dress that made the audience applaud. The music Eugenia had chosen was so contemporary and exciting that it added life to the girls striding down the runway. Eugenia came out and took a quick bow at the end of the show. She was always shy about it. Quinn noticed that a very beautiful young woman held the curtain back for her. She and Eugenia looked somewhat similar. She had a great figure and long blonde hair and was wearing black jeans and a black T-shirt. She looked like one of the models, but she wasn't dressed for the show and hadn't been on the runway with the others. She caught Quinn's attention immediately, and he nudged his father.

"Who's that?" He pointed seconds before they dropped the curtain and Eugenia disappeared backstage, and so did the beautiful younger woman. He doubted that his father knew, but he might. All he knew was that his father was dating Eugenia Ward, he didn't know anything else about her. And many of the models Quinn dated had been in her shows. She was a big deal in fashion, and his father had told him that she was in the process of reinventing herself, which seemed to be a common theme these days.

Patrick wasn't quite sure who he meant, and Quinn described the girl he'd seen behind Eugenia. "I'm not sure, I didn't see her for long enough," Patrick answered. "It might be one of her daughters. One of them was a designer for Balenciaga in Paris, and just moved back to New York. She's been helping her mother with the show."

Quinn laughed at his father again. "Listen to you, being up on all the big designers." It was a whole new view of Patrick, which Quinn thought was great. He used to be all about business, and lately he was having fun too. In the past, the only fun he had was on his boat. Eugenia seemed to be expanding his horizons, and Patrick was diversifying his interests because of her. "Is the daughter nice?" Quinn asked him and Patrick thought about it.

"I think so, she's very bright, and is good to her mother. I think she wants to go back to Paris, she's looking for a job. I've only met her twice."

When the show ended, Patrick wanted to congratulate Eugenia and tell her how great the show was. He stood up and told Quinn he was going backstage.

"I'll go with you," Quinn said, and his father smiled.

"What a good son you are," he teased him.

"Yeah, yeah, I know. I'm all heart." As father and son they got along well, and Quinn had long since forgiven his father for the times he wasn't around when he was young.

They had had some great times together in recent years on the boat and had taken several trips together.

Father and son pressed through the crowd to get to Eugenia. She was wearing white jeans, a plain white T-shirt, and sneakers, and Quinn could see she had a great body and a youthful face, and then he saw the girl in black standing right behind her. While Patrick was telling Eugenia how fabulous the show had been, Quinn said hello to the girl in the black T-shirt.

"Hi," he said to her amidst the din and the chaos, with people pressing to get on the stage to reach Eugenia. Quinn had been backstage at fashion shows before, but he somehow felt tongue-tied, talking to the tall beautiful blonde in the black shirt and jeans. "Do you work here?" he asked her.

"I'm just helping out," she said with a breathtaking smile.

"The show was great."

"It's a whole new direction for the designer," she said, which made him think she wasn't Eugenia's daughter after all. But whoever she was, she was gorgeous, and she seemed interesting and pleasant. He couldn't think of what to say to her, which was unusual for him. Normally, he had no trouble thinking up clever lines to pick up women, but his mind was suddenly a blank. There was no way he could ask her for her number with nothing else to say to her, it would seem so crass. And he turned and saw his father standing next to him. Quinn was taller and broader, but Patrick was a handsome man too. The beautiful woman's face broke into a warm smile when she saw Quinn's father.

"Hi, Patrick," she said to him, "how did you like the show?"

"Loved it! It was worth all the hard work you and your mother put into it. It was terrific. Have you met my son?" he said innocently, and suddenly Quinn came to life. She was the designer's daughter, and just trying to be professional and discreet. "You and your mother will have to have dinner with us sometime. Things ought to slow down a little now that the show is over." Eloise laughed at the suggestion.

"Yeah, for about five minutes. She's busy on Cotton Candy now, and we're taking that and this collection to Paris to take orders there during Paris Fashion Week. We leave in two weeks. She never stops for long."

"I'm getting to know that. Maybe we'll see you there," Patrick said. They were being jostled by the crowd, and she looked at them both with a friendly expression.

"I'd better rescue my mother. She looks like she's being eaten alive by the crowd. It was nice to see you," she said to Patrick and glanced at his son, "and nice to meet you," and then, clutching her clipboard, she disappeared into the crowd. The two men found their way off the stage, and Patrick smiled at Quinn on the way out.

"You looked like you needed a helping hand." He grinned at him, and Quinn looked sheepish.

"I didn't know what to say to her, I couldn't figure out if she was the designer's daughter or not. Let's take them both to dinner sometime."

"Ah, so we're now a father and son act," Patrick teased him.

"Maybe I will come to Paris with you. That might really be fun." Quinn had dated several French models, and had been to Paris Fashion Week before, and gone to some of the shows when his dates were in them.

"You'd better be nice to me if you expect me to introduce you to my women friends' daughters." That had never happened before.

"Not women, or daughters, just that one. She's got a nice real look, not all the phony crap that goes with models. And most of them are teenagers, too young for me."

"I suspect you're in a much better position to know about models than I am. I haven't dated a model in about twenty years."

"You've moved up in the world, Dad. You're dating

designers. Maybe I'm ready for the next step too." They left each other outside the venue, and they both went back to their offices smiling. They'd had a good time.

Patrick spent the night with Eugenia that night at his house, since Eloise was still staying with her.

It was the first relaxed evening they'd had in weeks. Now that the show was over she could breathe again, and she hadn't fallen asleep at dinner.

"Guess who I introduced my son to today," he said, and she couldn't guess. "Eloise. We saw her when I was looking for you backstage. He was very taken with her. He thinks we should go to dinner together sometime. What do you think?"

"I'd love to meet him, and have dinner with him. But Eloise is unpredictable and not very social. She works so hard, she rarely goes out, though now that she's working for me for a little while, she's not working quite as hard. She's very shy and she gets anxious. Daphne tried to introduce her to people for years and finally gave up. Eloise just turned thirty, and I think she's perfectly happy staying single forever."

"She's so beautiful, that's a terrible waste. She looks just like you. He even said he might come to Paris with me, if I go to see you." She smiled at the idea of introducing their children to each other. Usually those attempts were never successful, and children usually hated their parents' friends.

She'd tried when they were younger, unsuccessfully.

"You're welcome to try. It would be fun if they like each other, and it might be a nice introduction for Quinn to meet the others." She'd been thinking about it lately and Patrick liked the idea. He liked her children, and Eloise might be a nice friend for Quinn, if nothing else.

They had a good time talking to each other that night, since they'd had so few opportunities to see each other for the past two weeks, between the wedding and the show. He was getting to know her. She was going to take her two new lines to Paris and take orders there, and be busy again. She was a moving target.

"I like the idea of coming to Paris, by the way," Patrick said to her, but he didn't want to crowd her when she was working. "Would you have time to see me?" He didn't want to bother her if she was too busy. He knew what that was like, and wanted to be respectful of her commitments.

"It won't be as crazy there, since I'm not doing a show, just a presentation in our sales office. It would be fun to see you," she said, and kissed him.

"Then maybe I'll come," he said, pensive. They held each other close when they fell asleep that night after they made love. He had missed her while she was so busy, but now he had Paris to look forward to.

*

277

They had breakfast together the next day, after making love again in the morning. They were well suited and had a great time in bed. At breakfast, Patrick was reading *The Wall Street Journal* and Eugenia was reading *The New York Times* on her iPad when she stopped and stared at a photograph and read the headline above it. She looked up at Patrick in astonishment.

"You're not going to believe this."

"Try me." She handed him her iPad and he stared too, and then he whistled, read the article, looked up at her, and said, "Wow!"

"Holy shit, Patrick. Now what do I do?"

"You exercise your morals clause," he said simply. Austin Wylie had been indicted on federal charges for selling missiles, automatic weapons, and other comparable weapons of destruction to three countries in the Middle East, and two in Africa, all of whom were hostile to the United States. "You know, I always had a feeling about him. I thought there was something smoky about his oil business. He was too rich just for oil. I figured he was doing something illegal. This is exactly what I thought. I'm shocked but not surprised."

"Do I have to give him back his money?" Eugenia looked suddenly disappointed. "I need that money, Patrick. Things are going well, but I'm not back where I was yet. I'm trying to rebuild my business, and I can do it with the twenty million he gave me. Without that, I'm going to be broke again. What do I do?"

"You can't keep tainted money to run your business," he said wisely. "That will come back to haunt you at just the wrong time, and you could lose everything. They could accuse you of knowing where it came from, laundering money, or being part of the deal."

"Shit. When do I have to give it back?"

"Soon. Now. You have to register your displeasure with him, and publicly refuse to do business with a dangerous criminal. He'll go to prison for this. The faster you give him his money back, the better for you." Patrick thought for a moment and looked at her. He trusted her completely and he dealt in much bigger amounts than what Wylie had loaned her. "I can loan you twenty million for a while, until you find new investors."

"I'll have money after Paris, but not twenty million. I don't want to take money from you, and I don't know when I could pay you back."

"You need to find investors to replace him. Just know that if you need me to cover you for a while, I can."

"Thank you." She was genuinely touched. It was a very generous offer.

She thought about it on her way to work, and called Stefano when she got to the office, telling him her dilemma.

"Patrick's right," he said to her. "That's liable to turn into a really dangerous mess, Mom. Who knows what else he was selling? Military secrets, whatever he can get his hands on."

"I thought he was harmless," she said.

"Well, clearly he's not."

"Patrick was uncomfortable about him all along."

"He's a smart guy," Stef said. "And he's right, you need to give Wylie his money back. He's going to need it for lawyers. But unfortunately, I don't know anyone I think would invest in the fashion industry. No one's ever asked me for that." Eugenia had taken out two loans during the pandemic, and she didn't want to add more debt to her books. Another investor was the only way. But who? "You know, Mom, you should talk to Liz. I know you were uncomfortable about her at first, but she's really smart, and she likes you, and she knows all kinds of investors. She's much better at networking than I am," he said.

Eugenia hated to call Liz after all the things she and the girls had said about her. She felt like such a hypocrite. But without Austin's money, she was still at risk of losing her business, and things were going so well, heading in the right direction. And if she got big orders in Paris for her new lines, she wouldn't be able to produce them without more money, if she had to give Wylie back his.

With some trepidation, she called Liz, who listened to

what she had to say. She expected Liz to tell her to get lost. Instead, she stunned her mother-in-law, and leapt into action. She was more than willing to help her.

"Give me a few days," she said to Eugenia. "I'm going to shake the trees and see what I can come up with. I have some ideas." She didn't hesitate for a minute. She dove right into the deep end of the pool to save Eugenia and her business. Stef was right. And Eugenia was grateful for her efforts, even if she didn't find any investors. Liz promised to call her by the end of the week, which sounded too fast and unrealistic to Eugenia.

She called her banker and lawyer after that, and arranged to return Austin's twenty million by the next day, without penalty, just as their contract said, thanks to Patrick's good advice.

She sent out an email blast informing everyone she dealt with that Austin Wylie was no longer an investor in Eugenia Ward, Princess Eugenie, or Cotton Candy, and that his money had been returned. The press talked about it and commented on it the next day. She was worried about her business again, and distracted, but as promised, she got a call from Liz on Friday afternoon.

"Two down and one to go," she reported in a voice of victory.

"Two what?" Eugenia thought Liz was talking about her

Cotton Candy dress order, which was large and had just been sent to her.

"Two investors, of course. One is a really sweet guy in the garment district who owns four factories in New Jersey and loves what you do, and one is a shut-in who was a designer in her youth and loves fashion. She married a wealthy man and retired early, and now she's a widow. The first one gave us ten million, the second one gave us five. I've made some good investments for them and made them a lot of money. I can get you another five million easily. It's a small amount of money and you're a big, important brand. They're really excited to invest in your business, and want to help you out." Eugenia couldn't believe that her rhinestone-studded not-so-genteel little daughter-in-law had gotten her fifteen million dollars in two days. And the third investor was sure to come. Five million was not a big investment for anyone to make and Liz would find it.

"Liz, I can't tell you how grateful I am," Eugenia said to her.

"It was fun. I loved it. I'll get you the other five within a week."

Eugenia was floating on a cloud at the store that afternoon, thinking about the money and how efficient Liz was. And then suddenly she looked up and Natasha was there. She seemed tired and worried, and Eugenia realized how unpleasant this was for her. She probably had had no idea what Austin was up to, and certainly not the scale to which he was implicated. Her whole life must be upside down now too.

"So we are not partners anymore?" Natasha said sadly. And even if she was vulgar and badly dressed, she was harmless and smart, and she loved Eugenia's brands, and was so proud to be part of the business.

"I gave the money back," Eugenia told her. "It's already on its way to Austin's account. My daughter-in-law just found two investors for me. I still need another one," Eugenia said candidly.

"For five million, how much partnership do I get?" Natasha looked mischievous as she said it. She didn't appear to be too sympathetic about Austin's fate. Eugenia wondered if she even liked him. Maybe not. Maybe she'd even turned state's evidence against him. They were a tough crowd.

"For five million, you get five percent ownership. Don't waste your money, Natasha, it's not worth it." She might need the money now with Austin in prison, where he was sure to end up.

"Five percent is good. I'll give you five million. I can afford it. And I can work in the store whenever you want me," Natasha said, smiling. Eugenia wanted to hug her. And then she thought of something.

"Did Austin give you the money? Originally?" If he had,

it would still be dangerous for her if they traced it. Natasha smiled mysteriously.

"No, this is my money. Not Austin's. I get it from selling the jewelry he gives me. It's all expensive and I don't like it." It struck Eugenia as funny, but the money was clean. The jewelry belonged to Natasha, according to their prenup, and she had a right to sell it if she wished.

"What's going to happen to you now if Austin goes to jail?" Eugenia asked her.

"My lawyer says he will. I'm going to divorce him," Natasha said matter-of-factly, with no look of regret. And then she lowered her voice so no one could hear her, except Eugenia. "I have a boyfriend. He's much richer than Austin. He's Russian like me. And very smart." Eugenia couldn't help wondering how girls like Natasha managed to always land on their feet. It was a business to them, and they were good at it. She smiled at Natasha.

"I'm happy for you," and she meant it.

"I'll transfer the five million to you on Monday. And we're partners five percent. My lawyer will draw up contract. Everything is good now. And Austin is gone." Natasha shook Eugenia's hand, hugged her and kissed her, and left a few minutes later.

Eugenia called Liz to tell her that she had found the last five million herself. And Natasha seemed like an honest woman. With magic powers to use on wealthy men. Eugenia was back in business, and by next week should have twenty million in her bank account again for her brands. Patrick had saved her with the morals clause he had insisted on in her contract with Austin Wylie. And Natasha had turned out to be an unexpected blessing. She was a very smart woman, and not the mindless trophy wife she appeared to be. Eugenia actually liked her and they were "partners five percent."

Chapter 13

Eugenia flew to Paris for Fashion Week with Patrick on his plane. Ten days before, they had had dinner with Quinn and Eloise, who had hit it off remarkably, and on the spur of the moment Quinn decided to come. Eloise flew with them. She was going to help her mother with the presentation and the orders. The presentation was too much for Eugenia to do alone, running both brands, though she had a small staff in Paris, an assistant in the office and three women who worked with him. And Eugenia had Eloise there to help her with the Cotton Candy orders. Guy was fun to work with, and Eloise liked the Paris staff. They were excited about the new lines too. Eugenia preferred working with Pam in New York, but she didn't speak French, so the Paris office staff handled the orders in Europe. Eloise was fluent, so she was a big help to her mother, and she knew the new lines. Eugenia thought it would be good for Eloise's self-confidence to be back in Paris, working with a successful brand, and not depressed at her apartment, unemployed. Eloise hated to give up her Paris apartment, which she loved. She still didn't know whether she wanted to stay in Paris and look for a job, or try to find one in New York. She had contacted headhunters in both cities. In the interim, she could work for her mother's lines, until she found a new job. It was working out well for both of them.

Eloise and Quinn had had dinner alone once, after the dinner with their parents, and Eloise said she had fun with him. He had a great sense of humor and was handsome, smart, and successful, but she could sense that he was a player, and she didn't want to be part of a chorus line, so she refused to take him seriously, which sparked his interest even more.

They sat next to each other on the plane and talked. Then they both watched a movie, and eventually fell asleep.

Eugenia smiled, watching them, and whispered to Patrick, "It's funny having our children with us, isn't it? I love working with her, but she needs a real job. She's a talented designer and should have an important job like the one she had, not being my assistant."

"Maybe she needs a break for a while. There must have

been a lot of pressure in her last job. You said she was always anxious, so maybe this is what she needs, a little while under your wing, with no big decisions to make." Eugenia thought he might be right, and she wondered if anything was going to happen between her daughter and Quinn romantically. There were definitely sparks, but Eloise refused to fan the flames. She was afraid to get involved, and she didn't even know if she was going to stay in New York. Quinn seemed like a complication to her, and she was being cautious, which made Quinn want her all the more. He was dazzled by her beauty, and she was talented and smart and a nice person.

"I was like him at his age," Patrick admitted to Eugenia on the flight, and he had before. "I was divorced and having too much fun to get deeply involved with anyone, and by the time I realized that wasn't the right answer for the long run, I'd been alone for too long, set in my ways, and a deep committed relationship seemed like too much trouble. I was more comfortable alone. I could do what I wanted, go where I wanted, didn't have to answer to anyone. And then you came along, and turned my safe lonely world upside down, and now I'm happy." He smiled at her. "Happier than I've ever been before. I'm sorry I waited this long." They'd been together for two months, and everything was going smoothly, and he was understanding about the demands of her job and how hard she worked. The previous men in her life had always resented it, or been jealous of her success. Patrick had his own. And he had a heavy workload too. They were evenly matched.

"I did the same thing, I filled my life with my work and my kids," she said. "I felt safe that way. And now the kids are gone, and work isn't enough. I want more. But I didn't know that was what I wanted until now." She had never known anyone like him. He was the exact opposite of Umberto in every way. He was solid, responsible, kind, a good father, and he tried to take care of Eugenia when she let him. She was independent and self-sufficient, but she loved being close to him. They had the best of all possible worlds and he admitted that in the past, he would never have taken a week off to go to Paris for fun. He had been married to his business for forty years. And now he loved being with Eugenia, and he was fine about her work when she was busy. He couldn't wait to be in Paris with her, his favorite city in the world, other than New York.

"Do you think Eloise will move back to Paris?" Patrick asked her quietly.

"I think it will depend where she finds a job she loves."

"You don't want to hire her to work for you?"

"She deserves more than that," Eugenia said honestly. "I don't want her to live in my shadow. She needs her own world."

"That's why I never encouraged Quinn to work for me. He needs to be his own man." Eugenia agreed, for both of them. She wished that something would happen between them, but it was up to them. She thought Quinn seemed like a good man, like his father.

Eugenia had invited Gloria to meet them in Paris, but she was in London, working seriously on her book, and said she didn't want to lose the impetus again. She was hoping to come to New York for Thanksgiving, and that was only two months away. She didn't want to stop now. And she felt awkward being around her mother, after all the things she had said. She had meant them at the time, encouraged by Geoff, but she regretted them now and she couldn't take them back or erase them.

Eugenia had a feeling that Brad and Sofia would get engaged over the holidays, but he hadn't said anything about it officially to Eugenia yet, and he seemed like the kind of man who would. He had made it clear that he had the intention, but she had no idea when, and Sofia was young, although mature for her age.

When they got to Paris, Patrick stayed at Eugenia's apartment with her. Eloise stayed in hers, and Quinn was at a hotel. He liked the George V and could afford it, so he had booked a room there, and invited Eloise out to dinner. She gave a small informal dinner party and introduced him to a few of her French friends. He could see why she loved her life there. He liked her friends. They were all French but spoke English. She had a lovely apartment, and she loved the city. She was sad she had lost the job and didn't know if she'd find another one of the same stature in Paris.

When she wasn't busy with her mother, Eloise took Quinn to her favorite haunts, little cafés and typical French restaurants, shops on the Left Bank, and galleries. She showed him a whole new world, and a side of Paris he'd never seen before and loved discovering with her.

"Do you think you could be happy living in New York again?" he asked her one day, and she thought about it.

"I don't know. It depends on what else is in my life, like if I find a job I love."

"Don't you want to settle down?" he asked her, curious, as they lay on the grass in the Bois de Boulogne on a warm late September day.

"Not really," she said honestly. "I hated watching my parents' marriage. My father was never there, my mother had all the responsibility. She never complained, but her life was hard while we were growing up. I can't remember my mother having fun, except with us. My father hates responsibility. All he wants to do is go to parties and play. His life would bore me to death. I'm more like my mother.

I love my work. And kids grow up and move away. You can't count on them. I saw my sister tear my mother apart this summer over her stupid wedding. She really hurt my mother deeply. What's the point of that? It was like watching her get mugged and beaten up. I don't want kids who would do that to me."

"But she has the rest of you."

"There's always one rotten apple in the barrel who spoils everything," she said. "I'm happy as I am."

"You're the first woman I've ever met who wasn't dying to get married and have kids," he said, startled by her. She was a mystery to him. She was a locked door, and he couldn't find the key.

"Those girls are just too lazy to get a job," she said and he laughed. "They want to spend someone else's money. And kids are so much harder."

"Maybe you're scared to get married and have kids," he suggested, and she thought about it.

"Probably. And I'm too young to have kids. I'm thirty. I have my whole life ahead of me."

"It goes faster than you think," he said, wise for his years. "Yesterday I was thirty. Now I'm thirty-five. And suddenly you blink and you're our parents' age. I think my father is sad that he's alone now. He says it's too late. Or at least he said that until he met your mother. He's like a kid now, or a young man. I've never seen him that way. Your mom is good for him," he said warmly.

"She says the same about him. I think they're good for each other, it's nice for them." They were lying in the grass, talking, and Quinn couldn't resist anymore. He'd been circling her for weeks and she was keeping him at bay. He rolled over in the grass next to her, leaned gently toward her and kissed her. She looked startled at first, and then she kissed him back until they were both breathless and had to stop. He was terrified of her reaction afterward. Maybe she would never see him again. She lay on her back, looking up at the sky for a few minutes, and didn't say anything. She loved the sky in Paris, it was always beautiful, filled with giant puffy clouds, or pearl gray in the rain. The sky was luminous. And then she turned to look at Quinn. "Why did you do that?" She wasn't angry, she was curious, referring to the kiss. She hadn't expected it.

"Because I'm crazy about you, and I couldn't stand it any longer," he said honestly. She was so close and so out of reach at the same time. "I've wanted to kiss you for weeks, and you always stay just distant enough that I was afraid to upset you."

"I'm not upset, or scared," she said, and he kissed her again, and this time she responded even more passionately, with their bodies pressed together until she could feel that he was aroused, and she wanted him too. "Let's go back to my apartment," she whispered. Lying there, listening to him, she had made a decision. She had unlocked the door, and was willing to open it to him. She didn't know what else she was going to do with her life now, but whatever it would be, she wanted him in her life too. She didn't want to make any promises, she wanted to see how they were together and figure it out as they went along. She didn't want to make a mistake, as her parents had. She'd been afraid of that all her life.

When they got to her apartment, they raced each other up the stairs, laughing. She liked having fun with him. He acted like a kid sometimes and she liked that. Most of the time, he seemed very grown up. The building was old and full of charm. She unlocked the door, they walked in, and they never made it to her bedroom. They made love on the battered vintage leather couch in the living room, in a big comfortable chair she had bought at the flea market, finally on her bed, and in the shower afterward. She had held back for so long, that she realized now that she was starving for him. He had no idea what had finally given her the courage to let him in, but she abandoned herself to him, and that night they clung to each other, sated, in a private world all their own. They ate cheese and a baguette, naked in her kitchen, and shared a bottle of red wine. They fell asleep with his arms around her that night, and he knew he had come home, to the place and the woman he wanted to be with. He had been looking for her and never found her until he met Eloise. The first time he had seen her he knew she was special.

He checked out of the hotel the next day and moved in with her. She loved sharing her apartment with him, although it was small, but she loved the smell and feel of him, his touch, his skin. After keeping her distance at first, she was the most passionate woman he had ever known, and she knew she had been waiting for him too. The walls she had built around her heart to protect it were crumbling as she opened herself to him.

His father called him that night on his cell, sounding worried.

"Where are you? They said you checked out of the hotel."

"I did," Quinn admitted, without further explanation. Eloise was lying naked next to him.

"Are you okay?" Patrick asked him, but he could hear that Quinn was peaceful and content. Patrick didn't know where Quinn was, but he hoped he was with Eloise, and Eugenia felt the same way.

"Do you want to have lunch tomorrow? Eugenia wants to have lunch at a bistro she loves, and she'd like to know if you and Eloise would join us."

"We'd love to come," Quinn said cryptically, and Patrick smiled. He could guess the rest. If Quinn were with a girl other than Eloise, he wouldn't have brought her to lunch with them. His father told him the name of the bistro. And Patrick reported the call to Eugenia when he hung up.

"Well, we'll see who he brings to lunch tomorrow," she said, smiling.

When Quinn and Eloise walked into the restaurant together the next day, they tried to look casual, but everything they felt for each other was written on their faces. Eugenia wished that she could freeze the moment forever as she watched them. She could tell instantly that something had changed. She and Patrick held hands under the table, as they watched their children and smiled. Quinn and Eloise had found each other, and there was a tangible intimacy between them that didn't need words. The rest was up to them.

The orders they took at Eugenia's office were phenomenal. Cotton Candy outsold the daywear line two to one, but the new daywear was a big hit with high-end stores. Cotton Candy had done brilliantly in Europe, Asia, and the States. It was the look every young girl wanted. Eugenia couldn't believe how much they sold.

They flew back to New York after a week, and Eloise

decided not to give up her Paris apartment. She hoped that she and Quinn would come back there again often, whenever they could. And she was still open to the idea of a job in Paris.

She moved in with Quinn three weeks later after they returned to New York. Patrick and Eugenia were alternating between his house, her apartment, and the boat on weekends. They had an abundance of possibilities. The boat was where they had the most fun, and the choice of her place or his depended on their mood and their meetings the next day.

Patrick and Eugenia went skiing in January, instead of Eugenia showing her couture line in Paris. She had decided to take a season off from haute couture to build her two successful ready-to-wear lines and make them even stronger. She was going to present her new couture collection in July, and expected to be financially stable again by then. Maybe even more so than before. The decision not to show for a season was the right one, and she thought the world would be going to parties again by summer. She had a terrific time skiing with Patrick. They were both good skiers, and spent a week trying out different trails in the three valleys near Courchevel. It was the perfect trip for them, healthy, relaxed, and fun.

*

Sofia and Brad had gotten engaged at Christmas, which didn't surprise anybody, and they were all happy for her. They were going to wait a year to get married.

Gloria had finished her book by then and came home for Christmas. But she wasn't ready to leave London yet. She hadn't dated since Geoff, and she didn't feel ready for that yet either. She was taking her time to get over the trauma of the canceled wedding and seeing him pursue another woman on the eve of their wedding. She hadn't run into him since in London, and hoped she never would. She was taking the time she needed to heal. And she had a lot of fences to mend when she was ready. Eugenia had forgiven her, but Gloria needed time to understand how she had fallen prey to a man who didn't love or respect her, and only cared about himself, and why she'd been so willing to embrace all his opinions and abandon her own.

While Patrick and Eugenia were in the Alps, Eloise texted her mother that she had found a job, designing for a new label that someone was starting in New York. She said she would be traveling between Paris and New York, which suited her perfectly. She was glad she had kept her apartment in Paris. The job felt like a perfect fit and she hoped she was right. She said she would miss working with her mother. It had been fun and exciting, but now it was time to move forward. Eloise was ready. And she was going to continue living with Quinn when she was in New York. She loved him and wanted to give the relationship a chance to see where it went. She thought they were headed in the right direction, while respecting themselves and each other. She was in no hurry to marry, and didn't want anyone controlling her life. Quinn was well aware of it and respected her boundaries. Their relationship was working well so far. And now she had a job she was excited about too. Eugenia was happy for her.

Chapter 14

Eugenia showed her couture collection in Paris in July, for the first time since the pandemic, just as she'd planned. There were a few day pieces in the couture line now too. But most of it was the elegant evening gowns she was known for. There were thirty-five looks in the collection, one more beautiful than the next, and a magnificent bride at the end. The fashion critics loved the collection, and especially the wedding dress as the finale.

All her children had come to the show and they were all going to the south of France afterward, on Patrick's boat.

It was a glorious July day with a perfect blue sky. They sailed out of the port in Monaco at sunset with the priest from one of the local churches on board. Eloise was dressing in her cabin, with all her sisters and her mother around her, fussing with the dress, her veil, and her hair. The dress just reached her ankles, and Eugenia had had white shoes in the same lace made for her to go with it. It was the perfect touch. Daphne was there in a pale blue silk dress, and had gotten her figure back. The twins were ten months old, Charlotte and Alexander. Gloria was wearing a red silk dress she had bought in Italy, and she was the most striking of the group. Her book had just been bought by an American publisher. She had taken nearly a year off from dating, and had just met an Italian photographer she'd had dinner with twice and liked a lot. Liz was wearing a dress Eugenia had made for her. There was just a dusting of tiny rhinestones on the collar and the sleeves and she looked very chic. Eugenia had made it as a gift from her haute couture line.

Umberto was there, alone for the first time, and he seemed very subdued, more so than Eugenia had ever seen him. He was waiting outside the cabin for Eloise to be ready and emerge. Predictably, he had recently asked Eugenia to lend him some money, and she had refused. After that, he had asked Daphne, who had turned him down too. Eugenia strongly suspected Patrick would be next, and she had warned him not to fall prey to Umberto's charm. Whatever Umberto got, he blew through in months.

They all looked serious and elegant standing on the deck.

The deck had been lavishly decorated with white orchids. Eugenia was wearing a dress from her own couture line in a delicate lavender, and was standing next to Patrick in a hat that matched her dress. He looked proud beside her and she looked serene and happy.

The boat sailed out of the port and they anchored in Saint-Jean-Cap-Ferrat, as everyone chatted and drank champagne.

Eloise emerged from her cabin then and took her father's arm, and Quinn emerged from the captain's quarters, where he'd been hiding so as not to see Eloise all day.

Eloise was wearing a simple white organdie and lace gown her mother had designed for her, with a short veil, and carried a bouquet of lily of the valley. Quinn had a sprig of it on his lapel. They had chosen to marry with only their family and a few of their closest friends present.

Quinn's mother was there, and Umberto was charming and attentive to her. She was an attractive woman, and had just turned sixty, like Patrick, and they were on civil terms.

Eloise and Quinn looked so happy that the mood was contagious and included them all. It was exactly the wedding they both wanted, discreet, private, and small, and Patrick was lending them the boat for their honeymoon. He had rented a house in Saint-Jean-Cap-Ferrat for the month for him and Eugenia and any of her children who chose to join them. Daphne and Phillip and their children were planning to stay for a week. The others planned to come too for a short stay. Brad and Sofia stood together and were planning to marry at Christmas.

Patrick and Eugenia stood side by side to watch their children get married. She had been living in his house since February. Umberto walked Eloise down the aisle, bordered by white orchids and fragrant lily of the valley. The priest stood in front of them, and they repeated their vows after him. The vows were traditional, the same ones Eugenia had spoken when she married Umberto, Daphne when she married Phillip, Liz when she married Stefano, and Patrick with Quinn's mother. They glanced at each other and smiled with the distance of history. Patrick and Eugenia held hands as they listened.

"For better for worse . . . for richer for poorer," which had a whole new meaning to Patrick and Eugenia after the hard times they'd been through for nearly two years, "to love and to cherish, to have and to hold . . . until death do us part." The words had deep meaning to all of them as Eloise and Quinn stood beaming at each other, waiting for the future to unveil its mysteries, as they vowed their lives to each other and exchanged rings.

After he kissed her, Quinn gave a shout of joy, the musicians Patrick had hired started to play, and the champagne was poured plentifully, as Patrick looked into Eugenia's eyes and they smiled at each other, knowing how far they'd come. Their world was safe and secure again, thanks to them and the fates that brought them together. In the year that they'd known each other, good things had happened and they knew they belonged together.

They danced on the deck that night, in the moonlight under the summer stars. Umberto danced with each of his daughters and Quinn's mother, as Patrick and Eugenia slipped away to a quiet place on the deck where they could be alone for a few minutes away from the others.

"You've made me the luckiest man in the world," he said to her softly. "I have a family, a woman I love. Our children are happy. A year ago, I thought my life was over, but it started the day I met you."

"You saved me, Patrick," she said, her voice filled with emotion and the love she felt for him.

"No, you saved you, and your kids, just as you always have. You're the bravest woman I know. You make me brave, and you made me realize what life could be with the right woman, 'for richer for poorer, for better for worse.' It's what we have, which is better than everything else," he said, pointing to his heart and then hers, and then he kissed her.

They were strong people who had come far, on their own, had found each other, and were brave enough to love each other, whatever it took, wherever it led them, in darkness and in light.

They kissed again for a long time, and went back to the others, feeling peaceful and grateful. They were just in time for the cake. And Gloria caught the bouquet, which was as it should be. Patrick and Eugenia smiled at each other and she made no attempt to catch it. They already had everything they needed and wanted, and were wise enough to know it. Their love for each other and life together was a living vow, to love and to cherish, for better for worse, for richer for poorer.

THE PORTRAIT

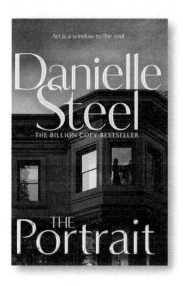

Art is a window to the soul . . .

Portrait artist Devon Darcy has a talent for capturing the souls of her subjects on canvas, and has built a successful career despite a devastating past. Entrepreneur Charles Mackenzie Taylor has given up on romance. But when the two meet at a New York gallery, Charlie is haunted by Devon's beauty and talent and approaches her to paint him.

Over the course of a summer in the Hamptons, their connection deepens. But the ghosts of their pasts are not easily put to rest. And after an accident endangers Devon's career, they must decide what their future will hold . . .

Coming soon

PURE STEEL. PURE HEART.

ABOUT THE AUTHOR

DANIELLE STEEL has been hailed as one of the world's most popular authors, with a billion copies of her novels sold. Her many international bestsellers include *A Mother's Love, A Mind of Her Own* and *Far from Home*. She is also the author of *His Bright Light*, the story of her son Nick Traina's life and death; *A Gift of Hope*, a memoir of her work with the homeless; and the children's books *Pretty Minnie in Paris* and *Pretty Minnie in Hollywood*. Danielle divides her time between Paris and her home in northern California.

daniellesteel.com
Facebook.com/DanielleSteelOfficial
Instagram: @officialdaniellesteel